Changeling Press LLC

ChangelingPress.com

Python/Joker Duet
A Dixie Reapers Bad Boys Romance
Harley Wylde

Python/Joker
A Dixie Reapers Bad Boys Romance
Harley Wylde

ISBN: 978-1-60521-927-1

Publisher:
Changeling Press LLC
315 N. Centre St.
Martinsburg, WV 25404
ChangelingPress.com

Printed in the U.S.A.

Editor: Crystal Esau
Cover Artist: Bryan Keller

The individual stories in this anthology have been previously released in E-Book format.

Table of Contents

Python (Dixie Reapers MC 18)
A Dixie Reapers Bad Boys Romance
Harley Wylde

Galina -- All my life I've been taught to obey men without question, but when I find out my father has offered my hand in marriage to Dima, a man who's already killed two women, I know I've had enough. The Vor offers me a chance to run, and I take it. Living with the Dixie Reapers MC was supposed to be temporary. When I see one of the club girls harassing Python, I step in. Maybe I shouldn't have. I never thought something so simple would become a complicated situation.

Python -- All I wanted was to enjoy the single life forever. Didn't matter if the pretty little Russian caught my eye. I wasn't the type to settle down. Then she went and claimed me in front of a club girl. The officers in my club are having far too much fun with this. I'd planned to keep her at arm's length -- until I found out she was in danger. With trouble breathing down her neck, I don't have a choice. I'll make her mine in every way that matters. Anyone dares to touch her, even the Bratva, and I'll bury them.

Prologue

Lina

A cabinet door slammed, then another. It wouldn't surprise me if he'd broken them again. I heard my father's steps as he stomped his way around the house. The crash of a vase. The rattle of the silverware drawer. More glass breaking that made me wonder if he'd just smashed the family pictures. It wouldn't be the first time. The steps drew closer, and he pounded his fist on my bedroom door.

"Galina, open the door."

No matter how scared I was of my father, there was someone I feared more. The Vor. He'd promised he'd get me out of here. I knew of my father's plans. He wanted a connection to the Belov family and planned to use me to do it. I'd been raised to obey without question. I'd have done it this time too, except the Vor had come to me. The Belovs only had one son - - Dima. He looked perfect on the outside. Inside lay a monster. The whispers among the women in the Bratva said he'd killed more than one whore, and even a girlfriend or two.

My father didn't care what happened to me. As long as he could line his pockets, nothing else mattered. If he knew Vadim Ivanov had contacted me with a way out of this nightmare, he'd have forced me to be with Belov even sooner. Instead, he'd arranged for an engagement ceremony to take place in one week.

Our family was much lower in rank than the others. In fact, my father was nearly at the very bottom. Our home was a modest size and couldn't compare to the mansions the higher-ups lived in. I knew it was my father's dream to climb his way to the top. It was a pity he only had one child. Me. Once I escaped, he'd lose his bargaining chip.

The door rattled on the hinges as he banged on it again. "You little slut, open the fucking door."

I pressed my lips together and remained silent, refusing to engage with him. Easing my phone from my pocket, I texted Vadim. *I need help immediately.*

The message showed he'd read it. He wouldn't risk texting me back and my phone making any sort of noise. The man was too smart for that. No, he'd send someone to extract me from the house. I had faith in him. The Vor would make sure it was handled silently.

More glass broke from somewhere in the house. My father continued to curse and yell, until everything went quiet. I didn't dare move. It could have been a trap to lure me out. A gentler knock sounded at the door.

"Miss Kuzmin? My name is Artem. The Vor sent me."

Did I dare believe him? "Where's my father?"

"He's alive, but unconscious. Please open the door, Miss Kuzmin. We need to get you to safety as quickly as possible."

I stood and crept closer, pressing my ear to the door. I had no way of knowing if he spoke the truth. Wait. The Vor! I text him again. *Did you send someone named Artem to get me?*

It only took him a moment to answer. *Da. Go with him.*

Opening the door, I stared at the young man on the other side. He didn't seem much older than me. He tipped his head toward my room. "You should pack anything you don't want to leave behind. You won't be returning here."

It didn't take me long to pack a bag with the only picture I had of my mother, a few precious items she'd given me before her death, and some clothes. Everything else could stay for all I cared. As long as I was free of my father, and preferably the Bratva, then nothing else mattered. The Vor hadn't said where he'd send me, but it had to be better than here.

"I'm ready."

He took the bag from me and led the way to a blacked-out car in the driveway. He helped me into the back seat, then climbed into the passenger side up front. The driver's gaze met mine in the rearview mirror and the emptiness sent a chill down my spine. If ever there was someone with a killer's eyes, it was this man. For a brief moment, I wondered if I'd made a mistake. Had I put my trust in the wrong person? The Vor seemed genuine when he'd said he'd help me escape my father and the Bratva. I didn't understand why he'd made the offer. What if I'd just put my life in the wrong hands?

"We'll be on the road for quite a while. Did the Vor tell you where you'll be going?" Artem asked.

"*Nyet*."

He gave me a slight nod and flashed a smile. I had a feeling he was trying to set me at ease. It worked, slightly. The man at least seemed human compared to the driver. I wasn't sure the other man felt anything at all.

"Alabama and a group called the Dixie Reapers. They weren't expecting you quite so soon, but I know they'll find a place for you. It's the only way to keep you out of your father's hands, and Belov's."

"I appreciate everything you're doing for me."

Maybe this would be okay. At least I now knew where they were taking me, as long as they hadn't lied.

With no one to contact, I had no choice but to put my life in their hands. Thanks to my father, the only friends I had were ones he'd handpicked. If I talked to any of them, they'd only tell him where to find me.

Crap! I pulled my phone from my pocket and tapped Artem on the shoulder. "Um, should I have left this behind?"

He saw the device in my hand and let out a muffled curse before taking it from me. He popped out the battery and sim card before tossing the phone out the window. I was going to take that to mean I'd fucked up. We hadn't been on the road for very long, so it wasn't likely my father had tried to track me. He might not even be awake yet, depending on how Artem knocked him out.

"How will I contact the Bratva?" I asked.

"You won't," Artem said. "This is a new start for you, Galina. A new life. Once we leave you with the Dixie Reapers, the Bratva will be a thing of your past."

"The Vor is really going to let me leave like this?" I asked. "There's no catch?"

"Only a select few people know of this. The Vor isn't happy with the way things have been run, the way fathers use their daughters. It hasn't been long since things changed. You have Viktor and his wife to thank for this."

I knew of Viktor but hadn't met him before. He was too high up for me to have ever moved in the same circles as him or his wife. I didn't understand what he had to do with any of this, but I wasn't sure Artem would answer if I asked. If he'd planned to tell me more, he'd have given me a better explanation already.

I sat back and watched the scenery pass, wondering what this new life of mine would look like.

Chapter One

Python

I didn't know what the hell the club officers were thinking. Yeah, I knew the club had agreed to work with the Bratva when it came to helping women in distress. I got it. They had my support one hundred percent. But I'd thought we'd give them money, a new identity, and move them along. So, why was this girl still here? In the past year, none of the women had stayed longer than a night or two.

"What crawled up your ass?" Sticks asked.

We'd both patched in at the same time and had started prospecting together as well. It had taken both of us a week or two to stop using our real names around each other. There were times I still thought of him as Will.

I pointed to the Russian girl. "Why is she still here?"

"You'd have to ask Grimm, or more accurately, his wife. Oksana took a liking to Galina. It's why she's over there so much."

"Isn't this just asking for trouble? It's no secret Oksana is here, or that we know where her mother and sister are located. What if someone in the Bratva comes nosing around? Oksana might be protected, but Galina isn't."

Sticks smacked me on the back. "Well, unless you're volunteering…"

Hell no. The last thing I needed was a woman. My gaze strayed to her again. I had to admit she was pretty. Not gorgeous or even what I would call beautiful. For some reason, there was still an innocence to her. How the hell she'd grown up around the Bratva and not come out the other side jaded was beyond me.

"Don't let Wire and Lavender see you eying her like that," Sticks said. "You know what happens when they even get a whiff of interest from one of us."

I nearly shuddered. Yeah, that was the last thing I wanted to happen. I tore my gaze away from Galina and went into the clubhouse. A cold beer was exactly what I needed.

In the past year or two, a lot of changes had occurred not only here, but with other clubs we called family or friends. Most had done away with the club whores or set up a separate building for family events since so many brothers were settling down. It made sense. If I did have a wife and kid, I wouldn't want them in the same space those dumb bitches spread their legs.

As for the Dixie Reapers, this building was the one place you could still find a woman. At least, after Wire and Lavender vetted them. Anyone wanting to hang with us went through a background check these days. Too many little ones running around to risk letting the wrong sort of person in. It had happened too often already.

I grabbed a cold bottle of my favorite beer from behind the bar and sat at a nearby table. Only two women were here at the moment, and I didn't want anything to do with either of them. Anna was the least clingy of the two. Once I'd told her I wasn't interested, she'd mostly left me alone. Unless she thought I was drunk enough to give her a shot. The other... Penny was a menace. The woman always latched on and wouldn't let go.

I'd no sooner thought her name than she spotted me and headed over. If I wasn't trying to keep away from Galina outside, I'd have left the building like my ass was on fire. Anything to avoid the bitch who wanted a property cut. And yeah, we all knew what her end game was, even if she denied it. We could see it in her eyes.

"Did you come here to see me?" she asked, leaning toward me. The woman practically shoved her tits in my face, and I barely dodged.

"Nope. Wanted a beer."

She batted her eyes. "You could have had one of those at home. You know you don't have to be shy. I'll give you anything you want."

I'd bet she would, and probably something else I most certainly didn't want or need right now. A baby in her belly. Bitch was crazy as fuck, and I wouldn't put it past her to get pregnant on purpose. I finished my beer and got up to use the bathroom, hoping she'd be gone when I got back. No such luck. She'd not only made herself comfortable, but she'd gotten two beers. The way she licked at one of them told me it was hers. And if it hadn't been, it was now.

I stared at the open bottles. We always cautioned women not to accept open containers. Someone at the Hades Abyss had learned not too long ago men needed to be wary too. Cotton had gotten screwed over and still hadn't recovered from what happened.

"I didn't spit in it," she said, rolling her eyes.

"Wasn't my concern."

She huffed and took the bottle. After swallowing a mouthful, she handed it back to me. "Not poisoned either."

Fine. I might very well regret this later, but I didn't want to make a big deal out of it. Slayer and Royal were both across the room. Last thing I needed was them calling me a little bitch or some shit. I drank the beer quickly, then stood.

"I'm afraid I'm not good company today." I made my way to the front door. Partway there, the room started to tilt and spin. *What the fuck*?

I stumbled out onto the porch and down the steps. The entire world looked like I'd entered a funhouse tunnel. Shaking my head, I tried to make sense of where I was. The line of bikes blurred and I couldn't tell one from another.

A small hand gripped mine and I started to shake it off, until I heard the soft Russian accent.

"Let me help you."

Galina. I let her lead me away, but we didn't make it far before I heard Penny yelling out my name.

"Wait for me, Python!"

Galina put her lips near my ear and spoke in a low voice. "Do you want to wait for her?"

"No."

She gave a nod and helped me walk a little farther. I hadn't realized it before, but the car the club had given her sat at the end of the row of bikes. I didn't know why she'd parked there, but right now I was grateful.

"Hey, bitch! Where are you taking my man?" Penny screamed.

Galina stopped and I felt her turn. She didn't release me. Only switched to her other hand, as if she worried I might fall. She wasn't wrong. At any moment I could land on my ass. Although, I didn't think the pint-size woman was going to be able to hold me up.

"Your man?" she asked. She spit out a string of Russian that sounded like she was cussing the woman out and I couldn't hold back my smile. Even though I felt like shit, I had to admit I liked seeing this side of

Galina. "He's not yours. He'll *never* be yours."

Penny sputtered, and it sounded like she was coming closer. Galina managed to get me to her car and into the passenger seat. She slammed the door about the time Penny stopped beside her. I couldn't hear what Galina was saying, but I could tell from the tone she was pissed. She lit into Penny, and if I hadn't thought I might pass out or throw up, I'd have found it hysterical. She'd done the one thing I hadn't been able to. Mostly because I'd have felt like shit. Although, now that I was certain the bitch had drugged me, I wouldn't hold back. In fact, once this passed, I was going to talk to the Pres and get that woman booted permanently.

Galina got into the car and backed up. Penny ran around to put herself in front, and Galina revved the engine. I heard the tires spin right before the car shot forward. My eyes felt so heavy they slid shut, and I missed the look on Penny's face. Galina didn't slow for a few minutes. My house was toward the back of the compound, and the moment she came to a stop, I knew she'd brought me home.

She shut off the car and I heard her get out. She opened my door and placed her hand on my arm.

"Can you stand?" she asked. "Should I get help?"

Oh fuck no. "My brothers will laugh if they know about this."

Shit. That's right. If I told the Pres, then... I'd have to think about it tomorrow. Right now, I wasn't sure how much longer I'd stay coherent, or able to stand. Galina helped me from the car, and we walked up to my door. I couldn't seem to get my keys out of my pocket.

I felt her hand slide in and grasp the keyring, but

it wasn't all she touched. Groaning as my cock went rock-hard, I wondered if I'd just been dumped straight into hell. She froze and I could feel her staring at me, even if I couldn't manage to open my eyes.

"Sorry," I muttered.

She pulled out my keys and got the door open. I tripped over the threshold and barely stayed upright. Her small hand grasped mine tightly as she led the way through my home. It was almost as if she knew exactly where she was going. When we reached my bedroom, I sank onto the side of the bed, and she kneeled at my feet. Fuck if that didn't screw with my drug-addled brain.

She set my boots beside the nightstand, then helped me get my cut off. I tried to watch her, but the world was spinning too much. Closing my eyes, I fell back on the mattress. My legs still hung off the side, but I didn't care.

"Python, what happened? Should I get someone?"

"Drugged." At least, I tried to say it. Not sure how it sounded to her. I could tell my words slurred and my tongue felt heavy. What the hell had Penny planned to accomplish with me in this state? Then again, I'd gotten hard when Galina brushed against my cock. It seemed that part of me worked, even if the rest didn't.

She did her best to get me all the way onto the bed, and I heard her panting for breath when she'd finished. I didn't know what Penny had dosed me with, so I had no clue how long this would last. The thought of lying here alone, unable to even get up if I needed to puke or take a piss, bothered me. That bitch was going to pay when I got through this.

"Stay," I said, or tried to. Galina seemed to

understand. I felt the bed dip as she sat beside me.

My movements were clumsy, but I managed to pull her down beside me. I attempted to wrap my arm around her, to hold her closer, but failed miserably. She sighed and inched closer.

"When I thought of my first time in bed with a man, this wasn't what I had in mind," she said.

My head felt too foggy for her words to really sink in. First time? Wait. "Virgin?"

She buried her face against my side. "Stop. Don't make fun of me."

Before I could say anything else, the darkness started to pull me under.

* * *

My mouth felt like someone had stuffed it full of cotton. Hammers pounded against the inside of my skull. I tried to shift, but I couldn't. Prying my eyes opened, I winced and slammed them shut again. It took a few tries before I could stand the daylight pouring in through the windows. At least I'd survived the night.

Looking down my body, I realized why I couldn't move. Galina curled against me, her leg thrown over my thigh and her head on my shoulder. She'd put her hand over my heart. I watched her sleep and wondered how the hell we'd ended up like this. I could only remember bits and pieces from last night. Not much past getting into her car after that bitch, Penny, drugged me.

Her clothes, and mine, were intact so at least nothing had happened between us. The fact my cock was hard as fuck and trying to escape my pants was enough to make me move. I eased out from under Galina and managed to get out of bed. My legs weren't quite steady as I went into the bathroom and shut the door. It wasn't until after I'd taken a piss I realized I wasn't getting my jeans back on. Not in my current condition. Morning wood was bad enough for most people, but they called me Python for a reason. I rubbed my hand up and down the back of my head as I stared at my dick and wondered what the hell I was supposed to do. It wasn't like I could go out there in my underwear, or naked. Not with Galina in my bed.

"Shower," I mumbled to myself. By the time I finished, surely she'd be awake and have left.

I started the water and once it was hot enough, I stripped out of my clothes and stepped under the spray. It didn't take long to wash. I pressed my hands to the shower wall and hung my head, letting the water pound against my neck and shoulders. While I still didn't remember everything from last night, my head was slowly clearing. It wasn't until the water began to cool that I got out and dried off. Wrapping the towel around my waist, I stepped out into the bedroom and froze, eyes going wide.

"What the fuck?" I asked.

"That's what we'd like to know," Grimm said. He folded his arms and gave a pointed look from Galina to me. Shit. I knew what he thought.

"I didn't touch her," I said. "I had too much to drink last night, and she gave me a ride home so I wouldn't crash my bike." I should have talked to Galina about this shit before now. What would happen if she told them I'd been drugged? The last thing I wanted was to come across as weak. Although, I knew they needed to know about Penny... just not right this moment.

And what I said wasn't entirely a lie. I eyed Galina and she gave me a soft smile. Maybe she'd caught on that I didn't want to say anything right now.

The moment Oksana saw it, her eyebrows lifted. Great. If they blabbed, this wouldn't end well. I had to figure out how to keep them quiet.

"We're here because Penny was in the clubhouse going off about how no one told her you'd been taken already," Grimm said. "She mentioned a little Russian bitch. Since I knew it wasn't Oksana, that only left Galina."

"Penny saw me leave with Galina," I said. "That's all there is to it."

Galina's cheeks flushed and she looked away. Or maybe not. What the fuck had she said to Penny? I remembered her going off in Russian. Of course, Penny didn't know a damn word that wasn't English, and even then I sometimes had my doubts about how much she understood. Clearly "no" wasn't in her vocabulary.

"She was being pushy and made me angry," Galina said. "The way she spoke about you wasn't right."

"Galina, what did you tell her?" Oksana asked.

"That he couldn't be hers because he was mine." Her cheeks went even more scarlet. "I didn't think she'd tell everyone. I only wanted her to leave Python alone. It was clear he didn't want anything to do with her, and she was following him out of the clubhouse. I only meant to help."

Grimm rolled his lips in and I knew he was biting down on them to keep from laughing. I could see the humor in his eyes and his shoulders shook a little. Asshole. She'd gone and claimed me in front of a mouthy fucking whore, and now I knew I'd end up paying the price for it. Unless Savior gave us some slack since Galina had no idea what she'd done.

"So, you claimed him?" Grimm asked. "Seems

like I've heard of that happening once before. Who was it? Oh, right. Ridley laid claim to Venom, in the middle of Church no less."

"Fuck me," I muttered. Or maybe he wasn't going to let it slide. This was seriously fucked up. Galina didn't deserve this shit, and I'd make sure they knew it. "Do they know?"

"I think everyone does," Oksana said. "Penny wasn't exactly quiet this morning. Even Tempest had to come out and handle the situation."

I rubbed my hand down my face and wondered how bad this was going to be. Galina hadn't meant anything by it. At least, I didn't think so. I honestly thought she'd only been trying to help me, and now this might come back to bite both of us in the ass.

"Do I need to go talk to Savior?" I asked. "She has no idea what she's done. Galina is still learning what it's like to live here. Does it really sound fair to screw up her life because she was attempting to be nice?"

"Actually, he'll be here in a few minutes. Might want to put on some pants first or he'll definitely get the wrong idea." Grimm looked over at Galina again. "I'm still not sure I believe all this is entirely innocent, so I know he won't. You may be new here, but did you really think nothing would happen if you said Python was yours?"

Galina paled and looked away. Shit. The woman looked terrified. I wasn't sure if she was worried about being in trouble or scared of being mine. It could go either way.

"Great." I grabbed a pair of underwear out of the dresser and some jeans from the closet. Heading back into the bathroom, I quickly pulled them on before I opened the door again. Savior stood in my bedroom, along with Saint, Tempest, Royal, Viking, and Prophet. Well, all the officers were here. This didn't bode well. "How fucked am I?"

Savior didn't look amused. In fact, none of them did. Viking's jaw clenched, and I had a feeling he'd take a swing at me if I said the wrong thing. I'd noticed the way he watched Galina when he thought no one was paying attention. It was obvious she intrigued him. If he thought for one second I'd wronged her or taken advantage, I knew he'd do his best to put me on my ass.

"Penny has told everyone you have an old lady now," Tempest said. "Or rather, she told anyone at the clubhouse, and it spread like fucking wildfire because no one had heard a damn thing about it until now. I got stopped multiple times by brothers asking when you'd gotten an old lady."

Motherfucker! I wanted to gut Penny right about now. Not only had the bitch drugged me, but she'd run her fucking mouth and caused all sorts of trouble. Galina looked like she might hit the floor at any moment, and I could tell she was terrified. I also knew if I stopped to reassure her, everyone in this room would take it as a sign we were meant to be together. The fucking club was worse than a bunch of old women when it came to this shit. Especially Wire and Lavender. I hoped like hell no one had told the two of them yet!

"Galina just drove me home. I wasn't able to ride my bike because I was too fucked up and stumbling all over the damn parking lot. That's all there is to it," I said. "Penny was bugging the shit out of me and followed me out. I guess once Galina got me into her car, Penny must have said something that upset her, so she told Penny that we were a thing. She had no idea what she was doing."

"Then why is she still here and you're half dressed?" Savior asked.

And that's when I knew things weren't going to go my way.

Chapter Two

Lina

No matter how stressed Python appeared right now, I didn't regret what I'd done. Well, maybe the things I'd said, but Penny had made me so angry. Back home, I never would have said anything. I'd have meekly hung my head and gotten out of her way. Since coming to the Dixie Reapers, I'd become a bit bolder. I liked this new version of myself, but I didn't think Python felt the same right now.

"I worried he'd get sick during the night," I said. "I stayed to make sure he would be okay."

It wasn't entirely a lie. Omitting the part where he'd tried to pull me into his arms was probably for the best. The panic in his eyes told me he didn't like any of this. I didn't understand where the conversation was going, or what the issue was. Whatever was going on, Python wasn't the least bit confused. Only upset. Exactly what problem had I caused?

"Galina, the club promised to protect you and help you start a new life," Savior said. "The fact you're here in the house of a single man, and he's half dressed, doesn't paint the best picture."

I still didn't get it. Were they unaware of the things that happened in the Bratva? At least Python hadn't touched me. If I'd done this same thing with anyone back home, the results would have been vastly different. They'd have taken advantage. The only way it would have ended in marriage is if they were higher up than my father, and he'd wanted the connection. Otherwise, I'd have been used as a whore to advance his career. Or he'd have outright sold me.

"Why am I still here?" I asked. "I've enjoyed getting to know everyone, and I appreciate the fact you've given me a safe place to hide from my family."

"But?" Savior asked.

"Well, I've heard the whispers when people see me. They all want to know why I haven't left yet. You've helped others escape the Bratva, haven't you?" He nodded. Just as I'd thought. "And they didn't stay here as long as I have, right?"

"They didn't," Savior agreed.

So... why me? I didn't know why things were different from the other times. There wasn't anything special about me. Or did they think I couldn't survive on my own? I'd never know if I didn't try. While it was true I'd never lived alone, I thought I could handle it. At least, as long as my father couldn't find me.

Python shook his head and gave a humorless laugh. "I get it. I'd wondered the same thing. Didn't put two and two together until now. It's because of Viking, right?"

"What?" I glanced at the big man they called Viking. He held my gaze a moment before looking away. I didn't know what he had to do with anything. Was he supposed to find the place where I'd go from here? Had there been an issue? "I don't understand."

"He likes you," Python said. "Looked pissed as hell when he came and saw us. So, why haven't you manned the fuck up and asked her out, Viking? Far as I know, you haven't given a shit about women. Treat them with respect, but you might as well be dead below the waist. Haven't even seen you with the damn whores who swarm this place."

"That's enough," Savior said. "Back off, Python."

He lifted his hands and took a step back. "Fine. But tell me I'm wrong."

Savior sighed. "I was giving him time to make a decision. He didn't ask for it."

"You like me?" I asked the big man. He gave a brisk nod but wouldn't hold my gaze. I wasn't sure what to think of the situation. He seemed nice, and I hadn't had any issues with him. At the same time, his size was a bit off-putting for me. If I had to name my ideal body type, it would be Python's. He wasn't overly large, even though his muscles were defined. Being close to him didn't scare me, or make me worry he might break me in half.

"You're going to force her to be with me, aren't you?" Python asked. "All because things didn't go your way. Never mind what Galina wants. She's right. She should have been out of here long ago. If anyone is to blame for this situation, it's you, Pres, and you damn well know it."

The way he narrowed his eyes and glared at Python made me flinch. Perhaps he shouldn't have blamed the man for what happened. In all honesty, something bothered me about last night. The way Penny chased after Python and his condition... had she put something in his drink?

Python held my gaze, and I knew he didn't want me to say anything. I had no idea why, though. Did he worry the men would hurt Penny? Or was he concerned how they might view *him*? I knew my father would never admit a woman had gotten the best of him. Did Python share that trait with him? I wasn't sure how I felt about it. Thinking this man could have anything in common with a monster made me feel unsettled.

"What if... I mean, could we date?" I asked. "Even if it's just for a week or two. It might make the gossip die down, and then it wouldn't be obvious to

Penny I lied to her. I said Python was mine, but does it have to mean... whatever that phrase means here?"

Viking sighed and folded his arms. "It's not an awful idea. Galina is still new enough we could pass it off as a communication issue. Of course, then Penny will be after Python again."

"I'll deal with Penny," Python said. "Don't punish Galina. Being with me would be a fate worse than death for any woman."

I didn't know why he felt that way. He didn't seem like a bad man. I'd met my share of those. After living my entire life with the Bratva, and my rotten bastard of a father, the biker was more like Prince Charming. Although, the way he was talking, I didn't think he'd appreciate the comparison.

"When you say deal with her..." Savior eyed Python. "Something else we need to know?"

Python ran a hand down his face. As much as he seemed to want to remain silent, I thought it best to say something. Maybe it would defuse this entire situation.

"I don't think he was drunk last night." Python's head jerked my way and his jaw went tight. Yeah, I'd just pissed him off. Too bad. "The way Penny chased him, it was like she expected something to happen with Python."

Viking's gaze sharpened on me, and so did the other men's. "You saying she drugged him?"

"Yes! Damnit. I didn't want to say anything yet, but yes, the fucking bitch must have slipped something in my drink when I went to take a piss. Go ahead. I know you want to make fun of me for letting a stupid fucking whore get the best of me," Python said, his face turning red. I'd watched him off and on since coming here, but I'd never seen him this angry before.

Savior held up a hand. "First off, we'd never

make light of something like that happening. If you really think she dosed you with something, then we need to handle it. Bitch needs to go. Second, you should have fucking led with that shit."

"So, Galina was really just trying to help you?" Viking asked.

I swallowed hard and took a step back, putting Python between me and the other men. The last thing I wanted to do was cause more trouble, but if Viking asked me out, I'd have to turn him down. I wasn't sure how he'd take it, or the rest of the club for that matter. I reached out and put my fingers through Python's beltloop and held on.

"Um, if everyone thinks Python and I are together, I still think pretending to date for a week or two would be a good idea." I knew I was grasping at straws. Now that they knew what Penny had done, they'd explain the situation to everyone else. Then the rumors would die down and things would go back to normal.

Viking's gaze landed on my hand, the one now attached to Python's jeans. It was a shitty way to tell him I wasn't interested, but I still wasn't used to confrontation. After doing what I'd been told all my life, the freedom to be myself and say what I wanted was still new to me.

Python glanced down at me before focusing on the others again. "Her idea seems to be the easiest. I can take her on a few dates, invite her over, and as far as anyone will know we're a legitimate couple. Just keep Wire and Lavender from doing that shit where they marry people without asking."

Wait. What? How was that even a thing? Now didn't seem like the time to ask. I watched the others, waiting to see if they'd agree. Viking seemed resigned to the fact I wasn't interested in him. The others... I couldn't tell what they were thinking or feeling right now.

"Fine. Penny will be handled now and not later," Savior said. "I can't have her doing that shit to anyone else. She's clearly lost her fucking mind."

Tempest slapped him on the back. "I'll take care of it, Pres. Not sure your wife will like you getting your hands dirty with this one. Not to mention, you have enough to deal with already."

Savior sighed and pinched the bridge of his nose. "No shit. Ares is going to make me switch from beer to tequila at this rate."

"So, we're dating?" I asked. "Or rather, pretending to?"

"Yeah. You can hang out here a little longer today, and I'll make sure people see us going to lunch together," Python said. "You sure you're fine with this?"

"Of course. I wouldn't have offered otherwise. Besides, I assume the club needs time to get everything in order before I can leave, right?" I asked. Since I wouldn't be going out with Viking and my relationship with Python wasn't real, there wasn't any reason for me to stick around. It was past time for me to start my new life. I had to admit I'd miss the few friends I'd made since I'd been here.

"Oksana and I will go talk to Wire and Lavender. They'll need to know this isn't real so they won't meddle," Grimm said. "I'd say give it two weeks. Savior will have time to get Penny out of here, and then you can make a big production of breaking up. Something loud and with lots of witnesses."

Oksana studied me, and I hoped she couldn't see through me. I'd done my best to hide the fact I liked

Python. He hadn't interacted with me much since I'd been here, but the few times we'd spoken, he'd been nice. I had a feeling she saw more than I wanted her to. Python had already made it clear he didn't want a woman in his life. The last thing he needed was to have the club force him to keep me.

"If everyone could leave, I think Galina and I need to come up with a plan," Python said. "But thanks for busting into my house and shitting all over my day."

Tempest took a step forward and got right in Python's face. "I get that you're pissed about this situation, but you put yourself in it to begin with. Had you just told Grimm Penny had drugged you, the rest of us wouldn't be here. The issue would have been over before it even started. But you decided to be a little bitch and hide it so you wouldn't appear weak, am I right? So fuck you, Python."

I felt him tense and I leaned into him, hoping it would be enough to keep him from taking a swing at Tempest. I'd watched men fight enough times to know what was coming. At least, unless we could calm them down first.

"Get out," Python said. "This is as nicely as I can say it right now, but I don't want Galina getting mixed up in a fight."

"He's right," Grimm said. "Oksana doesn't need to be here for that shit either. I get where he's coming from. And I'm sure if he was drugged, his head is probably killing him. All this tension isn't helping anything."

Python reached down and pried my hand loose from his pants, then started shoving the men from our room. Grimm followed behind them, but Oksana lingered. The look in her eyes was a mix of pity and understanding.

"These men, they're different from what we're used to," she said. "It's easy to fall for them."

"I don't know him well enough for that," I said.

"But he makes you feel safe?"

"*Da.* You're right when you say they're not like the men we've known. I know he's strong. He wouldn't be here otherwise. But his strength, it doesn't frighten me. No matter how angry he gets, I don't think he'd hurt me."

"He wouldn't," Oksana agreed. "Your father can't get to you here, Galina. These men will defend you. The women will be your friends if you let them. And Python... maybe over the next two weeks, he'll see how amazing you are."

I shook my head. "No. He doesn't want a woman in his life, and I have to respect his wishes. I'll make some memories with him, and then I'll move on when it's time."

Oksana gave me a nod and left the bedroom. When Python came in a moment later, I wondered if he'd heard everything. The assessing way he gazed at me made me a little uncomfortable.

He walked over to the dresser and pulled out a shirt, then tugged it over his head. Leaning against the dresser, he looked like he had the weight of the world on his shoulders. He gripped the wood and stared at the floor.

"You heard me, didn't you?" I asked softly. He gave a brief nod, and my heart sank. This was why I hadn't wanted him to know I found him attractive. Now things would be awkward during the weeks we had to pretend to be a couple. "I meant what I said. When it's time for us to break up, I'll leave. Assuming they've set up my new identity and have a place for me to go. Either way, I'll make sure I stay out of your way."

He still didn't respond or look up. I swallowed hard and realized I'd messed up even worse than I had when I'd mouthed off to Penny. Maybe being strong and independent wasn't in the cards for me. I should have stayed with the Bratva and done as my father wanted. He'd said we'd make plans, but it seemed that wasn't going to happen now. I rushed past him and didn't stop until I was not only out of his house, but in my car and driving away.

"Perfect, Galina," I muttered to myself. "Now he knows you like him, and you've screwed up your chance at a new life."

Instead of going to the home where I'd been staying, I kept driving and left the compound. I didn't have a direction in mind. Before I'd realized it, I'd left town and was heading down the highway. Should I keep going? I wasn't sure I could ever face Python again. Not after I'd made a fool of myself.

Blue light flashed in my rearview mirror, and I cursed as I pulled onto the shoulder. The car stopped behind me, and a man walked up to my window in a Sheriff's uniform. Rolling down the window, I looked over at the passenger seat to grab my purse and realized I didn't have it with me. I'd left it at Python's house!

"Ma'am, do you know why I pulled you over?"

"Nyet."

He stared at me and glanced into the vehicle. "Can I see your license and registration, please?"

"I don't have my license. I was upset and forgot my purse, but the registration is in the console."

He sighed and took a step back. "Get out of the car, please."

I did as he said, and my heart raced as I wondered if I was about to go to jail. Was that something he could do simply because I'd forgotten my license? I answered all his questions and thought I might pass out when he put me in the back of his car.

No one had any idea where I was. What if I couldn't prove my identity? Even worse, it was possible my father would find me now. How had everything gone so horribly wrong? All I'd done last night was try to help Python. Now I was on my way to the Sheriff's Department, and I had a feeling I was in far more trouble than I realized.

Chapter Three

Python

What the fuck just happened? Galina liked me? Had she volunteered to be my pretend girlfriend in the hopes it would become real? It felt like everything was spinning. I'd never wanted to settle down. Especially after the fiasco with Savior's daughter, Ares. She'd had a crush on me, and I'd talked to her through text for a bit. Then the Pres found out and got pissed about it. Although, he'd technically given me permission to keep texting her, as long as I didn't do anything else until she turned eighteen.

I'd have been happy to do that. Ares had always been a good kid, and I'd honestly been flattered she liked me. Didn't mean I wanted to keep her forever. When Prophet made his move, I'd been only too happy to step aside. Of course, Ares was still underage so nothing had happened between the two of them. I wasn't sure if he was going to claim her or not. Only time would tell.

I knew I needed to clear things up with Galina. The way she'd run out of here, she'd either been embarrassed or terrified of my reaction. She couldn't help how she felt, and I didn't want her walking on eggshells around me. I'd just swung my leg over my motorcycle when one of the Prospects rolled up.

"Did Galina say where she was going?" he asked.

I froze and slowly turned my head toward him. "What? Are you saying she left?"

He nodded. "Took off toward the highway. I heard the two of you were together, but it looked like she was crying. Thought I should come talk to you."

"Thanks." Where the hell could she have gone? On the off chance she hadn't gotten very far, maybe I could catch up to her. I backed the bike out of the driveway and drove to the gate. The second it was opened, I pulled through and hung a right.

I watched for her car not only in the traffic ahead of me, but also in those passing on the opposite side. The more miles between me and the compound, the more anxious I became. Had she pulled off somewhere? What if something happened to her car? I'd been on the road for about a half hour when I saw her vehicle on the shoulder. I stopped behind it and got out to see if she was all right.

The moment I realized it was empty, my heart nearly stopped. I scanned the highway, checking to see if she might be on foot. If she had been, she was long gone now, or someone had picked her up. What if her father had found her?

I pulled my phone from my pocket and called Savior. He answered almost immediately.

"This better be important," he said.

"Hello to you too, Pres, and yeah, it's pretty fucking important. Galina left. She had a head start and by the time I caught up to her... All I can find is her car, Savior. It's on the side of the highway and I don't see her."

He started cussing, and I heard a door slam. "What the fuck happened?"

"She was talking to Oksana and I overheard them. Galina likes me. I didn't know what to say or how to process what I'd heard, and I guess she took it hard. She left the compound. I wouldn't have even known if Sam hadn't stopped by to tell me."

"Does she have her purse with her?" he asked.

"I didn't see it in the car."

"She doesn't know, but Wire has a tracker in it. I'll ask him to pinpoint her location. Give me a few minutes and I'll text or call back."

"Thanks, Pres. I need to make sure she's safe."

Within ten minutes, I received the text. *Purse is at the compound.*

Fucking hell. If she didn't have it with her, there was no way for me to find her. I couldn't help but think of all the things that could go horribly wrong. A tow truck slowed as it passed me, then pulled over in front of Galina's car. The driver backed up, then got out.

"I'm going to need you to step away from the vehicle," the driver said.

"And I'm going to need *you* to answer some questions. Like why the hell my woman's car is about to be towed. Where the fuck is Galina?"

He paused. "All I know is I got a call from the Sheriff's Department to tow it to the impound lot. Sounds to me like your woman got arrested."

Seriously? Little Galina? I couldn't imagine what she could have possibly done. Then I remembered Savior said her purse was at the compound, which meant she didn't have her license. *Shit.* I checked my phone for the nearest Sheriff's office and decided to go straight there. Even if that wasn't where they'd taken Galina, I could at least get more information.

I got on my bike and found the place after two wrong turns. Parking out front, I shut off the engine. I couldn't remember a time I'd ever volunteered to walk into a place like this. One look at my cut, and they might very well put me in the cell next to hers. I walked up the steps and into the building. The woman at the front desk eyed me, and not in a pleasant way.

"I'm looking for Galina Kuzmin. I think she may have been brought in for driving without a license," I said.

"I can't just give that information to anyone," she said.

"I'm her boyfriend. Found her car on the side of the road around the time the tow truck arrived. He told me the Sheriff's Department called him, so here I am. Scared the shit out of me when I realized the car was empty and I didn't see her anywhere."

One of the deputies approached, his jaw tensed and his shoulders pushed back. "Did you say you were looking for Galina Kuzmin?"

"Yeah. Is she here? Can I see her?" I asked.

"She is, and no you may not. Caught her driving without a license."

Uh-huh. I knew she didn't have it with her. Didn't explain *why* he'd pulled her over. Had he even explained it to her? I took out my phone and texted Wire. *Can you hack a body cam?*

He answered right away. *If you give me more details than that.*

I sent him the deputy's name, his badge number, and the county I was in. I had a feeling, he'd fucked up. Worked in my favor because it would mean Galina would be released. In the meantime, I'd just park my ass here and wait.

"Why did you pull her over?" I asked.

"I don't have to tell you shit. I suggest you get your ass out of here before I decide to lock you up too."

I hated men like him. Power trip from hell. He might be a deputy, but it didn't mean he could ignore the law, or bend it to suit him. If he wanted to be an outlaw, then he should ditch the badge.

My phone buzzed with an incoming text and I saw it was from Lavender. *She'll be released soon.*

I wasn't sure what that meant, exactly, but I'd take it. Getting her car from impound wouldn't be fun. I didn't like having to pay for someone else's fuckup, but I knew she'd need transportation. Of course, I could always get her something else. The one she had now was something cheap the club gave her. It hadn't been intended for long-term use.

"Think I'll wait. She should be coming out soon," I said.

"Look, asshole, that woman isn't leaving here. She's locked up, and that's where she'll stay until the judge sees her."

I smirked. "You sure about that?"

Another man opened a door along the far wall and Galina stepped through. The moment she saw me, tears filled her eyes and she rushed over, throwing her arms around my waist. I held her close and grinned at the deputy.

"See? Told you she'd be out soon."

He turned and growled, stomping over to the man who'd released Galina. "What the fuck is going on? I arrested her for a reason."

"Sheriff said to let her go. Something about you not following procedure and pissing off the wrong people." He glanced my way for a second. "Sheriff wants to see you. He seems furious."

The deputy pushed his way through the door and disappeared from sight. I gave the other one a nod and led Galina to the counter.

"We need whatever personal belongings were confiscated," I said.

The woman pursed her lips like she'd sucked on a sour lemon. It took a few minutes for someone to bring the envelope with Galina's keys. I pocketed them, knowing she wouldn't need them right now. Even if we drove to the impound lot, we wouldn't get her car. Not until the paperwork had been processed.

"You'll have to ride back home with me," I said. "We'll sort things out with the car tomorrow."

"I'm sorry," she said, sniffling a little. "I screwed up."

"Hey." I lightly touched her chin and she looked up at me. "None of this is your fault, all right? I should have stopped you before you left the house. I'm sorry for not reacting better. Let's go home and talk."

"You aren't mad at me?" she asked.

"Of course not, Lina." Her eyes widened and her gaze softened. "Come on, beautiful. Time to get out of this place."

I took her by the hand and led her out to my bike. After I got on, I helped her onto the back, and made sure she held on tight. Having her pressed up against me didn't feel as awkward as I'd thought it would. It wasn't like I'd never had anyone ride on my bike. Although, I couldn't remember how it had felt. I only knew this was different.

I placed my hand on her thigh and gave it a squeeze. "You need to stop for any reason before we get to the house, you tap my chest and I'll pull over."

"I'll be okay," she said.

I walked the bike out of the parking space and then pulled out of the lot and onto the street. By the time we got back to town, we'd need to eat lunch. Even though I'd said we were going home, I wondered if I shouldn't stop somewhere for food first. Best to do it back in my own territory. For one, if we were going to make people think we were dating, we needed the locals to see us. Didn't do us much good out here.

When we got back to town, I passed the compound and went down Main Street. As much as I wanted to take her somewhere better than the diner, I knew our chances of being seen by the club would be better there. It was one of the more inexpensive options in town, and the food always filled us up. It probably clogged our arteries too, but I'd worry about that later. I wasn't quite thirty yet and refused to not live life to the fullest.

I parked and helped Galina off my bike, then held her hand as we went inside.

"Thought you might be hungry," I said.

She nodded. "*Da.*"

"You don't speak Russian often. It's something I've noticed. Unless you're upset."

"Even though I was raised in the Bratva, I was born here in the US. My family spoke Russian at home, but I grew up learning both my parents' native language and English."

A waitress came over and greeted us with a smile. "Table for two?"

"Something by the window if possible," I said.

"Follow me." She led us to a nearby booth and placed two menus and two sets of silverware on the table. "Do you know what you'd like to drink?"

"Do you have lemonade?" Galina asked.

"I do." The waitress turned to me. "And for you?"

"Coffee and water."

"I'll be back in a few minutes. Special for today is meatloaf and the desserts are apple pie and peach cobbler." She took off, leaving us to peruse the menus.

"Get whatever you want, Lina. I know today was stressful for you." And I was at fault for some of it. I could admit as much. Never claimed to be perfect or all knowing. I was only human and I'd fuck up from time to time. This happened to be one of them.

The woman came back with our drinks and we placed our orders. After she left again, I reached across the table to take Galina's hand.

"Why do you call me Lina?" she asked.

"You don't like it?"

Her cheeks flushed. "No, I do. I'm just confused."

"About what?"

"When I left, I thought you'd never want to see me again. I know how you feel about being tied down. You don't want anything long-term, and I..." She bit her lip.

"One day at a time, Lina. The Pres gave us permission to date for a bit and make sure this is what you want. He may have made it seem like we're just putting on a show for everyone, but I know my club better than that. Those busybodies are hoping we'll end up together. I know things are very different from what you're used to, and there's still the issue of your father. I have no idea if he'll come looking for you."

"It's possible he now knows I'm in Alabama," she said. "He has connections with law enforcement. Since the deputy arrested me, it will show in the system, won't it?"

"Did they fingerprint you and process you all the way through?" I asked.

She nodded. "I was in a holding cell while they found clothes for me and figured out where to place me."

"Shit. Then yeah, it's possible he could find out. Since that town wasn't too far from here, it wouldn't take much for them to locate you. We'll need to be careful, and I'll ask Wire and Lavender to monitor your dad. If he makes a move, we'll know."

"Why would you do that for me?" she asked.

I tightened my hold on her hand. Two of the club whores came into the diner. Although, I barely recognized them without their make-up on and wearing more clothing. I winked at Galina. "Because you're mine. That's reason enough."

She sucked in a breath, and I worried I'd just given her hope. Then she saw the women walk by us and seemed to catch on. She gave me a slight smile. Yeah, I'd just dug my hole deeper. She'd play along, but at what cost? I felt like a dick knowing this would hurt her.

"When we get back, I think you should move your stuff into my place." She tugged her hand from mine. Yep. I'd definitely fucked up. "I want to make sure you're safe, Lina. If your father is going to come looking for you, I don't want to wonder if you're at your place or out somewhere."

"That's not a good enough reason to move in together."

It seemed she was going to be stubborn about this. I didn't want to do the caveman thing, but maybe I should. I leaned in closer and lowered my voice. "I can't protect you if you aren't with me. I'm not asking, Lina. I'm telling you to get your shit and move it to my house when we get back, and since you don't have a car right now, I'll have one of the Prospects come over with a truck."

She pursed her lips. "I don't have enough to warrant a truck."

Her accent became thicker, which confirmed it. I'd pissed her off. I'd know for sure if she went off on me in Russian. Either way, I was doing this for her own good. Whether she liked it or not.

"Still can't haul any bags on my bike. Unless you can carry it on your back," I said. "Stop being so fucking stubborn, Lina."

"I don't..." She shook her head and sighed. "If I move in with you, I may not want to leave."

It was a gamble I'd have to take. For one, it would make our story more plausible. And for another... well, waking up to her in my house hadn't been completely terrible. Didn't mean I wanted it to be every day for the rest of my life, but I could handle it for a little while.

I lowered my voice so no one else could hear us. "You can sleep in the spare room. I can't exactly set up a bed in there, but we could figure something out. Air mattress or futon. Something I could either smuggle in easily or explain as being for something other than sleeping."

"Fine. I don't think this is a good idea, but I'm clearly not winning this argument."

Our food arrived, and I steered the conversation to safer topics. The rest of our meal passed pleasantly enough, then it was time to go home. As I got on my bike and helped Galina onto the back, I noticed the club whores watching us through the window. Wouldn't take long for this news to spread, much like the rumor this morning. I only hoped this didn't blow up in our faces.

Chapter Four

Lina

I'd lost my mind. The moment he said I was going to move in with him, I should have fought harder. Being with Python every day would make it more difficult to leave. Instead, he'd helped me pack my meager belongings and haul everything to his house. I still didn't understand what happened today. The deputy never said why he'd pulled me over. The moment I'd spoken, he'd placed me under arrest for driving without a license. Since I technically had one, I'd hoped I would only get a fine.

Wire and Lavender sat at the table. Python poured two cups of coffee, one for him and one for Wire, before handing Lavender a soda. I already had a bottle of water. I'd met both of them before, but we hadn't really spoken much. I wasn't sure why they were here.

"How did you get Lina released so quickly?" Python asked.

Good question. I hadn't realized they'd had anything to do with it. No one had told me much of anything while I'd been there.

"The body cam footage proved he never explained why she'd been pulled over, and when he arrested her, he didn't utter so much as one word of the Miranda rights. It was an unlawful arrest that violated her rights as a US citizen." Wire took a swallow of his coffee and sighed. "That particular deputy was already on thin ice. He doesn't like people he considers foreigners. The moment he heard her Russian accent, even though it's faint, things went downhill. He's been in trouble multiple times for harassing people who aren't white."

"So, he's an asshole," Python said. "Already figured that part out."

"We alerted the sheriff about the issue with Galina's arrest, and he immediately released her. The deputy is getting fired. Like Wire said, it wasn't his first offense," Lavender said.

"Any idea why he pulled me over to begin with?" I asked.

"No. We may never know. The important thing is the situation was handled. However, we got a hit in the last twenty minutes. We think the Bratva knows you're here, or at least your father may be aware you were arrested in that town. It's possible he'll be on his way, or send someone for you," Wire said.

Since the Vor sent me here, I knew some people in the Bravta were already aware of my location. But that was different from my father or Dima finding me. The two shared a look. Python tensed. What was going on? I felt like I was missing something.

"We know the two of you are seeing each other," Lavender said. "The news is all over the place. There's only one way to protect Galina. As of right now, if someone were to snatch her, she'd be a missing person, but it could be argued she'd simply gone home with her father."

"Wait." Python held up a hand. "Didn't Oksana and Grimm talk to you about the two of us?"

"Were they supposed to?" Wire asked.

So it seemed they hadn't kept their word. I didn't know if something happened to distract them, or if they'd done it on purpose. Oksana knew I liked Python. Had it been her way of trying to help me? Except I didn't want to trick him into keeping me around.

"Then what's the guaranteed way to keep me safe?" I asked.

"You already publicly claimed Python. Why not make it official and get married?" Lavender asked.

"Um, what?" I asked. "You can't be serious. I only moved in here because he didn't give me a choice. We barely know one another."

"But you're a couple," Lavender said. "You don't expect us to believe you haven't slept together, do you? If you were together long enough for you to claim him in front of Penny, I don't see how you can consider yourselves strangers."

I glanced at Python. Was it okay to tell them?

"We haven't slept together," Python said. "We're dating, but that's all. You know I don't plan to settle down and start a family. Lina will be moving on sooner or later, starting her new life. We're just spending time together until then."

So, we were going with the partial truth. I could live with that. As long as it got these two to back off. The last thing I wanted was for Python to be stuck with me. He'd be miserable, and so would I. Of course, I actually liked him, but I knew he didn't feel the same. I refused to use him to save myself. There had to be another way to keep away from my father.

"I think we're missing something," Lavender said. "The two of you are all anyone is talking about. We were all shocked to hear Python had an old lady, and now you're saying none of it is true? Why haven't you stopped the rumors?"

"The officers know," Python said. "Savior said he'd handle it."

"This is about more than the two of you, isn't it?" Wire asked. "It has something to do with Penny. Savior asked me to run all kinds of shit on her, then told me to make her disappear in a way that wouldn't seem suspicious. So I left a paper trail of her leaving town and heading north."

"What happened?" Lavender asked.

"Lina saved me," Python said. "Penny dosed my drink and followed me to the parking lot of the clubhouse. Think she planned to take advantage and possibly get knocked up."

"Jesus," Wire muttered. "And we aren't telling everyone because why?"

"Would you want to be seen as the weak little bitch who got drugged by a whore?" Python asked. "Because I sure the hell don't."

"I brought him home and watched over him. Nothing else happened," I said. "But Penny wouldn't leave him alone, so I told her he was mine. I didn't know what would happen. I only wanted her to back off and leave him alone. It was clear she'd hurt him in some way. At the time, I hadn't realized he'd been drugged. I thought he was drunk the way he was stumbling around."

Lavender smiled faintly. "You know, it's always the men around here saving the women. Nice to see the reverse happen."

"Are the two of you really dating?" Wire asked. "Or is that just part of the story you want everyone to believe?"

"We're faking it," I said. If he'd told them about Penny, there was no reason to hide the rest.

"Are you sure?" Lavender asked. "Can you both honestly say you're both good enough actors to fool everyone this well? Or could there be some feelings neither of you wants to admit you have?"

Python stood and glared at her. "Enough of this

bullshit. Stop trying to force everyone into relationships. It may have worked for you and Wire, and possibly for the others, but that doesn't mean it's the right thing to do. One of these days you're going to meddle in the wrong person's life, and it's going to come back to bite you in the ass."

Wire shoved his chair back and rose slowly to his feet. "I may be getting older, but I can still put you on your ass. Talk to Lavender like that again, I'll knock your fucking teeth down your throat, then I'll wipe out your entire existence. Do you understand?"

"Then stop fucking with people's lives. This isn't a game. People can get hurt, and you won't be the ones to deal with that pain." Python pointed to the kitchen doorway. "I want the two of you to leave. If you even think of hacking into the county records and marrying us, you'd better hit the pause button. I don't want a wife. Don't need one. And you sure the fuck won't be doing Galina any favors."

He was back to using my full name. Great. I wasn't sure if he was so opposed to getting married to anyone, or if it was me in particular. It seemed as if he hated the idea regardless of who his wife might be. It made me wonder why he felt so strongly about it. Wire and Lavender left, slamming the door behind them. Python drank another cup of coffee, and I stayed in my seat.

"Can I ask you something?" I asked.

"What?"

"Why do you hate the idea of being married? And I don't mean to me. It seems as if you abhor the thought entirely, regardless of who your bride would be."

He sighed and closed his eyes a moment. "You're not wrong, and I do have my reasons."

"Too personal?"

"I've been a Prospect for this club since I was twenty-one. I haven't shared much about my past with anyone, and for good reason." He took another swallow of his drink. "In high school, I accidentally got my best friend pregnant."

"Um... I'm assuming your best friend was a girl."

He smiled faintly. "Yeah. We decided to get drunk off our asses when we were sixteen. Ended up sleeping together. When she told me she was pregnant, I freaked the fuck out. At first."

"And then later?" I asked.

"I didn't mind the idea of having of a kid with her. Got permission to marry her. I wanted our baby to have my last name." The smile slipped from his face, and his eyes darkened with the deepest sorrow I'd ever seen. "She died during delivery. Both of them."

"Wire and Lavender never discovered your previous marriage?" I asked. "If they're hackers, wouldn't they have run across something like that?"

He shrugged a shoulder. "Might have... if I still went by that name."

"Whoa. What's that supposed to mean?"

"All records pertaining to Dylan Harmon are fake. Really good ones, thanks to the government. I had to go into Witness Protection when I was seventeen."

"Why?" I asked.

"Jenny's father lost it when his daughter died. Tried to kill me. Since Jenny's mom talked him into allowing the marriage, he shot her. I think he planned to end all our lives that day, but I managed to escape. Unfortunately, so did he."

"So there's someone out there who wants you

dead?"

"Not anymore. Got a call from an agent when I was twenty. They found his body in the river. If it had just been him, then things would have most likely gone back to normal. Except Jenny's dad wasn't exactly law-abiding."

"Did you know that beforehand?" I asked.

"No. Neither did Jenny, or her mom. Found out when they arrested him that he was part of a gang. They weren't just local but had a nationwide reach... except for in a few states. Alabama being one of them."

I leaned closer. "So who were you before?"

"Dyson Hinley. Dylan Harmon was close enough to my real name to make it easy for me to answer to it."

At least I now understood why he didn't want to get married. He'd already taken that path before and it had destroyed his life. I didn't blame him for wanting to avoid marriage in the future.

"Why didn't you tell anyone?" I asked. "If they knew, I'm sure they wouldn't have pushed so hard."

He shook his head. "You don't know those two. They'll decide I just need to give someone a chance to heal my broken heart. I loved Jenny, but I wasn't *in* love with her, if you know what I mean. The fact she died haunts me. I feel responsible. It doesn't seem right for me to get the opportunity to have a family when she can't."

I didn't know Jenny, and I barely knew Python. Just the same, I didn't think she'd want him to suffer the rest of his life. What happened was a tragic accident. It wasn't as if he'd gotten her pregnant on purpose, and neither of them could have known she'd die while giving birth. I hated that he felt like he shouldn't be happy because of what happened.

The fact Lavender even mentioned us getting

married must have been painful. He'd tried to do the right thing before and it hadn't ended well. My heart hurt for him. I wished I could make them understand, but I wouldn't break his trust in me. If he'd wanted them to know, he'd have told them.

"Are you sure you want me here?" I asked. "It's not too late for me to go back."

"I'm sure. I think not knowing you're safe would drive me crazy. You really did save me from Penny. It's only right for me to return the favor."

Now it was payback and nothing more. Every word from his lips felt like a blow to my heart. It was too soon to say I loved him, but I did feel something for Python. He'd fascinated me since the first time I saw him. The feelings only got stronger the longer I remained here. If I didn't move on soon, it might be too late. Then Python wouldn't be the only broken one.

I stood and shoved my hands into my pockets. "I should unpack my things."

"Put them in my room," he said. "You can use the bed. I'll sleep on the couch."

"I'm not kicking you out of your room." I hesitated a moment. What I was about to say would only end up hurting me more. And yet... "We can share the bed, like last night. You're not attracted to me, so there's no reason we can't sleep beside one another. Besides, it would make the entire dating thing more believable."

"Fine." He cleared his throat. "But for the record, I never said I didn't think you were pretty. If I weren't unavailable, things might be different."

"Right. But they aren't because you'll always be Jenny's. She has a hold on you no one will ever be able to break. It's fine, Python. A week or two and maybe Savior will have things in place for my new life."

Then I'd leave and never look back. It was the only way.

Chapter Five

Python

Idiot. Stupid fucking moron.

I knew I'd hurt her. I'd seen it clearly stamped on her face. Would it have been better if I'd never said anything about Jenny? At the time, she'd seemed to genuinely want to hear what I had to say, and I'd thought maybe it would clear things up between us. Instead, I only ended up causing her more pain. This was yet another reason I never needed to get married. I didn't know how to communicate with women. The club whores were easy since they were only a place to stick your dick and get off. It wasn't like I needed to maintain a relationship with them.

The only reason I'd flirted with Ares about a year ago was because I knew she was too young for things to get serious. She'd wanted someone to make her feel like a woman. I hadn't seen the harm in it. I'd have dated her when she got older, as long as she understood it wasn't going to be a forever kind of deal. Savior had put me on the spot about it, and I'd said I'd take responsibility for my actions, but I knew it would only have made the both of us miserable. Ares deserved better. Truthfully, when Prophet stepped in and made sure we all knew he wanted Ares, I'd been relieved.

I'd done my best to project my happiness at being single. No one needed to know the reason why I didn't want a woman living in my house. Although, now I had Galina here. It wasn't the same, though. With her, things were different. I knew she needed me, and for some reason, I wanted to protect her. Every time I saw her, I felt the urge to be her shield. I'd felt that way about Jenny and look how it turned out. The best thing I could do for Galina was keep her safe while she was here, then send her on her way.

If only Penny hadn't pulled that bullshit at the clubhouse... We were only in this mess because of her. No matter how many times we stressed the fact they were only here for a good time and we weren't going to claim them, someone always caused problems. They always wanted more than what we were willing to give. I'd heard the Hades Abyss in Mississippi tossed their club whores. None were allowed at the compound anymore. I had to wonder if they weren't on to something.

There were days I didn't even want to see a woman. Caused too much trouble. Of course, I didn't think that applied to Galina. From what little I knew of her, she was sweet. Others would have taken advantage of the situation. Instead, she'd fought to keep things fair. Even though she liked me, she hadn't jumped at the chance to be mine. It would have been easy enough to tell Wire to go ahead and marry us. Instead, she'd tried to understand why I didn't want a family.

Now we were going to share the bed. Probably not the best idea. I had a feeling this wasn't going to go according to plan. Then again, nothing ever did. If I'd thought my world was fucked up and twisted, it was even more so for Galina. The Bratva didn't give a shit about their women. Not usually. Galina would be used by her father to further his career, and abused by her husband simply because he could. Animals were treated better. I'd do whatever it took to keep her from going back there.

Which was how I found myself in this

predicament. I refused to let Wire and Lavender play God and marry the two of us. It wouldn't end well. Didn't mean I wouldn't find another way to keep Galina safe. I had no idea how she'd held onto her sweetness and innocence in that brutal world. The fact she'd come out unscathed was a miracle.

Even though I knew Wire was pissed at me, I picked up the phone and called him.

"What the fuck do you want?" he asked, not even bothering to say a simple *hello*.

"I need to know the plan for getting Lina out of here. She was never meant to linger this long at the compound. Savior only dragged his feet because he knew Viking liked her, but she doesn't return those feelings. If her father has any idea she's here, then she's in danger."

"You think I'm not aware? It's why Lavender wanted the two of you to get married. As of right now, if they come for her, we're going to be protecting a stranger. At least in their eyes. She's not related to anyone here, not dating one of us, and not an old lady or wife. If she's married to someone here, then she's Dixie Reapers' property. Those men might think twice about trying to snatch her."

I snorted. "Have you lost your fucking mind? Do you really think they'll give a shit? No. They'll come here and try to take what they want, which in this case is Lina. Those men won't care if she's married or not. The only thing it would accomplish is pissing them off even more. Haven't you learned anything from dealing with the Bratva in the past?"

I heard the rustle of papers, the low murmur of Lavender's voice, and then it went silent. I knew I'd made them mad earlier, but someone needed to call them on their shit. Not all marriages ended in happily ever after. It didn't seem realistic to expect a fairy tale to happen every time they paired people up. Had it worked so far? Sure. Even I could admit their success rate was rather shocking. It was like they had the magic touch.

"We haven't been wrong so far," Wire said. "Lavender wants to talk to you."

Great. If I made her cry or upset her again, Wire really would come over here and kick my ass. Or worse, empty my bank account.

"I understand now," she said softly. "Why didn't you tell anyone?"

Fuck. Me. "You went digging, didn't you? Couldn't just leave things alone."

"Pretending the past didn't happen doesn't make it go away, Python. You could have told us. Do you think the club would have cared? Even if you had your reservations while you were a Prospect, you've been a patched member for six months. You didn't think any of us deserved to know the truth?" she asked.

"You going to tell everyone?"

"It's not my story. It's yours. Does Galina know why you're keeping her at a distance?" she asked.

"Yeah. I told Galina. She knows who I really am, and why I don't want a family. It seemed like the right thing to do. I know she likes me, but I'm no good for her or any other woman."

"Python…" Her voice sounded husky. Christ. Was she about to cry? "Do you think Jenny would want you to be miserable all these years later? She wouldn't have wanted her death to ruin your life."

"Too fucking late, and don't you dare say her name ever again."

"Am I allowed to say your son's name? If he'd lived, would it have given you the strength to move on? Think of your boy, Python. Sweet little Rhett."

Hearing that name nearly gutted me. It had been Jenny's choice. She'd always loved *Gone with the Wind*. Scarlett and Rhett were her two favorite characters of all time. I'd always thought Rhett was kind of an asshole, but she'd thought he was romantic. When we'd found out we were having a boy, I'd let her choose the name.

"Shut up, Lavender." I gripped the phone so tight I thought I might break it. "He's dead. They're both dead, and neither are ever coming back. Do you understand?"

It was quiet. When the line disconnected, I wondered if I'd pushed too hard. Was Wire on his way over? Or worse, would the two of them go blabbing to the club officers? I may have been patched in, but they'd done it based on lies. None of them knew who I truly was. Well, Lavender did now, and I assumed she'd tell Wire if she hadn't already.

I heard a knock at the door and knew it had to be one or both of them. I opened it, bracing myself for a fist to my face. Instead, they both appeared to be anxious as fuck.

"Guess you can come in," I said.

"We need to tell you something." Lavender handed me some papers. "Jenny may have died giving birth... but your son is alive, Python."

It felt like the ground fell away and I staggered, falling into the wall. "What? What the fuck are you saying right now?"

"Your father-in-law had connections. They bribed the hospital. Made it seem like Rhett died. He didn't." She tapped on another piece of paper. His birth certificate. Not the one they'd given for a stillborn baby, but one showing he'd been alive. Still was according to Lavender. "Rhett Hinley is alive and in foster care. He lives two towns over and is now eleven years old. Best we can figure, he wanted you to suffer before he ended your life. I don't think he'd have killed you right off."

"The way things played out, and how quickly, I think he had a contingency plan in place," Wire said. "A way to fuck with you if things went south. Of course, we can't say for sure. It's also possible they'd planned to get both Jenny and Rhett away from you, until she'd died. Without asking someone involved, all we can do is speculate."

My son hadn't died? I couldn't wrap my brain around it. All this time, why hadn't anyone said anything? Wouldn't the government officials have known? When they put me in Witness Protection and gave me a new name, wouldn't they have checked the hospital for Jenny and Rhett's bodies? I hadn't even been able to attend the funerals. Now I knew there'd only been one.

"We can get him for you," Wire said. "Bring him here. Change his last name to match yours. Maybe if you try to explain things…"

I'd missed eleven years of my child's life. He had to hate me. I knew if I were in his shoes, I wouldn't want anything to do with my dad. Unless someone told him he'd been stolen from me, which was doubtful, he had to think he'd been abandoned. Hell, I'd probably want to kill the bastard calling himself my dad if I were in Rhett's shoes. Lavender handed me another page. This one a photo. Jesus. He had my features and Jenny's coloring. A perfect mini version of the two of us.

"I admit I shouldn't have pushed so hard to marry you off to Galina," Lavender said. "I can't fix what I said or tried to do, but I *can* do this. Let me bring your son home."

"I don't know anything about raising a child," I said.

"I do. At least a little." I turned to find Lina standing a few feet behind me. Tears filled her eyes and spilled down her cheeks. So she'd heard everything it seemed. "Let me help. I'm not asking to marry you or stay here forever. You offered me your home as a place to stay while I hid from my father. The least I can do is help with your son."

"Fine." I stared at Lavender and Wire. "Bring Rhett here. He may hate me, but it doesn't change the fact he's mine and I love him. Never even got to see him except on an ultrasound, but he's part of Jenny and I can't let our kid be raised in the system."

"I checked and he hasn't been harmed," Lavender said. "He's been with an older couple the last two years, and before that he bounced around a bit. Couldn't find anything about bruising, missing school, or any other red flags."

"Just get him here. I'll prepare a room for him." I paused. "Any way to find out what size clothes and shoes he wears or what types of things he likes?"

"I'll text everything to you within the hour," Lavender said.

"And I'll head over to Savior's and tell him what we've found. I know you should be the one to explain your situation, and I also know you aren't up for it right now. Can't promise he'll give you space." Wire put his arm around Lavender. "You need anything, let us know."

Galina placed her hand in the middle of my back. I shut the door behind Wire and Lavender, then turned to face her. "You sure about this?"

She nodded. "Should we start with clearing the room he'll use?"

I took her hand and led her to the spare bedroom with the least amount of crap in it. I'd never thought I'd need either bedroom for anything, so I'd mostly been using them as storage. It wouldn't take much to move everything to one room or the other. I really needed to dig through all the shit and toss out things I didn't need.

The house had a split plan, so the master bedroom was in a different hall from the other two. It would allow Rhett a sense of privacy while he adjusted to his new home, and later when he became a teenager he'd appreciate the space. Galina helped me move everything to the back bedroom after we decided to give Rhett the one closest to the living room. The walls were plain beige, and I hadn't bought curtains. Then again, I didn't have any in the entire house.

"Where can we get a twin bed and dresser?" Galina asked.

"There's a discount furniture store down the highway. They usually have stuff in stock, and even put entire sets on clearance. It's where I got the stuff in the living room. It matches because the store sells it that way."

"Then should we start there? Or do you want to paint the room?" she asked.

Fuck. This was more difficult than I'd thought. My phone rang and I saw Savior's name. Looked like Wire had literally gone straight there and spilled everything. I'd thought maybe I'd have a little more time.

"Hello," I said when the call connected.

"You and I need to have a chat at some point, but I'm guessing now isn't the time," Savior said. "What do you need from the club?"

It felt like a weight had been lifted off me. "Lina mentioned painting Rhett's room, and we'll need furniture. After that, we'll have to fill in everything else. Bedding, clothes, shoes, toys or whatever he's into."

"I understand your aversion to getting married, but I need you to think about something. Galina needs protection, which marriage to someone in this club could offer her. Your boy will also need a mother. I'm not saying rush into anything. I'm only suggesting you keep an open mind," Savior said.

"Fine. I'll try," I said. "If it was for Rhett, I could do most anything. We'd just have to set some ground rules. Plenty of people get married without being in love."

"I'll send Sam over to paint the room. Sticks and Slayer will follow you to the furniture store in one of the club trucks. They'll haul back whatever you buy and get it put together, that way you and Galina can focus on the other things. But you can't shop while riding your bike."

"Her car is at an impound," I said.

"I'm aware. Borrow Emmie's SUV for today. We'll work on getting another vehicle for you. I'll call Tank when we hang up, so he'll know to expect you," Savior said.

"Thanks, Pres."

I ended the call and eyed Galina. While I might not understand why she wanted to help me, I was grateful just the same. I knew I couldn't do this on my own. I told her what Savior said, and we decided to walk over to Tank's house. He was standing out front waiting for us when we arrived.

"Use it for as long as you need to," he said,

handing me the keys. "With the girls all grown up and driving their own cars, might be time to downsize a bit. Can't have anything too small or I won't fit, but we don't' really need a third row anymore."

"Anything wrong with it?" I asked, nodding my head toward the SUV.

"Nope. In fact, just put new tires and brakes on it about a month ago. Why? You want it?"

"Let me know how much. I may just buy it from you. Saves me from having to shop for something. Might tell Savior, though. He mentioned something about finding another vehicle for me now that I'll have Rhett."

"It's a bit big for only you and one kid," Tank said. "Eats a shit ton of gas too. Drive it for today and then make a decision. I really don't think you'll want it. There's about a half tank of gas."

"I'll return it on a half, unless I decide to keep it," I said.

He smirked. "Sure. Why don't you try filling it up? That alone will make you give it back."

Jesus. How much gas could the damn thing take? I helped Galina into the huge vehicle and we drove over to the furniture store. They had quite a few options for twin bedroom sets. Since Galina was willing to help with Rhett, I also asked for her input when picking out items for him. We chose a walnut set with a nightstand and dresser. After I paid, I made sure they would allow Slayer and Sticks to load it up and haul it to my house, then left with Galina.

Lavender had already texted a list of things Rhett liked, as well as his sizes. Being in the foster system, I doubted he'd had many nice things. There was a chance he'd never even had the chance to wear anything brand new that was only his. I knew a lot of those families couldn't afford much. While there were people who did it for the money, others simply wanted to offer their homes to children who had nowhere else to go.

We spent the next several hours picking out everything Rhett would need, as well as things we'd thought he'd want. By the time we'd loaded the SUV and stopped for gas, I understood why Tank had said I wouldn't want it. I couldn't remember ever spending over one hundred dollars to fill a car with gas. Fucking ridiculous!

I only hoped I was doing the right thing for Rhett. I hadn't stopped to consider he might be happy where he was. What if this blew up in my face?

Chapter Six

Lina

As the night settled over us, I found myself lying in bed next to Python. The tension in the air was palpable, our proximity a constant reminder of our complicated situation. I tried to steal glances at him, searching for any sign he might be feeling the same pull between us that I felt. But he remained stoic, his gaze fixed on the ceiling.

Yeah. Nothing had changed. Even though we'd had a great day getting things for Rhett, I was still nothing more than an unwanted guest in his home. Finding out he had a son, when he'd thought he'd lost both Jenny and Rhett, couldn't be easy. I wished he'd share his thoughts and feelings with me.

I couldn't help but wonder what it would take to break down the walls he had built around himself. Every time I took a step forward, Python seemed to take two steps back. It hurt to know that he saw me as an obligation rather than someone he genuinely desired. But I wasn't ready to give up just yet. He'd need me now that his son was coming to live with him.

"You know," I said softly, breaking the heavy silence, "I understand why you feel the way you do about relationships. But not all love stories end in tragedy."

He turned his head slightly to look at me, his eyes searching mine. "Never said they do. Plenty of happy couples around here."

"But you don't think that will ever be you?" I asked.

He shook his head. "No. Things are going to be

different anyway. I'll have my hands full with Rhett. I imagine he'll be angry. No telling what he was told all this time. That I didn't want him. Left him and his mom. I don't know what I'll be facing when he comes here."

"You don't think he'll see the time and effort you put into his room and realize how much you want him in your life?" I asked.

"Lina, I had no idea he hadn't died with Jenny. They lied to me. If they gave me a falsified certificate of stillbirth, then it wouldn't be unreasonable to assume they lied to Rhett too. He had to have asked about his parents."

I leaned up on my elbow and looked down at him. "Did Lavender say when he went into foster care? If he's been in there from the beginning, it's possible no one has told him anything."

He ran a hand over his face. "You're right. I'm only speculating until I actually meet my son in person."

"What are you going to tell him about us? He's bound to wonder who I am to you and why we're sharing a room. It might have been better to clear out both the spare bedrooms so I could use the other one." I wondered if he'd thought that far. An eleven-year-old wouldn't hesitate to speak his mind. At least, the boys I'd known were like that. Then again, they'd been raised in the Bratva. Perhaps Rhett had a gentler upbringing.

"I don't even know when he's coming here," Python said. "Lavender and Wire were going to get everything in order. It could take a day, several, or even a week or more. The waiting is going to drive me crazy. He's so close yet so far away."

"You've gone eleven years thinking he'd died,

Python. A little more time won't make much difference," I said.

"You're right." He sighed. "We should get some sleep. In the morning, I'll place a grocery order for pick up and ask one of the Prospects to bring it to us. I want to make sure the kitchen is well-stocked, so we're ready whenever Rhett arrives."

I reached over and took his hand. Python tensed, and I worried he might pull away. After a moment, he relaxed and held my gaze.

"You're not alone. I'm here to help however I can, and you have the club. I can tell they'd do anything for you. There's no reason to be nervous, Python. You have far more help than you realize." I licked my lips. "These people are your family. Do you have any idea how lucky you are to have their support?"

"Right. I *am* lucky. I only wish you'd had people you could rely on. If you had, then maybe you wouldn't be in this situation right now. What confuses me is why the Vor sent you here. Couldn't he have just stopped your father? There had to be a reason he got you out of there instead."

I'd wondered the same thing. The Bratva might not be law-abiding, but they did obey their own rules. If my father hadn't done anything wrong in their eyes, then the Vor's hands would have been tied. It wasn't unheard of for a father to use his daughter to further his career. The fact Dima only had rumors about him and no hard evidence he'd killed those women complicated things. For the Vor to step in, he'd have needed proof of wrongdoing. Without it, it wouldn't have taken long for people to turn on him.

"I don't know all the facts. I can only assume my father didn't break any of the Bratva's rules, so the Vor couldn't officially do anything. Instead, he managed to sneak me out and sent me to the Dixie Reapers. It was probably the best he could do at the time."

"Is there a reason you never tried to escape?" he asked.

"I knew without the proper resources, my father would easily catch me. Running would only have resulted in a harsh punishment, or he may have even beaten me to death. Kind of defeats the purpose of getting away. When the Vor gave me a chance to escape, I took it. He promised there would be people to help me start over. Of course, I didn't realize I'd be here for so long."

"Wasn't the plan," he said. "Until Viking took notice of you. Sorry about that. Then Penny had to go and fuck with my life. You happened to find me at the wrong time. Maybe you should have kept walking."

I tightened my hold on his hand. "If I had, then Penny would have taken advantage of you and things would be even more screwed up. Besides, if you hadn't refused to let Lavender marry us, you might have never known about Rhett. She wouldn't have had a reason to dig into your past."

Honestly, I didn't want to think of what might have happened if I hadn't been in the right place at the right time. Despite what he'd said, I thought it was a blessing I'd found him when I did. If he thought Penny had been trying to get pregnant on purpose, it wouldn't have ended well for any of them. She didn't seem like the motherly type, and I knew Python would have resented her. No child should have to live in a home with two parents who hated each other.

I felt a bit nervous over meeting Rhett for the first time. He might not want me here. Even if he hadn't met his mother, what if he felt like I was trying to take her place? All I wanted was to help him settle in and assist Python in any way I could. Others might not see it the same, though. I'd claimed him in front of Penny, and the rumors around the club has us together as a couple. Only the officers, Wire, and Lavender knew the truth. Something told me this was going to be even more complicated after Rhett joined us.

"What are you going to tell your club?" I asked. "Us dating without a commitment was one thing when it was only us involved, but now your son will be here. Won't they try pushing for us to make things official?"

"They might, but since Savior knows the score, he'll hold them off. At least, I'm counting on him to do that."

I hoped he was right. I released his hand and put some space between us. He didn't even acknowledge that I'd moved away. I didn't know how this was going to work. It would probably be best if I left the Dixie Reapers sooner rather than later. I'd lend a hand with Rhett for as long as I could, but I needed to speak to Savior about lining up my next home and my new identity as quickly as possible. If for no other reason that the longer I remained here, the harder I'd end up falling for Python. I already found him fascinating and wanted to know everything about him. How much worse would it be in a few weeks or months?

His breathing evened out and I was thankful he'd fallen asleep. I watched him in the darkness. If Jenny had lived, would they have had a happy marriage? Would they still be together all these years later? There was no way of knowing. He'd said he hadn't been in love with her. There was a chance they either would have grown closer together or fallen for other people. I hated that he'd experienced such heartbreak. Not once had he mentioned his family.

What had they thought of all this?

"Are there parts of you that are still Dyson, or are you only Python now?" I whispered. "I'd say I wished I'd met you before your world fell apart, but I was only a child then. If you were seventeen when Rhett was born, and he's eleven now, then you're twenty-eight. There's nearly a decade between us."

It didn't matter to me. I might be nineteen, and maybe there was a lot I didn't know, but there was one thing I was certain about. I'd never meet another man like Python. Even though he'd been deeply wounded, he still put one foot in front of the other and faced each new day. In his place, I might have given up when Jenny died. What would I do if Python were to die tomorrow? It was a morbid thought, and I could acknowledge it as such, but it did make me wonder. Was I only staying here because he'd told me to? Or was I secretly hoping for something more?

"I wish you'd see me," I whispered. "No one ever has. I've only been a tool to be used. One day, I want someone to look at me and want me. Not because I can advance their career or because our children will have the right bloodline. Is it wrong to want something just for myself?"

"No, it's not," he said. I jolted, not having realized he was actually awake. He rolled to his side to face me. "You can do better than me, Lina. I'm so fucked up it's not even funny. Doesn't mean I don't see you, though. I do. Don't ever feel invisible."

"I know you don't really want me here, Python. I appreciate the fact you want to keep me safe, and that you weren't going to make me sleep on the couch, but how far are you going to take this? I wasn't kidding when I said Rhett would be confused. I'm an adult and even I can't make sense of all this."

"Maybe sometimes there are things that don't *have* to make sense, Lina. I never wanted a woman in my house, not after Jenny. Having you here isn't as awful as I thought it would be. In fact, when I woke up with you next to me the first time, I didn't exactly hate it."

"What are you trying to say?" I asked.

"Not sure. Just… can we take things one day at a time? I'm not looking for a wife or a family, but now my son is coming home, a boy I thought had died before he'd even been born. Having Rhett in my life is going to change everything I thought I knew or how I felt."

"Are you saying all that because you think he needs a mom?" I asked.

"Not exactly. I mean, you're not wrong. He could use a woman's influence. I don't know what he's been through or how he's been raised all these years. He might very well walk through the door and hate both of us right off. I guess what I'm trying to say is that I'm not ready to be alone with him. I need someone to hold my hand, like you were earlier."

"How much did it cost you to admit that?" I asked, smiling a little.

"More than you could ever know," he mumbled. "But hey, I already told the officers about Penny and how she nearly trapped me. What could be worse than that?"

"It doesn't make you weak, Python. She took advantage."

"I know. Logically, I get it. At the same time, I guess I was always taught men need to be tough. Invincible. Being vulnerable makes you a weak-ass little bitch."

"You don't talk about your family. What were

they doing while you dealt with Jenny and the pregnancy?" I asked.

"I got emancipated when I was sixteen. My dad was an alcoholic and my mom was never around. I pretty much raised myself anyway." He reached out to tuck my hair behind my ear. "Taking on a wife and kid wasn't as big a deal as it would have been to someone who relied on their family."

"Has anyone ever told you how amazing you are?" I asked.

"Can't say they have."

"Then everyone is blind. The moment you heard Rhett was alive, you made a place for him at the house. You spent the day getting things he'd like so he'd feel welcome, and you've lain awake in bed worrying about what he'll think of you. You may not have met your son yet, Python, but you're already a great dad."

He flicked my nose. "Call me Dylan. But only when the club isn't around."

My cheeks warmed. I knew what it meant to have permission to use his real name. I felt like we'd just taken a step in the right direction. Maybe my worries about where I'd go or how long I'd be here were all for nothing. Was there a chance he might open up to me? I'd learned so much about him in the last twenty-four hours. More than he'd apparently shared with his club. I felt... special.

"Have you ever dated before?" he asked.

"No. Even though we're fake dating, you're still my first boyfriend. My dad kept me home. Since I was a chess piece for him to move around the board, he didn't want me being with the wrong sort of people or falling in love and messing up his plans."

"Tomorrow we'll go out for breakfast. There's a café near the main strip I've heard is really good. Some of the ladies here like to eat there." He laced our fingers together. "I guess we both need to get on the same page. Create a united front. Us against everyone else."

"Why does it sound like we're going to war?" I asked.

"We kind of are. War against your family, my meddlesome club, and whatever else comes our way."

I wasn't sure what to make of his sudden change, but I was going to embrace it. Mostly because he was saying everything I wanted to hear. I'd trust him, and if it backfired, then I'd end up with a broken heart. It was a risk I'd have to take. It seemed like everyone in his life had either turned their backs on him, or not bothered getting to know the real Python. I didn't want to be like everyone else.

Because for me... he mattered.

Chapter Seven
Python

I couldn't remember a time I'd ever stayed up all night talking to a woman, especially in bed. Lina set me at ease, and I could tell she actually listened to me. Most women told me what I wanted to hear, or what they *thought* I wanted to hear. They either only cared about what was in my wallet or in my pants. The second one had never been an issue. I'd had fun with plenty of women since Jenny. At first, I'd felt guilty about it. Later, I'd realized I couldn't live the rest of my life like a monk. As for the ones who were interested in my bank account... Well, the only time I willingly gave up cash for someone was with Lina, or when we shopped for Rhett. I hadn't spent a dime on a woman other than her and didn't plan to start now.

The water heated and I stepped under the shower spray. I'd left her sleeping and decided to get ready before I woke her. I had to admit I was looking forward to eating breakfast with her. I bowed my head and let the water pound my neck and the back of my head. The past two days had been hell. One surprise after another. Although, discovering Rhett was still alive fell into the category of things I wanted to know. Being drugged by Penny was definitely not the highlight of my life. I wondered what Savior had done to her. If Wire had been asked to make it look like she'd willingly left, I had a feeling the bitch was dead. Wouldn't be the first time the club had bloodied their hands and wouldn't be the last.

I heard the door open and tensed, turning my head in that direction. Galina stumbled into the bathroom, her eyes not even all the way open. Hell, I wasn't sure they were open at all. She held her hands out, feeling her way over to the toilet. I bit my lip so I wouldn't laugh at the ridiculous situation I found myself in, and turned away from her, giving her as much privacy as I could. How the fuck had she not realized the shower was going?

The toilet flushed a moment later, and I gave her time to leave. Instead, I felt a cool breeze down my back. Turning, my eyes went wide when I realized she was getting in with me. Except... Shit. Was she doing all this in her damn sleep?

"Um, Lina?"

She staggered a little and shut the shower door behind her. With her hands outstretched, she came closer, and I backed as far to the wall as I could. The moment the water hit her skin, she stepped under the spray.

I could honestly say I'd never experienced anything like this before. What the hell was I supposed to do? Once she woke up enough to realize we were in the shower together, she'd most likely freak the fuck out. Couldn't blame her. I did my damnedest to keep my eyes on her face. Didn't mean I succeeded. The woman might be on the tiny side, but she had curves in all the right places. Her breasts were the perfect size to fill my hands, and my fingers itched to see if she felt as soft as she looked.

"Lina. Are you awake yet?" I asked.

She sighed and reached a hand toward me. I grabbed it, not sure what she wanted. The second she plastered herself to me, I knew I'd fucked up. My cock had already been semi-hard. Not anymore. It turned to steel and was more than ready for some action. *Fuck my life.*

"Best dream," she murmured, rubbing her cheek against my chest.

So she was still asleep, or mostly. And it seemed she thought she was dreaming she was showering with me. Was this something she'd dreamed of before? I knew she liked me, but I hadn't realized it went this far. I wasn't sure how I felt about it. Well, a certain part of me was liking it just fine. My brain, on the other hand, was telling me how wrong all this was.

"Lina. Honey, this isn't a dream," I said.

She tensed and her eyes slowly opened. I knew the moment she fully woke. Her cheeks turned scarlet. Her lips parted, and a dazed expression entered her eyes. Yep, she'd really thought she was dreaming. I didn't know what to make of it all. Had to say this was a first for me.

"Wh-what... where... Um." She had a deer in the headlights expression and seemed incapable of moving. As much as I wanted to put more space between us, I also didn't want to startle her. She could easily slip and fall in here.

"Think you came into the bathroom while you were still mostly asleep. Got in the shower with me. I tried to wake you up," I said. And technically, I had. Maybe not as well as I should have. Couldn't lie even to myself. I'd enjoyed this too much. No matter how much I wanted to keep my distance, it got harder and harder to do. All the reasons I'd told myself I'd remain single didn't seem quite so important anymore. For one, Rhett was actually alive. And Lina was right. Jenny wouldn't want me to be alone forever. It was mostly guilt driving me to keep my life the way it had always been. I didn't feel like I deserved to be happy.

She covered her face with her hands. "I can't believe I did this. I'm so sorry, Python. I know you don't want me like this. I'll, um… I should get out."

Jesus Christ. How blind could she be? Or did she equate sex with a forever kind of relationship? I tensed. Fucking hell. Was she a virgin?

"Lina, have you ever seen a naked man before?"

She gasped and, even hidden behind her hands, I could see her face turn even redder. "Of course not!"

"So you're a virgin?"

She peeked at me between her fingers. "Do I come across as someone who sleeps around? I told you I hadn't dated. Who was I going to do that with?"

"Dating and sex don't always go hand in hand," I said. "I didn't date any of the women at the clubhouse, but I've fucked them before."

I winced. Probably should have found a better way to make my point. All I'd done was paint myself in a bad light. Besides, now that I was a father, I'd need to clean up my act a bit. I'd have to set a good example for Rhett.

"I'm not those women," she muttered.

"I'm aware. I didn't mean anything by it, Lina. Guess I find it hard to believe someone as pretty as you hasn't ever been with a man before. Just so we're clear, I'm clean. Even though I've slept around, I've always gotten tested. It's been a while since I was last with anyone. It's not like I'm over at the clubhouse balls-deep in a club whore every night."

Shit. I really was an eloquent bastard, wasn't I? It was amazing she hadn't run from me already. What the hell was I thinking? Wouldn't it better if she did?

Her hands fell from her face. "You really think I'm pretty?"

That's what she got out everything I'd said? "I'd have to be blind not to notice. And I already told you once before. You didn't believe me?"

Her gaze skimmed over me and when she got to my cock, she gasped and covered her face again. *Too damn cute!* "Does that happen all the time?"

"You mean me being hard?" She nodded. "Well, morning wood is a thing, but I wasn't in quite this state until you pressed against me. Have to admit I find you rather tempting."

"Really?" She peeked at me again. "You're not just saying that?"

Before I could think better of it, I reached out and grabbed her hand, then placed it on my cock. "Does it feel like I'm bullshitting you?"

"I... I... Uh..." Her eyes nearly bugged out as she stared at me. "My hand is on your... your..."

"Cock," I said.

"Yes, that. Why is my hand here?"

I noticed she wasn't exactly pulling away. My dick throbbed, and no matter bad of an idea this was, I had to admit I was enjoying it. I loved the flustered look on her face, and the way she stammered. Hadn't been with anyone like her before. Even Jenny had been bolder.

"You can move anytime you want. Not stopping you." Probably should have chosen a different phrase. Instead of taking her hand away, she gripped me a little tighter and slid her hand down my shaft. My balls drew up and I fought back a groan. Fuck but that felt good. "Wasn't what I had in mind, Lina. You keep doing that and I'm going to come all over your hand."

Her gaze held mine, and hell if she didn't keep stroking me. I'd been wrong when I thought she wasn't bold. For a virgin, she was far more daring than I'd thought she'd be. I wondered where she saw this going. I braced a hand on the wall and watched the various emotions play across her face. The fact this turned her on was a given. I'd noticed the way she squeezed her thighs together.

"Have you ever made yourself come?" She shook her head. So, she didn't know what an orgasm felt like. Was it due to lack of curiosity? Considering our current predicament, I didn't think so. "Do you want to?"

"What do you mean? Touch myself like I'm doing to you?" she asked.

"No. We might be playing with fire a bit, but..." I pulled her hand from my cock and spun her around. Pressing my palm to her spine, I forced her to bend over a little. "Put your hands on the wall."

She did as I said without question. I nudged her feet apart, then slid my cock between her thighs. I rubbed against her pussy, the head of my dick brushing her clit with every thrust. It wasn't going to take much to get me off, and the way she was squirming told me she might already be close.

I braced one hand on her hip and palmed her breast with the other. Her nipple hardened and she pushed her hips back. Looked like little Lina was sensitive. It made me wish we could take things even further. I wanted to see her fall apart.

"Come for me, Lina. Give me your first orgasm."

Her fingers curled against the shower wall and I heard her breath hitch. She gave a soft cry as her body tensed and she threw her head back. I could feel the heat of her release and thrust faster. I didn't stop until I came, my cum splattering the wall and quite possibly Lina as well.

Once we caught our breath, I turned her to face me. I could see the remnants of what we'd done clinging to the curls between her legs. *Shit.* I had to hope none made it inside her. Although, a virgin pregnancy would be an interesting story around here. Probably a first.

"You okay?" I asked. She nodded and her cheeks turned pink again. "Maybe I shouldn't have done that. I took things too far."

"I liked it," she murmured. She shifted from foot to foot, and I angled the showerhead so I could wash her off. Or more accurately, get the rest of my cum off her. I ran my hand over her pussy to make sure I'd got it all, and she shivered, parting her legs a little more.

"Damn, Lina. You still want more?"

"Is that bad?" she asked. "I still feel all achy, and…"

"And what?"

"I liked how it felt. I want to do it again and again."

I could think of worse ways to spend a day than making a woman come for hours. Not the best idea for the two of us. Still… I worked my thigh between hers and rubbed it against her. She hesitantly jerked her hips. "That's it. Go ahead and ride me. Get yourself off."

"Is that something people do?" she asked.

"My sweet, innocent Lina. Stick around and I'll completely corrupt you. To answer your question, yes. I want to watch you get yourself off. Show me how pretty you are when you come."

It took her a few tries before she found the right rhythm. She'd no sooner come than she started moving again. By the third time, I knew I needed a different plan. Looked like Lina was the type to be addicted to sex. Couldn't blame her. Orgasms felt amazing.

"Is it time to stop?" she asked.

"Not exactly. I think you can keep going, but we're going to do things a little differently. You still want to come once we're out of the shower and back in the bedroom, then I'll show you other things we can do -- without taking your virginity."

She gave me a bashful smile. "I wouldn't mind losing it to someone like you, Python. I know it isn't what *you* want, though."

She wasn't wrong, and yet she was. After feeling her come on my cock, I had to admit I didn't like the idea of another man being intimate with her. I might not deserve her, but I also couldn't think of a single guy who did. What if she left here and got hurt by someone? As easily as she trusted me, she could end up falling for a complete asshole who'd take advantage, then dump her.

We made our way back to the bedroom, and I kept asking myself if I really wanted to go down this path. I had a feeling it would be a game changer for both of us. I had no idea how we'd come back from this. She wasn't the type to see it as nothing more than having fun. Hell, I wasn't sure even I saw it that way right now.

She lay back on the bed, staring at me with trusting eyes. I hoped like fuck I didn't end up breaking her heart. I didn't think I'd ever forgive myself.

"Are you sure?" I asked. "I know the orgasms felt really good, but you can get yourself off. Even if you haven't done it before, there's no reason you can't start now."

"Is it wrong that I want it to be with you?" she asked. "Maybe the reason it feels so good and I never want it to stop has more to do with you than the act itself."

It felt like she'd just driven another nail in my coffin. At this rate, I'd be hers before the end of the day. She looked beautiful. Her hair splayed across the pillows, and she'd crooked her knee slightly and had it leaning across her other leg. I knew she hadn't posed on purpose. She probably wouldn't have a clue how to act sexy. It just came naturally to her.

I ran my fingers up her leg, stopping at her knee. "What if this changes things between us?"

"I've already made it clear I like you, Dylan." Her cheeks flushed again. I liked the way her eyes brightened when she said my name. "Do you really think I'd be upset if you decided to give us a chance?"

Fuck. I knew I was on the road to my destruction, and yet I couldn't seem to stop myself. I joined her on the bed, and wondered if maybe she was a devil disguised as an angel... because I was gladly going to follow her, even if she took me straight to hell.

Chapter Eight

Lina

My heart hammered against my ribs, and I wondered if he could hear it. Never in a million years did I think we'd end up like this. I might have hoped we would, but he'd been so resistant I'd thought it would never happen. I didn't know if he had a magic touch, or if there was something wrong with me. This couldn't be normal, right? If women were this into sex, nothing would ever get done.

"What is it?" he asked, hovering over me.

"Is something wrong with me?"

"I'm not sure I follow."

I swallowed hard. This was difficult for me. I'd never discussed sex with anyone before, much less someone who was lying in bed with me -- naked. "You seemed surprised at how much I liked what we did in the shower. Am I... abnormal?"

He pressed his lips together, but I felt his body shaking in silent laughter. He pressed his forehead against my shoulder. I didn't understand what was so funny about my question, or this situation.

"Lina, any man with a woman as responsive as you would be thanking every god known." He lifted his head and stared down at me. "The fact you come so easily, and want to do it often, makes me feel like I won the lottery. I don't know any man who wouldn't love having a woman like you."

"You're going to confuse me," I said. "I know this isn't anything permanent and you didn't intend to ever be intimate with me. Then you go and say something like that..."

He rolled away from me, lying on his back. He flung an arm across his eyes and sighed. Great. There went my orgasms. Even worse, I may have just screwed up everything. Things would be awkward between us now.

His phone rang and Python got up to answer it. I only halfway paid attention to what he was saying, until I caught the name Rhett. Sitting up, I focused on him. Python ran a hand through his hair.

"You couldn't have given us a little more notice?" he asked. "Fine. Stall for about ten minutes if you can."

He ended the call and faced me. "Rhett is already here. Wire and Lavender will bring him here in the next ten minutes."

I got out of bed. "Then we should get ready."

We managed to get dressed with a few minutes to spare. I checked on Rhett's room, then double-checked the items in the kitchen. Python must have placed an order when I wasn't looking because a Prospect had delivered a bunch of stuff earlier. I didn't know what a little boy might like to eat or drink. Hopefully, we'd stocked the right things.

The bell rang and Python ran his hands over his clothes before opening the door. A miniature version of him walked inside, with Wire and Lavender right behind him. Even if I'd met this boy elsewhere, I'd have known he was related to Python. Rhett came farther into the house, looking around.

"Rhett, this is your dad," Wire said.

I gave Python a nudge and he dropped to one knee in front of his son. It put Rhett slightly taller than him, and the boy seemed to relax a little.

"I'm glad I finally get to meet you," Python said. "I only wish your mom could have been here too."

The little boy glanced at me. "She's not my mom?"

"I'm a friend of your dad's," I said.

"His girlfriend," Wire said. "You know what that is, right?"

Rhett rolled his eyes. "I'm not stupid. I'm eleven. Of course, I know what a girlfriend is."

I wasn't sure if we should be lying to Rhett. Python and I weren't really dating. How would the boy feel when it was time for me to leave? He'd already been uprooted several times. What would happen if he grew attached to me? It would be better if I kept my distance, and yet... how could I possibly do that when he looked just like Python?

"Do you live here too?" Rhett asked.

"Um, I do. If it makes you uncomfortable, I can move out."

Python stood. "No, she can't. This is Lina. Her father is a bad man and he's trying to find her. Think you can help me keep her safe?"

Rhett nodded. He looked at each adult in the room before focusing on his dad again. "What do I call everyone?"

"Um. Well, I'm your dad, but I know we've just met. You can call me Python like everyone else does, until you're more comfortable with me." Python looked at the rest of us. "Actually, you can just call everyone by their name."

It might have been subtle, but I caught the flicker in Rhett's eyes. I knew Python's words had come across as cold, even if he hadn't intended it that way. I reached out my hand to Rhett. "Would you like to see your room? Your dad wanted to make it perfect for you."

He grasped my hand, and I led him from the

room, shooting Python a quick glance. He needed to fix this, and I hoped he knew it. I let Rhett enter his new room ahead of me, and I waited in the doorway as he checked things out.

"You know, your dad means well," I said. "He's new to all this and he's going to struggle a bit. It doesn't mean he isn't happy you're here. You should have seen him when he found out you were still alive."

Ah, I had Rhett's attention now. "He really didn't know about me?"

"He really and truly didn't. Your mom died when you were born, and they told your dad you'd passed with her. Then some bad things happened. Your dad had a hard time. What I can say for sure is that he loves you, Rhett. You were always important to him, from the moment he found out your mom was pregnant."

He looked around the room again. "I've never had a home before. Everyone was nice to me in their own way. I know some kids are worse off than me. I guess when they told me I was going to live with my dad, I thought…"

"You were worried they were wrong and you'd end moving homes again and again?" I asked. He nodded. "That's not going to happen, Rhett. Your dad found out as much about you as he could to make sure this place was just right. He picked out everything here himself."

"Only him?" Rhett asked.

"Well, mostly him. I did help." I smiled at him. "Your dad picked the color and his club painted the room for you and brought the furniture here while we got everything else."

Rhett went to sit on his bed. I picked up the handheld game system Python bought for him, as well as the three games. Giving them to Rhett, I waited to see if there was anything else he needed to say or ask. He remained quiet, staring at the items in his hands.

"You good here for a bit? Did you have breakfast?" I asked.

He glanced up. "Like a meal we cook here?"

I nodded. "Exactly like that. Your dad and I haven't eaten yet, but if you're not up for breakfast food we can make something else. Today is your day, Rhett. You tell us what you'd like to do, and we'll do it."

He smiled a little. "Breakfast sounds good."

"All right. I'll call you when it's ready." I ruffled his hair and left the room. Wire and Lavender were still with Python.

"Everything okay?" Lavender asked. "He seemed tense on the way here."

"He's good. In fact, he's hungry. Thought we could make breakfast and eat together."

Lavender grinned and tugged on Wire's arm. "That's our cue. Time to head home to our own kids and leave these two with their boy."

I opened my mouth to correct her, but Python reached down to take my hand. The other two left and Python led me to the kitchen. He pulled eggs, milk, biscuits, and bacon from the fridge. I wasn't sure what sorts of things Rhett would like to eat, but I wanted today to be extra special.

"Should I make pancakes too?" I asked. "Or maybe mini waffles?"

"You just want an excuse to use the waffle maker you got yesterday," he said.

He wasn't entirely wrong. "Maybe. Doesn't mean Rhett wouldn't enjoy them too, though. I even got the waffle maker with the changeable plates with the different cartoon characters."

"Fine. Make the waffles while I handle the rest. I'm sure Rhett will love it."

I had to admit I liked making breakfast with him. Even though our morning had quickly unraveled, it felt like things might be back on track. At the very least, there wasn't the dreaded awkwardness between us. I really liked Rhett, and I wasn't looking forward to the day I'd have to leave this place. He seemed like a sweet kid.

By the time we'd finished making everything, and I'd set the table, I was anxious to see what Rhett thought about our breakfast. I went to get him and discovered him playing a video game while stretched out on his bed. He'd taken off his shoes and made himself at home.

"Ready to eat?" I asked.

He set the game system down and leaped off the bed. "Are we all eating together?"

"Of course. I've already set the table."

He grinned and followed me to the kitchen. He picked the place where he wanted to sit, then I filled a plate for him, giving him a waffle on the side. I placed the syrup in the middle of the table and checked to make sure he didn't need anything else. Once Python and I had made our plates, we joined him.

I nudged Python with my foot under the table, hoping he'd talk to his son. At the rate the two of them were going, Rhett might graduate from high school before they got to know one another.

"Do you enjoy school?" Python asked.

"I guess so. Do I have to change to a different one again?"

"How many times have you had to move to a new school?" Python asked.

"A few. I don't have many friends, so it's okay if I need to do it again. I don't mind." He twirled his fork in his hand. "That man, Wire, said there are other kids here. Are there any my age?"

"Tate and Theo are your age. There are quite a few who are a year or two older than you, and some who are younger." Python studied his son. "Theo is Sarge's son. He's similar to you in the fact his dad didn't know about him. Although, Sarge didn't even realize Theo's mother had been pregnant, so I guess you aren't quite the same."

"You said the other boy's name is Tate?" Rhett asked.

"Yes. He's Saint's son. Saint is the Vice President for this club. Tate's a good kid."

"Would you like to meet the two of them? I'm sure we could set something up for later today or tomorrow," I said. It would be good for him to get out of the house and see the compound, not to mention he really needed friends his age. It sounded like he hadn't had a support system all this time. I didn't want him to feel rushed, or overly stimulated, but I also worried he'd feel like he had more freedom if he saw more of his new home than the literal house he'd be staying in.

"Can I?" Rhett asked.

Python nodded. "Sure. There's a playground here at the compound. I can ask their parents to meet us there. Want to go after lunch today?"

"Yeah!" Rhett grinned and dug into his food. It was nice to see him so happy.

"Do you like your room? Anything else you need?" Python asked.

"I haven't checked everything out yet, but I like the games you got me," Rhett said.

"We weren't sure what types of books you might

like," I said. "If you want to make a list of your favorites, or ones you'd like to read, we can get them for you."

"But I don't have a bookshelf," he said.

"Easy enough to fix. If you enjoy reading, I'll get a bookshelf and you can get as many books as you want." Python hesitantly reached over and placed his hand on Rhett's head for a brief moment. "I want you to be happy here, Rhett. If I'd known about you sooner, you'd have been here from the beginning. You were always wanted by both me and your mom."

I might have been wrong, but I thought Rhett was taking things a little too well. He'd been uprooted multiple times, and then discovered his father had been alive all this time, and actually wanted him. I couldn't imagine how he felt, or what he was thinking. I'd keep an eye on him today and speak with Python when I had a chance. If Rhett had been moved around so much, he might be used to putting on a happy face and pretending everything was fine, even if it wasn't. We needed to make sure he knew he was safe here, and that this was his home forever.

After we finished eating, I stood and shooed them from the room. "The two of you should go watch a movie together, or play ball or something. Go do whatever boys do while I get the dishes cleared."

"I don't mind helping," Python said.

I shook my head. "Go! You need this time with your son. It will be good for the both of you. When I'm done in here, I'm going to go soak in the tub, so take your time."

Python looked slightly panicked at the idea of being alone with Rhett, but I knew he'd figure things out. The thought he'd put into everything he'd bought for Rhett said plenty. He loved the boy. I also knew actions spoke louder than words, and while the room showed he'd prepared for Rhett to move here, spending time with him today would be the best way to prove Python wanted him.

"Go on. I've got this," I said. "Isn't there a football in Rhett's room? Maybe the two of you can toss the ball, or whatever you want to call it."

"I've never played with a football before," Rhett said.

"Want to learn how to throw one?" Python asked.

"Yeah! Sounds fun." Rhett ran off. Python lingered a moment.

"The two of you need to bond," I said. "You're his father and I know you love him. Now it's time to show him. Some quality time will go a long way in building a relationship with him."

"Fine. Just don't overdo it, all right? All this stuff can wait."

"I don't think dishes will exhaust me."

He left and a minute or two later, I heard the front door open and shut. I cleared the table, rinsed the dishes, and loaded the dishwasher. It took a little extra time to clean the waffle iron before I could put it away. Once I'd wiped down the table and counters, I went to run the water for my bath.

I'd soak until the water was too cold, and then I'd check on Python and Rhett. If it seemed like they needed more time alone, then I'd hide in the bedroom for a bit. I wouldn't say no to a nap. After all the orgasms he'd given me this morning, I felt more tired than usual. I wondered if that was normal, but I wasn't about to ask him. I still felt mortified over my earlier question, the one that nearly ruined everything.

For now, Python thought he needed me. When

the day came for me to leave, I didn't want to have any regrets. I would do my best to pretend this morning didn't happen. I'd keep to my side of the bed, and...

You're a dummy. You're already falling for him.

Actually, I was pretty sure within a week I'd love both of them. Rhett was an adorable little boy, who looked just like his daddy. How could I not adore him?

I was in so much trouble.

Chapter Nine

Python

I knew Galina had given me space with Rhett so we could bond. I got it. Didn't mean I liked it. It felt wrong to exclude her. She'd helped prepare for his arrival just as much as I had. I might have paid for everything, but she'd picked things out or given her input when I couldn't decide on something. It looked like Rhett had taken to her already as well.

After being intimate with her, the lines between fake and real were starting to blur. I hadn't planned on settling down. Of course, I also hadn't realized Rhett was still alive. Having my son back in my life changed things. I didn't want Galina to feel like I only wanted her here because of Rhett. At the same time, I could tell she'd be good for him. He needed stability and a mother figure.

If the two continued to grow close to one another, would it be fair to send her away? She'd been planning to move on all this time.

Deep down, I knew Galina deserved better than the life I could offer her. Secrecy, danger, the possibility I wouldn't come home. Not to mention I wasn't sure I was capable of loving her. It had always been the plan for her to start a new life somewhere, but now, with Rhett in the picture, everything was more complicated.

Galina watched Rhett with a tenderness in her eyes. At breakfast, I'd noticed she had a way with him, a natural instinct that made it clear she was meant to be a mother. It tore at my heart to think of taking that away from both of them. At the same time, I wasn't sure I was ready for a family. Although, having Rhett changed everything. The life I'd planned had been turned upside down. I didn't regret it. Finding out he was alive was the best thing to ever happen to me.

As the days passed, I knew the bond between Rhett and Lina would only grow stronger. And if I managed to convince her things were fine between us, I knew we'd have more mornings like this one. I'd enjoyed that closeness with her. Knowing I was the first man to bring her pleasure had been more satisfying than I'd thought it would be. I also wanted more. Watching her as she came had turned me on more than porn or any other woman ever had.

Even now, I found myself craving her touch, and seeing that vulnerable side of her. If we were alone, I'd have been tempted to drag her to the bedroom and pick up where we'd left off. Until the moment she'd said if we kept going she'd grow even more attached to me, I'd felt better than I had in a long time. Almost as if I were whole and no longer missing part of myself.

I knew I had to make a decision, and it wasn't going to be an easy one. On one hand, I wanted to protect Galina from the dangerous world I lived in. She'd run from the Bratva and had every right to live a normal, happy life. While the Dixie Reapers weren't as wild as they'd once been, we didn't exactly go hand in hand with the words *law abiding*. She deserved a fresh start, far away from the ugliness of the world. But on the other hand, I couldn't deny the growing connection between us, and the undeniable bond she seemed to be forming with Rhett. As much as it hurt to admit it, he seemed to like her more than me.

Until this morning, I'd been able to deny the fact I wanted to keep Galina in my life. When she'd talked about how I didn't want an actual relationship with her, it had made me pause. Actually, it felt like a mule had kicked me right between the eyes. I'd been lying to myself all along. How could I possibly resist her? She was everything I never realized I needed or wanted. After losing Jenny and Rhett, I'd closed myself off. Finding out Rhett was alive, and having Galina in my house, was making me rethink a lot of decisions I'd made recently. Mostly the things I'd said to Galina.

I'd hurt her by pushing her away. Then I'd probably confused the hell out of her this morning. But now, after watching her with Rhett, I knew I needed to fix things between us. Spending time with him on my own gave me a glimpse of what the future looked like without Galina in it. It had felt like something was missing, and I thought Rhett might have felt the same. Even though we were both strangers to him, I could tell he liked Galina and trusted her.

I couldn't stand the thought of sending her away. Not only because Rhett needed her, but so did I. Maybe it was time I faced my fears head-on and allowed myself to open up to the possibility of a future with Galina.

We'd decided to go ahead and introduce Rhett to Tate and Theo. The boys were playing and seemed to be getting along. Sarge and Saint stood off to the side, watching the kids and also giving me and Galina a little space. I slowly reached for her hand and gave it a squeeze.

"Lina, there's something I need to say."

"Everything okay?" she asked, turning to face me.

"I... I want you to stay, to be a part of my life and Rhett's."

Her eyes widened and her lips parted slightly. "What?"

I took a deep breath, gathering my thoughts. "I've been a fool. I was so wrapped up in the past and what I thought my future should look like that I've never given anyone a chance. I've been pushing you away because I thought it was for your own good, and that it was also what I needed, but seeing you with Rhett... it made me realize we need you."

"Are you only saying this because of your son?" she asked.

"No, although he did point out I've been an idiot. This morning, I didn't turn away from you because I wanted to put space between us. It felt like you'd smacked me over the head. Hearing you say that I didn't want you in my life permanently was painful, and I hated myself for hurting you."

"Are you sure?" she asked.

"Let's keep dating for a week or two. The club thinks that's what we're doing anyway. It will give Rhett time to settle in more and adjust to both of us and give us the chance to explore if this is what we really want."

She nodded. "All right. Does that mean we can have more time together like this morning?"

I leaned in closer and lowered my voice so only she could hear me. "Is this your way of saying you need more orgasms?"

Her cheeks flushed and she didn't respond, but I saw the heat in her eyes. "It hasn't even been a full day. You may decide you don't need me. Rhett should be your priority."

"He is," I said. "You both are. I can't be concerned about both of you?"

"I'm worried about Rhett."

I looked over to watch him playing with the other two boys. "He seems fine to me."

"That's my point. He's *too* fine. Having his life turned upside down is normal for him. It has to be tough for him to pick up and move so much, not to mention changing schools and feeling as if it's not safe to make friends because he'll have to leave them behind. It's too much for an eleven-year-old little boy to handle, and yet he's smiling and acts like life is perfect. You don't find it odd?" she asked.

Since she'd pointed it out, he did seem more adjusted than I'd expected. I'd only thought he was being mature for his age. It never occurred to me he could be showing us a mask. If the boy was hurting, I wanted to know, even if I was the one responsible for causing him pain.

As Galina voiced her concerns about Rhett's seemingly perfect facade, a pang of guilt washed over me. She was right. I had been so focused on my own desires and fears I hadn't taken the time to truly understand what Rhett was going through. I turned my gaze back to the boys, watching them as they played, their laughter filling the air.

He seemed genuinely happy right now, and he probably was having a good time. But the rest of the morning, had he only been putting on an act?

"You're right, Lina," I admitted. "I've been blind to what Rhett might be feeling. It's clear he's been through a lot and has learned to cope by putting on a brave face."

Galina's eyes softened as she looked at me, her concern mirrored in her expression. "We need to be there for him. He deserves to feel safe and loved. I'm sure the people in his life up to this point did the best they could, but he wasn't their son. They probably had a lot of children in their homes. I don't think he's ever been anyone's priority."

I nodded, feeling a renewed determination to be the father Rhett needed. "You're absolutely right. I'm only sorry I wasn't the one who saw it. See? You're already proving how much we both need you. He needs a mom who will love him, and I need you to knock me upside my head when I'm being an idiot."

Galina smiled softly, her hand reaching up to cup my cheek. "I'll knock you upside the head as many times as it takes, Python. But I also need you to promise me something."

I furrowed my brow, curious about what she was about to ask of me. "What is it?"

"I want you to let go of your guilt," she said, her eyes searching mine. "You couldn't have known what Rhett was going through before, and you're doing everything you can now to make it right. Blaming yourself won't do anyone any good. You accepted their lies about his death, and it's understandable. You'd just lost Jenny and her father wanted to kill you. No one could ever blame you for what happened."

Her words hit me hard, and I realized she was right. Holding onto my guilt wasn't going to change the past or help Rhett moving forward. It would only hinder our ability to create a better future for him. I needed to focus on Rhett and building a relationship not only with him, but also one with Galina. I had a feeling she was going to be an important part of our family.

Rhett came running over. "Tate and Theo need to leave."

"Did you have fun?" Galina asked.

Rhett nodded. "Can I play with them again sometime?"

"We live at the same compound. You'll have plenty of chances to play with them and to meet the other kids," I said. "As for your concern earlier about changing schools, you don't have to if you don't want to."

"Theo and Tate said they ride to school together sometimes," Rhett said.

"They do. A lot of the kids here carpool. So if you want to move to the same school as them, we can take care of that Monday morning. Since it's the weekend, you'll have more time to get to know everyone here," I said.

"Why don't we head home for now?" Galina asked. "You can take a bath while your dad and I figure out dinner."

Rhett nodded eagerly, his eyes shining with excitement. "Yeah, that sounds good. Can we have pizza for dinner?"

I chuckled and ruffled his hair affectionately. "Pizza it is. Homemade or delivery?"

His eyes went wide. "You mean we can have something other than the frozen ones?"

It hurt, knowing he'd been deprived of the simple things. "Yeah. Just pick what you want, and I'll make it happen."

Galina elbowed me. "Your dad means we'll make it together, unless you want him to order one. We're fine with whichever you prefer."

"You can really make one?" he asked.

"Galina bought all the ingredients we'd need. I haven't made one from scratch before. If we mess it up, we'll get one delivered. How's that sound?" I asked.

"Good."

As we walked back to the house, Galina slipped her hand into mine, intertwining our fingers. It felt natural and right. The warmth of her touch spread through me, melting away the last remnants of doubt and fear. Now that I'd told her I wanted her to stay, I needed to show her what life would be like with me and Rhett. We could figure out how to be a family together.

Once we arrived home, Rhett eagerly ran to take a bath while Galina and I prepared dinner in the kitchen. I still worried about how happy he seemed. Although, to be fair, the boy had just discovered he had a dad who wanted him. If our roles were reversed, I probably would have been thrilled. We'd keep an eye on him and make sure he was okay. If need be, we could always find a therapist for him.

It wasn't long before the scent of tomato sauce and melting cheese filled the air. Thankfully she'd bought a premade crust, and she'd looked up a sauce recipe online. It hadn't taken long to put the pizza together, and soon it would be ready. Hopefully Rhett would be done with his bath by then.

"He should have a bedtime, right?" I asked. I didn't know a damn thing about kids.

"Yes. I was an only child, so I don't know anything about raising kids based off experience, but I did often listen to the conversations around me. I know the mothers always set a bedtime for the kids, made sure they brushed their teeth before bed, and had a bath after they came in from playing."

"Well, one of those is handled," I said. "What's a good bedtime for an eleven-year-old?"

She shrugged. "It's a Friday so there's no school tomorrow. Maybe nine or nine-thirty for Friday and Saturday nights? Eight-thirty for school nights?"

"Let's start with that and see how it goes," I said. "I should have asked Sarge or Saint about this kind of stuff. Theo is Saint's second child, so he's been through this twice already. Theo is Sarge's oldest. Well, technically Pepper is but she's an adult and has a family of her own."

Her jaw dropped a little. "Wait, he has an adult daughter *and* a son who's the same age as Rhett?"

"Yep. He didn't know about Pepper until she showed up at the gates one day. Didn't know about Theo either, now that I think about it."

Her eyebrows lifted nearly to her hairline. "So he makes it a habit of knocking up a woman and taking off before she can even say she's pregnant?"

"It's a long story. I'm sure the women will tell you about it sometime. I'm going to check on Rhett. The pizza should be done soon."

He was already out of the bath and putting on his pajamas when I knocked on the door. He opened it a crack and peeked through.

"Ready to eat?" I asked.

"Yeah! Did you really make the pizza yourself? You and Galina?" he asked.

"Yep. Although Lina did most of the work. Let's eat, then we can watch a movie until it's time for you to go to bed."

Our first family dinner went over well. Rhett loved the pizza, and he told us all about his time with Theo and Tate. It was nice to see him relaxed and content. I only hoped the rest of our days would go half as well.

Chapter Ten

Lina

Rhett had been an amazing buffer. Now that he was in bed, it left me alone with Python. We'd talked about making the dating thing real and giving a relationship a chance. This morning had been spontaneous, but tonight... if anything happened between us now, it was going to be somewhat planned and an acceptance that things were changing between us. I wasn't sure how I felt. Excited? Terrified? Perhaps a bit of both.

The door opened and Python stepped inside the room. He stared at me, and I could feel the tension in the air. Was he feeling every bit as conflicted as me? I knew he had more experience with women and sex. I'd never even seen a naked man until him.

"Are you sure about this?" he asked. "If we take things all the way, then you're mine. There's no second-guessing yourself later, or deciding you want to leave. So I need you to be certain before things progress too far. Doesn't mean I can't still give you orgasms like this morning. But if we go a step farther, then it changes everything."

"I understand, and I can't say for sure if I'm ready for us to have actual sex. What we did this morning was okay. I think I do want more of that, and to explore things between us. I already adore Rhett, and I've enjoyed my time with you. I just don't want to do anything that could wreck one or all of our lives."

He nodded. "I get it. If you want to just sleep tonight, then that's what we'll do. No pressure. I enjoyed this morning every bit as much as you did.

Saying that, I'm not expecting us to do that sort of thing all the time. Although, if you decide to stay forever, then I can't promise I'll be able to keep my hands off you."

My cheeks warmed. "You make it sound like a bad thing."

"You'll think it is after the first time we have sex. You're a virgin and have no idea what you're getting into. I'm surprised the size of my cock didn't scare you. Most women can't handle it."

My brow furrowed. "I don't understand. Is there something wrong with your size?"

"Are you being serious right now? I know you said you hadn't seen a naked man before, but you don't really think my cock is normal, do you?"

I shrugged a shoulder. I had no idea what to think. It wasn't like I had anything to compare him to.

"They call me python because of my dick," he said. "It's ten inches, which is not the biggest by far, but it's quite a bit larger than the average -- which is around five inches in case you were wondering. Mine is bigger than that when it's *not* hard."

"Are you trying to tell me it won't fit?" I asked. All he'd done was make me want to test the theory. The fact he had a son told me some women could handle it just fine. Clearly Jenny had been one of them.

"I'm saying you're a virgin, which means your first time might hurt even with someone much smaller than me. It won't matter how much I try to prepare you. It's going to hurt, and there's not a damn thing I can do about it. You're built to stretch, but even then some women can't handle a dick over seven inches. Not to mention I'm pretty thick too."

"If this is your way of saying you'd rather not touch me, then it's fine. We can just go to sleep."

He tipped his head back and growled. "Damnit, Lina. That's not even close to what I'm saying. I'm... I want to fuck you, okay? Touching you and making you come is fun, and I enjoyed the hell out of our time this morning, but I want more than that. The problem is I can't have more until you're sure this is the life you want. I'm not wearing a condom. I'll come inside you, fill you up until you're overflowing, and make you mine."

"You just got Rhett back after thinking he was dead. Your plan sounds like an excellent way to get me pregnant. Do you really think, even if I did say I wanted to be with you forever, that a baby would be a good idea right now?" I asked.

"Maybe not. But I'd rather leave it up to fate. If we're meant to have a baby now, then we will. Something to keep in mind."

"If you aren't ever going to use a condom, and I'm assuming you have an aversion to me using birth control as well, do you plan to have twenty kids?"

"I'd want at least one child that's part you and part me. I love Rhett, and I can tell how much you already care about him too. Having another child won't take away from that. I'd be lying if I said the thought of you giving birth didn't scare the shit out of me. Jenny died and there wasn't anything I could do about it. But I said I wasn't going to live in fear anymore, and that includes having a child with you."

It felt like he'd gone from *I'm going to be alone forever* to moving at warp speed and wanting to knock me up. I wasn't sure how to feel about it. Was he worried if we didn't jump in with both feet right away he might change his mind?

"Aren't you worried Rhett might need us in the middle of the night? It's his first time in a new place," I said. "What if we're naked and he comes into the room?"

Python pointed to the knob. "It has a lock. No reason we can't use it."

"But he could hear us if he's outside the door."

"Lina, if you don't want to do anything, just say so. I'm fine with it. Making excuses isn't going to change anything. You're either in the mood to do something, or you aren't. But if you're genuinely worried about Rhett hearing us, then it means we'd never have sex until he's out of the house and living his own life."

I chewed on my bottom lip, glancing at the door. He wasn't wrong. I knew parents had sex with their kids in the house all the time. If they didn't, everyone would only have one.

"Could we do it in the shower again like this morning? I think I'd feel more comfortable with the sound of the water muffling any noises we'd make. At least this first time. I can't help being nervous."

"I'm fine with that. I'll still lock the door just to be safe. I need to pick something up real quick, and I'll check on Rhett again before I come to the bedroom. Wait about fifteen minutes and start the water. If Rhett's asleep when I come back, then I'll join you in the shower. If he's not, then it's a great time for you to explore your body and figure out how to make yourself come."

I felt my cheeks heat and knew I had to be bright red. The thought of touching myself like that... I couldn't say I was entirely opposed to it. Would he enjoy watching me? I'd heard some people were into that sort of thing. Or rather, I'd eavesdropped on some of the conversations at Bratva events. Then again, there were plenty of things I'd heard the men say that I either hadn't understood or didn't ever want to try.

He left the bedroom, and I heard the front door open and shut. The sound of his motorcycle starting made me wonder where he needed to be at this time of night. It didn't seem like he was planning to be gone for very long. I stared up at the ceiling, listening intently for any little sound in the house. I couldn't hear anything, so I assumed Rhett was either asleep or at least being quiet in his room. Python said he'd check on him, but I needed to see for myself.

I got up and quietly walked to Rhett's room. The door stood partially open, and I peeked inside. He'd already fallen asleep, one foot sticking out from under the covers, his arm up over his head and the other across his belly. I smiled, thinking he looked rather cute. Backing away, I paused in the living room and parted the blinds so I could peer outside. In the darkness, I couldn't see much of anything. I also didn't hear a single motorcycle.

Python had said to give him fifteen minutes, but I felt restless. I wasn't sure what to do with myself while I waited. Heading into the kitchen, I made sure I'd put the clean dishes away. With nothing left to do, I decided to go ahead and start the shower. He'd either get back and join me before the water ran cold, or he wouldn't.

I shut the bedroom door, then froze. *Crap.* I couldn't very well lock it while Python wasn't home, or he couldn't get in the room. If I left it unlocked, Rhett could wake up and wander in here. Although, I didn't think he'd be so bold as to come into the bathroom when the shower was running. I deliberated for another minute or two before deciding I'd take the chance.

Making sure the bathroom door had shut all the

way, I started the water and stripped out of my clothes. While I waited for it to warm, I brushed my teeth and ran a brush through my hair. I tested the water, then stepped under the spray. Tipping my head back, I closed my eyes and did my best to relax. Steam began to fill the space and I breathed it in, taking long slow breaths.

The bedroom door opened and shut, making me tense again. When Python came into the bathroom, I let out a sigh of relief. "I thought you were Rhett."

"He's sound asleep." He placed a bag on the counter. "I locked the bedroom door. Still want me to join you?"

I eyed the sack. "I guess it depends on what you brought home."

He grinned. "I'll show you if you're brave enough to move things to the bedroom when we're done in here. Otherwise, you'll have to wait."

Well, that sounded… intriguing. I watched as he undressed and joined me. I took a few steps back, giving him some space and letting him under the spray. The water cascaded over his shoulders and down his chest.

I couldn't help myself. I reached out to run my fingers over the hard muscles. If I were an artist, I'd have loved to draw him. Sadly, I couldn't even make a stick person. Well, not a very good one at any rate.

"Last chance to back out," he said.

"No. I'm ready. You said earlier you couldn't keep living in fear. I need to be stronger and braver. You aren't the only one who has something to overcome."

"Why don't you start by washing?"

"Are you trying to say I stink?" I asked, smiling a little.

"No. I want you to move slow, taking your time soaping every inch of yourself." He leaned in closer and lowered his voice. "And I'm going to watch."

I sucked in a breath, heat flaring inside me. It looked like I'd found something that turned me on, other than him touching me. The mere thought of him watching me shower changed something mundane into an erotic experience. It was my first time considering such a thing.

I got some shower gel and rubbed it between my hands before starting to lather my neck and shoulders. I washed each arm, then slid my hands under my breasts. His eyes darkened and I saw his cock getting hard. I cupped the mounds and then... I wasn't sure what to do. Normally, I've have quickly soaped them along with the rest of me, then rinsed and gotten out.

"Don't forget to wash your nipples," he said. He reached out and lightly ran a finger over one. It hardened under his touch and my clit pulsed with need. "Unless you want me to do it for you?"

Oh. Oh! Yes, I very much wanted that. I nodded and let my hands drop back to my sides. Python moved in closer, crowding me against the shower wall. He rasped his palms over my nipples, teasing them in circles. The roughness of his skin scraped against them in the most delicious way.

"How does that feel?" he asked, his voice low and husky.

"Good. Really good," I murmured.

"Give me more than that. Do you ache anywhere?" I nodded. "Tell me. Use your words, Lina. Where does it hurt? Where do you need me to touch you?"

I couldn't bring myself to say it. Instead, I took his hand and placed it between my legs. "Here. I want you to touch me here."

He used his finger to part the lips of my pussy, and he stroked my clit. His slippery, soapy fingers slid over the hardened bud, driving me crazy. I parted my thighs a little more and arched into his touch. He lightly pinched my nipple, and I nearly came. When he did it again, and put a little more pressure on my clit, I fell headfirst into my first orgasm for the night.

"Look at you. I love how responsive you are," he said. "Want more?"

"Yes!"

"Hmm. Then I guess you better rinse and give me a second to get cleaned up. If you want to come again, we're going to the bedroom."

I wanted to say I'd changed my mind, but I couldn't. I did as he said and dried off while he washed and rinsed. Not knowing what else to do, I went into the bedroom and sat on the bed while I waited. He came in a few minutes later, with the bag he'd brought home.

"Are you going to tell me what's in there now?" I asked.

"How about I show you?" He took two items out of the bag, and some batteries. Wait. Had he gone to a store and bought vibrators? He held up a strange U-shaped thing that looked like it was made of silicone. "I'm going to charge this one so we'll use the smaller one first. There's one more, but we'll see how you like these first."

I watched as he plugged it in, then added a battery to the other one. It looked like it was close to the size of a tube of lipstick. What exactly was he going to do with it?

"Lie back and spread your legs," he said.

I knew he wouldn't hurt me, so I did as he said.

Although, I did still find it a little embarrassing to lie like this while he stared at me. I felt like I needed to cover myself. He turned it on, and it made a loud buzzing sound. The moment he placed it on my clit, I nearly lifted off the bed.

"Holy crap!" I sucked in a breath, my eyes going wide. "That's... It's..."

He circled the toy over my clit. "Come for me, Lina. Show me how pretty you are when you're coming apart."

His words triggered my orgasm, and I bit my lip so I wouldn't cry out. He teased and tormented me for what felt like forever. I came so much I could feel the bed getting soaked beneath me. He took the other one off the charger and held it up for me to see.

"This part goes over your clit and the other end slips inside you. It might burn a bit since you're a virgin." I eyed it and then his cock. Yeah, maybe it would, but it was way smaller than his cock. "Want to give it a try?"

"I do, but you aren't getting anything out of this."

"How bold are you feeling?" he asked.

"Um. I don't know. What did you have in mind?"

"I won't fit in your mouth, but it doesn't mean you can't stroke me like you did before. Maybe lick it a little, if you're up for it."

Oh wow. Was I? I wouldn't know unless I tried. "Okay."

He turned on the toy and eased it into place. I winced at the stretch I felt as the fatter part slid inside me. Once he had it in position, I nearly bit my tongue. The vibrations over my clit were amazing, but it was also hitting a spot inside me that had me whimpering and coming almost instantly.

"That's my girl," he murmured. "Fuck but you're gorgeous!"

He managed to flip me onto my hands and knees. My thighs trembled as the toy buzzed mercilessly, making my orgasm seem endless. He stroked his cock, and I saw a bead of moisture on the tip. Without consciously thinking about it, I flicked my tongue out and licked it off. A salty taste burst in my mouth.

"Holy shit! Do that again," he begged.

I licked the head again, then the shaft of his cock. I wrapped my fingers around the bottom half, sliding them up and down. I fitted my lips around the head and took as much of him into my mouth as I could. Shifting into a more comfortable position, the toy pressed tighter against my clit and my eyes nearly crossed. I came so hard I screamed around my mouthful of cock. My entire body shook from the force of my release.

"Jesus. I can't take it." He tossed me onto my back and pulled the toy from inside me. He threw it to the other side of the bed, and I felt his cock slide against my pussy. He rocked against me until the heat of his release sprayed across my belly and breasts. "I think you just reduced me to a teenage boy who can't control himself."

"That was..."

"Fun?" He smiled and winked at me. "Want to keep going? I might need about twenty minutes, but I can make you come all night long."

"Not sure I can handle that." But on the other hand, it might be enjoyable to give it a try.

"I'll clean you up while you decide." He leaned down and pressed his lips to mine. It was my very first kiss and I reached up to place my hand on the back of his neck. I held him in place, making his mouth linger on mine. "Then again..."

He eased down my body, shoving my thighs even wider apart. Before I could process what he was doing, I felt his tongue against my clit. I squealed and tried to close my legs, but he held me open.

"Just enjoy it," he said before lapping at me again. The crazy man made me come twice more before he went to get a washcloth to clean the cum off my body.

My heart raced and I felt a little dizzy. I also felt happier than I'd ever been before. It didn't matter how much time he gave me. I'd already decided. I wanted to be his. Any man who would pay so much attention to my needs without asking for more was a keeper. Or so I'd heard.

Yeah. I was going to hold onto this one. He was exactly what I'd been missing in my life.

Chapter Eleven
Python

I couldn't remember a time I'd ever moved so slowly with a woman. Then again, I hadn't dated one since high school. Jenny had been my best friend, and our one night had been a mistake. I didn't regret marrying her, or the fact we had Rhett. It had changed me, and not necessarily in a good way. After her death, I'd not wanted another relationship. One-night stands or easy pussy at the clubhouse were all I'd known since then. None of the things I would have said or done in those situations would work with Galina.

I'd spent the night wearing her out. She slept like the dead at the moment, and I couldn't help but smile. She looked pretty damn cute with her tangled hair in disarray, her lips slightly parted, and a soft snore escaping her every now and then. For someone who had worried so much about Rhett walking in on us, she'd finally let go and enjoyed herself. By the end, she'd even been screaming as she came.

Knowing she worried about Rhett, I'd gone to check on him once she'd fallen asleep. He hadn't woken up regardless of how loud Lina had been. Either the day had been exhausting for him, or he took after his mother. I'd always joked and said Jenny would sleep through an earthquake.

Lounging in the bed, I watched her as the sun came up, filtering through the blinds. I'd let her sleep as long as she wanted. Things had been changing between us ever since she'd rescued me from Penny's clutches, but it felt like we'd covered a lot of relationship miles in the past twenty-four hours. To some, we were probably going too fast. Those people hadn't met the members of my club. Preacher knocked up Kayla the night they met. Bull claimed Darian within a day of meeting her, and quite a few others had done the same with their women.

They'd always said I would know when I found the woman meant for me. At the time, I'd had to refrain from telling them about Jenny, and I'd blown off their words as a bunch of bullshit since I'd planned to stay single. Looked like the joke was on me.

I heard movement in the house and figured Rhett was up. I got out of bed and made my way to the front part of the house. Rhett stood in the living room, rubbing sleep from his eyes. He yawned widely and jolted a little when he saw me watching him.

"Morning. You sleep okay?" I asked.

"Good morning. I woke up because I was thirsty."

"Come on. Let's get you a drink. If you're still tired, you can go back to bed. Or if you're hungry, I'll make something for you."

He nodded and followed me. I poured him a glass of apple juice and handed it to him. He drank a few sips before sitting at the table. After I got the coffee brewing, I sat across from him.

"So, yesterday was a busy day. You found out about me, met Lina and several other people, and were basically dropped into an entirely different world. It's a lot for an adult, much less a kid."

"I'm okay," he said, not even hesitating.

"Uh-huh. I guess what I'm saying is that most people *wouldn't* be, and that's fine." I studied him while he drank more of his juice. "I'm new to this parenting thing, but there's one thing I know for sure. I will love you regardless of what you say or do. If you're hurting and need to cry, then that's what I want you to do. If you're confused and have questions, then ask them. This is a safe place for you, Rhett. It's your home."

"I've had those before," he mumbled. "They never last."

"Those weren't your home," I said. "Those people were paid to take care of you. I'm not saying none of them cared."

"But they weren't my real family?" he asked.

"Exactly! If they were, then you wouldn't have been moved around so much. You're my son, Rhett. If someone hadn't told me you died, then you'd have been with me all this time."

"What was my mom like?" he asked softly.

"Jenny was my best friend. She could be funny and sweet, unless you got on her bad side. It took a lot for her to get mad, but once she did you'd better be able to outrun her." I smiled at the memories flooding in as I thought about her. "We were in high school when we got married. Your mom was so excited to welcome you into the world."

"But she died?" he asked.

"Yeah, she did. You know what, though? She'd have been so happy you made it. She was always reading to you, singing songs, or just holding her hand over her belly so she could feel you move. A light entered her eyes every time she thought of you and the life the three of us could have together." I didn't even have a picture of Jenny I could show him. Everything from that part of my life was long gone.

He remained quiet, staring at his now empty glass. I knew he probably had more questions, doubts, and even some fear. What I didn't know was how to get the kid to open up to me.

"I'm not sure when Lina will be up. If you're not sleepy anymore, want me to make some breakfast?" I asked.

"Do you think she likes me?" Rhett mumbled.

"Lina? Of course, she does."

He looked away, his lower lip protruding a little. "But she's not my mom."

"Well, there are different kinds of families, Rhett. For instance, this club is my family. The two men you met yesterday, Sarge and Saint, are my brothers. We aren't related by blood, but it doesn't make a difference. Even though Lina didn't give birth to you, she can still love you."

"The kids at school always had a mom and dad, or at least a mom. I never had either."

"Now you have a dad," I said.

"I want a mom," he said. I noticed tears gathering in his eyes. It didn't take long before the first one spilled down his cheek. It was like a floodgate opened. Once he started crying, he couldn't stop. I pulled him into my arms and held him.

I caught movement from the corner of my eye and saw Galina in the doorway. She pressed her lips together and looked like she might join Rhett's sob fest at any moment. I held out a hand to her and she joined us.

"Look. Lina is awake," I said. Rhett sniffled and looked at her. "Was there something you wanted to ask her?"

"Can I… can I call you Mom?" Rhett asked.

Lina bit her lip. "I'd really love that, Rhett."

"If you're going to call her Mom, does that mean you'll call me Dad?" I asked.

He nodded. I hugged him again, then handed him to Lina. She cuddled him closer and kissed the top of his head. When her gaze met and held mine, I knew I needed to make a call, or at least send a text. Because as of now, Lina was my woman. I didn't have to worry about her leaving or changing her mind about us. She'd told Rhett he could call her Mom, and I knew she'd never do anything to hurt him. If she left now, it would tear his heart in two.

I went to the bedroom to get my phone and shot off a text to Savior. *Lina is mine. Make it official.*

It didn't take long for him to respond, despite how early it was on a Saturday. *Official as in property cut only, or want me to let Wire and Lavender do their thing?*

I didn't even have to think about it. *I want her to be my wife. She needs the same last name as me and Rhett.*

I saw he'd read the message even if he didn't respond again. Good enough for me. Now I just needed to get Lina a ring. I wondered if Rhett would want to help pick one out.

"I was about to make breakfast, but I have a better idea. Why don't we all get ready and eat out somewhere? Then Rhett and I have something we need to do," I said.

Lina narrowed her eyes at me. "He just asked to call me Mom and now you're leaving me out?"

"It's a surprise *for you.* So while we run our errand, you can browse some of the shops on Main Street. It shouldn't take more than a half hour. Go shower first while I talk to Rhett."

She rolled her eyes and walked off. It was the first time I'd seen her do such a thing, and I had to shake my head. It looked like the ice had finally broken and I was going to see the real Lina. Not that I thought she'd been hiding or anything. She seemed more relaxed, more certain of her place here.

I whispered to Rhett in case she lingered nearby and could hear us. "Now that Lina is going to be your mom, I need to get her a ring. I want you to help me pick it out. What do you think?"

He tipped his head slightly, as if thinking about it. "She seemed sad to be left alone. Maybe I should stay with her while you get it."

Hmm. I could work with that. "Then what color stone should I get in the ring? Here, we'll look up a few rings and you can show me the type you think she'd like. I can try to find one similar."

His eyes lit up as I pulled up a Google search for wedding sets. It didn't take him long to narrow down the choices to either an emerald or amethyst, and he thought she'd like a square cut stone. I was certain I could find something in town close enough to the ones he'd chosen. Just to be safe, I took a screenshot of them so I could show the jeweler.

"You had a bath before bed, so all you need to do is brush your teeth, wash your face, and get dressed." I shooed him off to his room. "Wait in the living room for us when you're done."

I heard the shower running when I got to the bedroom. Lina had already placed a change of clothes on the bed. Now that she was officially mine, I needed to get her more things. She'd made do so far, but what she had wasn't nearly enough. Besides, she'd need clothes appropriate for riding on the back of my bike as well.

We still had Tank's SUV out front. The one Wire tried to get for us had fallen through, and he was searching for something else. We didn't want one that was too large, yet big enough I wouldn't feel cramped in it. Also needed good safety features.

I put my own clothes out on the bed and went to

join Lina in the shower. Except, when I got in there, I decided I should wait. If I got my hands on her right now, I wasn't sure I could hold back. We'd made it this long only playing around. When I finally took her virginity, I wanted it to be after I had a ring on her finger and we had a marriage certificate. Those things hadn't been important to me before, but I wanted to prove to Galina that she was different from anyone I'd ever been with.

She got out and I handed her a towel. Even now, her cheeks turned pink when she noticed the way I eyed her. How could I have not realized sooner how tempting she was? Ignoring the fact my cock was now hard as a rock, I got into the shower and washed up quickly. By the time I'd finished and dressed, both Lina and Rhett were waiting for me in the living room.

"Ready to go?" I asked.

We loaded up into the SUV and headed for the main part of town. I hadn't bothered asking where they wanted breakfast. The diner seemed like the perfect choice. There were a lot of places for Rhett and Lina to shop while I got her ring. It was our first outing as a family, and I couldn't remember a time I'd felt more at peace than I did right now.

My phone buzzed and I checked the screen. I opened the text from Wire. *Congrats you're now married. Should have just let me do it earlier.*

Fucker. He just had to make a comment about that, didn't he? *I'm sorry if you thought I was being a dick before. Not all of us move at warp speed like you.*

I saw he read the message and he responded almost immediately. *While I appreciate the SciFi reference, please don't do that again. It's weird coming from you.*

There was no pleasing him. I could admit I'd probably not handled the situation better before. I knew Lavender and Wire meant well, even when they meddled in people's lives. While they *did* need to hear what I'd had to say, I could have said it a little nicer. They'd just pissed me off so much at the time.

"Order anything you want, Rhett," I said. "Today is a special day."

Lina smiled at me. I knew she thought I meant because of our talk this morning. I'd tell her we were married once I had her ring. I wanted to do this the right way. Well, as much as I could. It wasn't like anyone in my damn club did anything the normal way. Even Torch. He might have had an actual wedding, but he'd married a stranger who wasn't even an adult yet, all to offer her his name as protection. Took him and Isabella years to get on the same page, and now they were a solid couple who clearly adored each other.

After we ate, I'd get Lina's ring, then take the two of them to the local park. There was a pretty gazebo in the center. I thought it would be the perfect location to give the ring to her and tell her we were married.

Things were falling into place.

* * *

Lina

Breakfast had gone well, and now I found myself alone with Rhett. I hadn't explored the town much, so I wasn't sure what types of stores were in this area. I walked down the sidewalk, Rhett's hand clutched in mine. We passed a storefront with Legos in the window and I paused.

"Would you like to go inside?" I asked.

"Are you sure it's okay?"

"Of course! Your dad gave me some money." I had no idea how much the Legos would cost. Surely it wouldn't be too expensive for small plastic blocks.

We went inside and Rhett looked at every single item. I noticed a few things he'd circle back to and check out a second or third time. Picking up one of the sets, I nearly dropped it when I saw it was over one hundred dollars. They had to be joking, right?

He'd given me a few hundred dollars, but I hadn't thought I'd end up using it nearly all on one item. But if it's what Rhett really wanted, then I'd get it for him. It wasn't like he'd be spoiled all the time. There were so many things he'd need over the next few weeks.

"Is this the one you want?" I asked, holding it up.

"Um. I do, but I think I like this one better. I can make anything with it."

I went to see what he'd found. It was a large plastic tub of the different blocks. It also cost roughly half what the other set had. I carried it to the register and paid, then handed the bag to Rhett. It was nice seeing him smile. While I'd thought he was forcing it yesterday, today I could tell he was genuinely happy.

"Well, well. And here I thought we'd have a hard time finding the little bitch." The Russian accent not only caught my attention, but the man's words also sent a chill down my spine. I slowly turned to face him. No, *them*. Three large men stood only a few feet from us. "Dima will be pleased. Time to go home to your master."

My master? "No. I don't belong to Dima. Never have and I never will."

I pushed Rhett behind me, wanting to shield him from these monsters. The men circled us, and I worried Rhett was going to get hurt.

"Grab the boy too," one of the men said. "I'm

sure Dima will find a use for him."

"No! You can't touch Rhett!" I gave him a push past the men. "Run, Rhett! Go find your dad."

He didn't even make it three steps before they snagged him. One of the others grabbed my arm and wrenched it behind my back, twisting it at an angle that made it feel like it might break at any moment. I had no choice but to go with them. I looked around, hoping someone would step in and do something. The few people on the sidewalk all looked the other way.

As they forced us down the sidewalk and past the diner, I glanced inside. Our waitress saw me and her eyes went wide. I mouthed the words *help us*. She ran to the back, and I hoped she was going to call the police.

The men shoved us into a blacked-out car and slammed the door shut. One rode on the other side in the back seat while the other two got up front. I looked out the window, hoping and praying for a miracle.

I saw Python and began beating on the window and screaming for him. He glanced up, scanning the area. The moment he saw the car, the blood drained from his face and he rushed toward us. But it was too late… The car sped up, took the next right, and didn't stop until we needed gas what felt like an hour or more later.

Please find us, Python.

Chapter Twelve

Python

What the fuck just happened? I stared at the car racing away and ran to the SUV. By the time I followed them around the corner, the vehicle was long gone. I pulled to the side of the road and called Wire.

"How's married life?" Wire asked instead of saying the typical hello.

"I need you to hack the traffic cameras around town. Someone just took Lina and Rhett," I said.

"Wait. What?"

"They were in the back of a blacked-out Lincoln. Turned the corner at Main Street and Pine. I lost them after that. I don't know who has them, but I'm going to assume Lina's father found her."

Wire cleared his throat. "Savior was supposed to tell you. Her dad is dead. We got news last night his body was found floating in a river. So if the Bratva did snatch them, it's probably Dima Belov."

"I need everything you have on him, but first find Lina! There's no time to waste."

"Already on it." I heard the keys clicking in the background. "I'm getting off the phone to work on this, and I'll ask Lavender to find everything she can on Dima Belov, including his current location. Call Savior and tell him what's going on, then come back to the compound. We'll find them, Python, but we can't have you running around trying to track them like a damn bloodhound."

"Fine. Just… help me get my family back." As badly as I wanted to race after Lina and Rhett, I knew Wire was right. I went back to the compound and called Savior on the way. The phone only rang twice before one of the little kids answered.

"Hewwo."

"Judd, can you please give the phone to your daddy?"

I heard him running through the house, then the murmur of Savior's voice as he got onto him for not walking.

"Hello," he said as he came on the line.

"It's Python. I called Wire first and he and Lavender are already working on the issue, but... someone kidnapped Lina and Rhett while we were in town."

My hands shook no matter how hard I gripped the steering wheel. What the hell was happening to them right now? Where had they been taken? I needed to get them back.

"Holy fuck, are you serious?" Savior asked.

"I left them alone long enough to go into the jewelry store. I wanted Lina to have a ring. When I came out, they were in the back of a car. I heard her beating on the window and screaming my name."

"Hang on." I heard more voices in the background. "Viking is here. The waitress at the diner called him. She saw three men grab Lina and Rhett."

I didn't even want to know why the waitress had his number. The fact she'd called someone in the club was enough for now. I also didn't want the police involved. There was no way they could handle this matter, especially if the Bratva had taken them. Since I hadn't pissed anyone off lately, and neither had the club -- that I knew of -- it only left the Bratva.

With Lina's father out of the picture, like Wire said, the only other person who could possibly want to kidnap Lina was Dima Belov. He'd thought he was going to marry her, and it had to hurt his pride knowing she'd run from him. I had to hope Rhett had only been snatched because he'd been with Lina. As monstrous as Dima seemed, he could easily hurt my son, or worse.

Please hold on. I'm coming for both of you.

Whatever it took, I'd get them back. I pulled through the gates at the compound and went straight to Wire's house. Knocking seemed pointless since they were both supposedly working. I entered the house and checked the kitchen first. It didn't surprise me to see not only Lavender and Wire there, both with their laptops, but also Atlas. The boy couldn't do what his parents could -- yet -- but he was just as smart when it came to computers. They'd most likely given him a small task to do, so he'd feel like he was helping.

"What do we know so far?" I asked.

Neither Lavender nor Wire looked up from their screens. Atlas, who was only about a year older than Rhett, shoved a stack of papers over to me. "They printed these off a minute ago."

I flipped through them and froze. The traffic cameras had managed to catch the car, but it was on the way out of town. From the direction, I'd say they were taking her back home. I went through more and paused when I saw footage from a gas station.

"Are they really this close?" I asked.

"Yes and no," Wire said. "Check the time stamp."

I looked and saw it was from ten minutes ago. They most likely weren't obeying the speed limit, which meant they had a good head start on me. I checked the location and knew what I needed to do.

"I need a vehicle big enough for me, Lina, and Rhett, and fast enough to overtake their car." Lavender had paused her typing and I held her gaze. "Whatever it takes, find it for me and I needed it ten minutes ago."

Her fingers flew over the keys, and within five minutes, she was grinning. "Police impound has a Dodge Challenger. Hellcat model. I'm going to set up the paperwork for them to release the car to you. Start driving over there now."

I stood and only made it to the doorway before Wire stopped me. "Python, use the red key."

"What?" I had no idea what that meant.

"Hellcat has two keys. Red one is the one you want. You need to catch up to that car? Then that's how you do it. We'll do our best to keep any cops out of your way."

I pulled the keys from my pocket and went out to the borrowed SUV. It took fifteen minutes to reach the police impound lot. When I got there, I showed them my ID and signed the papers for the car. They handed me the keys and pointed out the direction I needed to take. The moment I saw the vehicle I let out a low whistle. What a beauty!

I eyed the keys and saw there were really two, and one was red. I didn't know how powerful the vehicle would feel with the regular key, so I decided to start with that one. True to his word, Wire kept the cops away. By the time I reached the edge of town, I was ready to change keys. I shut off the car and took a breath before using the red one.

Revving the engine, I steeled myself for how fast the car would go. I floored it, and the car shot off down the highway. Zero to sixty in less than four seconds. The car topped out at two hundred three miles per hour, and I gripped the wheel tight. I'd never felt so much power before and knew it would be addicting.

The vehicle the Bratva used to kidnap Lina and

Rhett had been a Lincoln Continental. Far as I knew, those didn't go nearly as fast. Without stopping to check the information on the car, I was going to assume they wouldn't go faster than a little over one hundred miles per hour. Maybe one-fifty at the most. They could easily be one hundred miles from town, but at my speed, I'd be to their current location within thirty minutes. As long as I didn't run out of gas, I thought I could catch up to them within roughly an hour.

The car ate up the miles, and I knew Wire had to still be helping because I didn't see a single law enforcement vehicle. I flew past any cars traveling the same way and didn't even slow down. Not until I saw a blacked-out car ahead. I glanced at the clock and realized I'd been close. It had been nearly an hour since I left town, and I knew in my gut that was the same car. Now how the fuck did I get them to pull over?

I gave my phone the command to call Wire and put the call on speaker.

"Did you find them?" he asked.

"I see what I believe is their car. Now how do I get them to stop without causing a wreck and possibly injuring both Lina and Rhett?"

"You don't. Stay far enough behind they won't realize you're following them. I'm going to text you the address of Dima's home. There's no doubt in my mind that's where they're headed."

"And when I get there?" I asked. Even I didn't want to try taking on the Bratva by myself.

"I'll have reinforcements ready for you."

Vague as fuck, but I'd take it. I ended the call and kept the car in my sight. When they stopped for gas, so did I. Except I chose a different gas station. I could still watch them, but hoped it was less obvious I was tailing them.

As Wire predicted, they entered Bratva territory and went to the address he'd texted me. The place wasn't quite the fortress I'd expected. I did see a few men wandering around outside, most likely armed. The car pulled up to the house and all three men got out, pulling Lina and Rhett out of the back seat. I parked the car and shut off the engine. Until Wire made good on his promise to send help, I'd sit and observe. All I could do right now was wait.

My phone vibrated and I checked the message. *On your six.*

Checking the rearview mirror, I saw two vehicles pull up behind me. Four men got out of each and approached my car. Since it seemed Wire knew them, I got out.

"Wire said these assholes have your wife and son," one of them said. "My name's Trick. Just tell me what you need from us."

"We have to get into the house and find Lina and Rhett, unless there's surveillance inside that Wire can hack. And that Dima asshole is mine. I don't care who else you kill, but hands off that bastard."

Trick nodded. "We're on it. Give us about twenty minutes to come up with a game plan and get into position. We'll get them back."

It felt like all I'd done since seeing Lina in the back of the car was hurry up and wait. My patience was about gone. I had no idea if they'd hurt Lina and Rhett. The glimpse I'd caught of them getting out of the car hadn't been enough. Not to mention, what the hell could Dima do to them in the twenty minutes it took these guys to get ready for an extraction?

The minutes passed slowly and when Trick and his team were finally ready, I followed them into the house. Two of his men took out the guards out front, while another two went around the back. Trick opened the front door. Two men inside drew their guns, but he was faster. He shot one between the eyes, and before the second man could get off a shot, Trick took a knife and stabbed him in the throat.

He handed the knife to me. "Figured you might be unarmed. Wire said you didn't seem to be thinking straight. Want this?"

"Yeah. All I could focus on was getting to Lina and Rhett. Now I need to find them."

"Our intel from Wire said this place has a basement. My money is on them being down there. Can't promise I'm right, though. I did place a call to Wire while we were planning. If this place has cameras, he couldn't hack into them. Only the exterior ones."

"I take it he pulled up the plans since you know there's a basement?" I asked.

"Yep. Now go find your family. We'll get rid of as much vermin as we can to clear the way for you."

I found the stairs that led down to the basement and crept as quietly as possible. The dim lighting didn't help matters. When I cleared the last step, I stopped and listened for signs of life. A scrape along the floor caught my attention, and I eased closer to it, clinging to the shadows.

The glow of a cigarette shone brightly. Not caring who it was, only certain it wasn't Lina, I rushed forward and plunged my knife into their chest. The man's eyes went wide and blood trickled from the corner of his mouth as he fell to the ground. I had no idea if there were more men down here or not.

It took me an entire lap around the area before I found the hidden door. Pushing it open, I found another set of stairs. How many levels did this place have? As I descended into the depths, I prayed to any god who would listen, asking for my family to be all right. If I didn't find them soon, I worried that none of us would make it out of here. How long could Lina and Rhett survive in a place like this, trapped with a madman who murdered people because he found it to be fun?

Chapter Thirteen

Lina

The only thing I could think of the entire time was how much I needed to protect Rhett. I knew exactly what sorts of monsters had taken us. The Bratva would do whatever the hell they pleased and could easily kill us without losing the teensiest bit of sleep. For that matter, Dima would get off on it, or so I'd heard.

Dima watched me, like a predator eyeing his prey. His gaze flicked over to Rhett and my stomach dropped. I knew Rhett hadn't been part of his plan. If he saw him as disposable, I wasn't sure how to keep the child alive.

"What to do with the little one," he muttered. "Who is Galina to you?"

Rhett pressed closer to me. "She's my mom."

Dima snorted. "Not hardly. She'd have been a child when you were born."

"He may not be mine biologically, but it doesn't mean I'm not his mother," I said.

"She's married to my dad," Rhett said. I winced, knowing Dima wouldn't like hearing those words. Rhett was probably trying to help me, or maybe he just really wanted me and his dad together. Either way, it was the wrong thing to say to Dima. I'd have to play along for now, though. I didn't need Rhett getting any more upset than he already was. If he needed the three of us to officially be a family to get through this, then that's what we'd be.

"Married?" His gaze narrowed on me. His next words came out in rapid-fire Russian. "What's he babbling about, Galina? You're mine, you fucking whore. How could you go and spread your legs for someone else?"

"I didn't agree to marry you. My father was forcing me into the marriage. Can you blame me for running?"

He smiled. "So, you do have some spirit. Good. I'll enjoy breaking you of it."

My heart hammered against my ribs. With Dima, I knew he meant it literally. Would there be anything left of me when Python found me? I had to hope I could find a way to stall him. I knew someone would be searching for me. Possibly the entire club, especially since the idiots had grabbed Rhett as well. Did they not realize they'd most likely signed their death sentence with that one act? There was no way Python would let anyone take his son away now that he'd finally discovered he was alive.

"I'd thought the boy would be good for business. I'm sure I could earn a lot off him." He eyed Rhett again. "But instead, I think he has a better use. For now, at any rate."

"What are you going to do?" I asked.

"Oh, it's not what I'll do. It's the fact you're going to agree to anything I demand because if you don't, I'll take it out on the child." He leaned in closer, placing his lips near my ear. "So if I decide I want to fuck you, and you deny me, then maybe I'll make you watch as he takes your place."

Bile rose up in my throat and I couldn't hold it back. Turning my head, I threw up all over the floor. I'd never met anyone as disgusting as Dima.

"Oh my. It seems you have a weak stomach," Dima said. "Your father didn't train you as well as he claimed."

"If you hurt Rhett in any way, you're going to regret it," I said.

"And why is that?"

"Because Python and the Dixie Reapers are going to kill you and every other person in this house, as well as anyone involved in the plan and kidnapping of the two of us."

He threw his head back and laughed. "And why would that filthy biker care about the two of you?"

"Did you think we were lying? I really am married to Rhett's dad... who happens to be a Dixie Reaper. They're going to come for us, and I hope they send you straight to hell." Honestly, Python would come for me just because he was a decent man. That and because his son was here with me.

He hauled back his hand and slapped me across the face. Fire bloomed in my cheek and my eye throbbed. My teeth had cut the inside of my mouth and I tasted blood.

"It looks like I need to begin disciplining you immediately." He grabbed my arm and yanked me across the room. Shoving me at a padded table that was as high as my waist he pointed to it. "You either pull your pants down and bend over that, or I'll make you."

"Please. Don't make Rhett watch this. He's just a little boy," I begged. I hated asking anything of this sadistic bastard, but I wanted to spare Rhett as much suffering as I could.

"Face the wall, boy. Close your eyes and cover your ears if you must. By all means, protect your innocence while you still can." Dima smirked at me. "There. See? I can be a reasonable man."

My hands shook as I complied with his demand. Tears gathered in my eyes. Terror and humiliation filled me as I leaned over the table, my bare ass on display. I gripped the edge of the table and braced myself for whatever was going to happen. I felt the heat of his body as he came closer, then the fabric of his clothes brushing against my skin. He leaned over me, whispering in my ear.

"For every question you don't answer, I'm going to use my belt to add a stripe to your ass cheeks. Do you understand?"

"Y-Yes."

"I want to know just how much of a whore you've been. How many dicks have you had in your mouth?"

"One," I said.

"Hmm." I felt his hands working his belt free, then the brush of the leather against my thigh. "And how many in your cunt?"

I nearly swallowed my tongue. I couldn't believe he was asking me such questions. "None."

"You're married and I'm to believe he hasn't fucked you? Or does he prefer your ass? How many dicks have you had there?"

"N-None. We were just married. We haven't had sex yet."

"I'll have to punish you for sucking his cock, but I'll go easy on you since you're still a virgin. You were meant to be the perfect broodmare. Prove to me you're worth the trouble, and I won't hand you off to my men."

He stepped away from me and I nearly screamed as the belt landed against my ass cheeks. He swung the leather again and again, each strike hurting more than the last. My skin felt like it was on fire, and I wondered if he'd hit me hard enough I might be bleeding.

"When I'm done, you're going to strip all the

way down. I'll be nice enough to use a bed for your first time, but I'm going to fuck you for hours. Next time you sit down, the stripes on your ass won't the be the only reason you wince." He growled as he hit me twice more with the belt. "Fuck, but I'm getting hard just thinking of pinning you down and shoving my dick inside you."

"Please let Rhett go," I pleaded.

"Don't worry. I have the perfect cage for him." I heard a pop and then another. Dima cursed. "What are those idiots doing up there?"

I hoped he'd go check it out and leave me alone. He wandered off, and I thought I'd gotten a reprieve, until he returned less than a minute later. Thankfully, I hadn't dared to move. If I had, something told me I'd be hurting far more than I was at the moment.

Dima grabbed my arm and hauled me into another room. I struggled to keep up and not trip over my pants, which had fallen to my ankles. I tried not to think of the horrors that may have happened within the walls of what appeared to be some sort of torture chamber. A bed took up a corner with handcuffs hanging from both the headboard and footboard. A tripod was on the other side of the space with a camera. As my gaze scanned the area, the other items in the room nearly had me ready to faint.

"Strip and lie face down on the bed," he said.

I tried to stifle my sobs as I obeyed him. I crawled onto the mattress. Dima locked the cuffs around my wrists, then spread my legs and did the same to my ankles. I couldn't stop crying. If it weren't for Rhett, I'd have done my best to fight him off. But I wasn't going to do anything that might put that sweet boy at risk. As long as I gave Dima what he wanted, I hoped he'd leave Rhett alone.

Dima unzipped his pants and I felt the bed dip. "Going to mark you as mine, then I need to take care of some business."

I didn't understand what he meant, until I heard him grunting and then felt the heat of his cum as it splattered over my lower back and the top of my ass cheeks. I shuddered, and knew I'd temporarily dodged a bullet. I stared at the opposite wall, wondering if I would ever get out of this house. Did he plan to keep me here in this room? He'd said something about breeding me. Was I to be locked up here like a caged beast?

"Be a good girl and I'll return soon," Dima said. "Cause any trouble and I'll make you watch as I hurt the boy."

"I'll be good," I whispered. Anything to keep Rhett safe.

I heard the door shut behind him, and I waited for what felt like ages. So many sounds filled the house. Shouts. More of the popping sounds that I now thought might be gunfire. The stomping of feet as if people were running in multiple directions. The door slammed into the wall and I jolted. Dima sprawled on the floor and my breath caught when I saw why. Python stalked him, entering the small space. The moment he saw me on the bed, the devastation on his face made my stomach drop. I knew what he had to be thinking.

"So, you've found your little whore," Dima said. "Don't worry. I've been showing her what it's like to be with a real man. Not some pussy like you."

"You kidnapped my wife and son, dared to put your hands on them, and you still have the balls to taunt me? If it's your way of asking for a quick death, request denied."

"See, Galina. He's no better than me or your father. This man is every bit as savage." Dima grinned, and Python hauled back his fist, nailing him right in the mouth. Dima spat out blood and a few teeth, but the arrogance didn't leave his face. I hoped Python destroyed him. Even if my new husband didn't want anything to do with me after this, just knowing he'd made Dima suffer would be enough to keep me going.

"Make him hurt," I said.

"Oh, I'm going to, Lina. You might want to close your eyes."

I shook my head. "No. I want to watch everything you do to him."

Perhaps it would be enough to keep the nightmares away. Once I left this place, I'd do my best to put this incident behind me. But something told me it wouldn't be quite so easy.

* * *

Python

I couldn't think about Lina right now. If I did, I was going to completely lose my shit. I'd taken my time with her, easing her into things, and now he'd... I didn't even want to complete the thought.

"You're lucky it looks like you only smacked my son a time or two. Or was it your goons who did it? Either way, none of you are leaving this place alive."

Dima laughed. "Only for now. I had plans for that one. After using him to control Galina, I was going to break him a little at a time. It would have been fun to make her watch."

"Sick assholes like you are what's wrong with this fucked-up world. I'm going to make you suffer, and if you pass the hell out, I'll wait until you're awake to start again."

"You good in here?" Trick asked, entering the room.

I whirled to face him. "Get the fuck out!"

His eyebrows shot up, the moment he saw Galina on the bed, understanding lit his eyes. He covered them with his hand and held the other one out palm up. "Get me the key. I'll release her."

"Where is the key?" I asked Dima.

He pulled it from his pocket, gave a bark of laughter, then tossed the damn thing into his mouth and swallowed. "Now you'll have to break her wrists or cut her hands off to get her out of here."

I wanted to beat the hell out of him, rip him open, and take the key out. I held up the knife. "Guess I'll have to go in after it."

"Not to stop your bit of fun," Trick said, "but it's not going to reach a spot anytime soon where you could cut it out, assuming that's what you meant. I'll pick the locks on the handcuffs. I won't look anywhere other than at her wrists and ankles. All right?"

"Fine. Get her and Rhett out of this house, Trick. Take them to my car and have someone guard them. I'll be there as soon as I'm done here."

"I swear I didn't look. Once I realized what was going on, I shut my eyes when you told me to leave. But... I did see enough to know she's not going to sit in a car comfortably. I don't think she's able to lay in the back seat of that Challenger either."

"I'll do it," Galina said. "Whatever it takes to go home, just please get me out of here. Assuming he still wants me to go home."

I froze and slowly turned to face her. I'd done my best not to. Seeing what the bastard had done made me want to throw up. I'd failed to protect her. "Why wouldn't I want you to go home with us? We're a family, Lina."

Tears fell from her eyes. "Because of what he's done to me. He wanted to make sure you see a filthy whore when you look at me."

I closed my eyes and took a breath, trying to calm myself. "I don't think that at all, Lina. Trick will get you and Rhett safely out of the house. Once Dima is dead, I'll take the two of you home."

Trick moved closer and knelt at her feet. He touched the cuffs, then pulled something from his back pocket. I snorted when I realized what it was.

"You always keep a lockpick with you?" I asked.

"Never know when you'll need it. Like now." It didn't take Trick long to free Lina. He wrapped her in a blanket and got her out of the room. I heard them speaking to Rhett and waited another few minutes.

"Now it's just us." I faced Dima and gripped the knife a little tighter. "You realize fighting is pointless, right? No matter how much you struggle, you aren't getting out of here."

"This is all her fault, you know? If she hadn't run off, then your boy wouldn't have been caught up in this."

"Lina still would have been hurt. Someone like you doesn't know how to treat a woman."

Dima smiled. "I'd have given her everything she wanted, as long as she gave me sons."

"And if she didn't or couldn't have kids?" I asked.

He shrugged. "Then I'd have let my men have her. I don't like useless things."

"Useless." I turned the knife in my hand, twisting the handle. "Right. Like you. I can't think of a single reason for a piece of shit like you to stay alive. Besides, you swallowed the key I needed. I might as well help retrieve it."

That had his attention. I saw the flash of fear in his eyes as he tried to bolt past me. I slammed my fist into his temple. Once. Twice. The third time, he fell to the floor. Dragging him toward the bed, I used the handcuffs to secure one of his wrists. At least he wouldn't be going anywhere now, unless he took the bed with him.

"Now. Let's have a little fun. You enjoyed playing with Lina, right? Now I get to play with *you*." I cut his shirt from his body, then trailed the knife down the center of his chest. A trail of blood beaded on the skin. I dug it in a little deeper. Not enough to completely slice him open, but he knew I meant business. "Since my wife and son are waiting for me, let's get this over with."

I slammed the blade into his gut. He screamed and cursed at me. Dima grew silent as I carved a jagged line across his abdomen. He'd paled and looked like he might be seconds from passing out. Reaching into the hole I'd made, I removed some of his organs, leaving them on the floor beside him. It didn't take long for him to breathe his last. Once I knew he'd never hurt anyone ever again, I got up and found a bathroom. I wasn't about to go out to Lina and Rhett looking like this. I cleaned myself up, then decided to let Trick and his crew handle the rest.

"You done?" he asked when I got to the car.

"Yeah. He's dead. Made a mess, though."

"We'll get it cleaned up. Get your family home safely."

I thanked him again and got into the Challenger. Rhett sat in the front seat, his eyes fearfully watching Galina. Thankfully, the blanket covered everything. When we got home, I'd need someone to watch Rhett so I could take care of her. But I didn't want him to be scared or feel like we were leaving him out.

"Rhett, I have a favor to ask."

"What is it, Dad?" he asked.

"Lina needs my help when we get home, and I'm not sure she'll like that you saw her like this. Would you be okay going to either Tate's or Theo's house for a little bit? Not overnight, unless you want to stay until morning. I need an hour or two with Lina."

"Okay." He eyed her again. "I love you, Mom."

Whatever hell she'd been through, now that she knew she was safe, she'd fallen asleep. I didn't know what sorts of nightmares she'd have after this. Whatever it took, I'd make sure she knew I loved her.

Chapter Fourteen

Python

I dropped Rhett off at Saint's house. Sofia got a bath ready for him and loaned him some of Tate's pajamas. When I got to the house, I lifted Lina from the back seat and carried her inside. I'd burn the fucking blanket tomorrow. We went straight to the master bathroom. I turned on the shower and somehow managed to strip out of my clothes without letting Lina fall. She'd woken up but seemed to be dazed.

I carried her into the shower and shut the door behind us. As gently as I could, I washed her. I could feel her body shaking as she silently cried. There wasn't a single thing I could think of to say to her. What could ever make this right?

"If you want to talk, I'll listen," I said. "But I'm not going to force you to tell me what happened."

"He didn't... didn't..." She buried her face against me.

"Are you trying to say he didn't rape you?" She nodded. Relief flooded me. At least she'd been spared that much. "But he beat you?"

"Used his belt on me," she said softly. "Then he cuffed me to the bed and came on me. He'd planned to do more, but you got there before anything else happened."

"You're going to hurt for a while," I said. "We'll treat your wounds when we get out. Rhett can stay the night at Saint's house. I'd told him he could come home tonight if that's what he wanted, but I'll message Saint and see if his kids can convince him to stay until morning. I think you need a quiet evening."

"Is he going to be okay?" Lina asked. "I tried to protect him as much as I could, but I don't know what he managed to hear or see while we were there."

"He's mostly worried about you, I think. I'll get someone to take a look at him tomorrow. There's a psychiatrist the club has used several times over the years. It wouldn't hurt for both of you to speak with him."

"Him?" she asked.

"Yes, it's a man. He happens to be gay, so I can promise you're not in any danger. But if you want me to stay with you the entire time, then that's what I'll do." I kissed the top of her head. "It scared the fuck out of me when I realized you and Rhett were being kidnapped."

"I told him to run. I tried really hard to keep him away from those men, but they decided he'd be worth something. Dima only wanted to use him as a way to control me. It's why I gave in to all his demands. As long as I did that, then Rhett wouldn't be hurt."

I held her tight, wishing like fuck I could erase everything that happened to the both of them. If we could have a do-over for the day, I never would have taken them into town. I'd have gone to get her ring by myself, and we'd have celebrated here. Of course, without knowing danger was lurking in town, we'd have eventually left the compound and she'd have still been a target. At least this way, I'd been able to witness the two of them being kidnapped, and I'd called Wire fast enough for him to track them.

"I shouldn't have left you alone," I said.

"You said you had an errand to run. It seemed important. Besides, how could you have known what would happen? This isn't your fault."

How the hell could she be trying to comfort me

at a time like this? After what she'd endured, she should be screaming at me. They had to have been waiting for the three of us to split up, or for me to be distracted long enough for them to snatch her.

"Wait here for just one second. I'm coming right back." I got out of the shower and wrapped a towel around my waist. When we'd gotten home, I'd noticed the SUV was in the driveway, which meant someone retrieved it for me. Good thing, since I'd left the ring in there. I got it out of the passenger seat, then went back to Lina.

She wasn't looking my way. Her eyes were closed, with her head bowed. I hoped like hell she wasn't still crying, but it was understandable if she was. The woman had been through hell today. I took the ring from the box, dropped my towel, and got back into the shower. Taking her left hand in mine, I slid the ring onto her finger.

Lina gasped and looked up at me with wide eyes. "Dylan? What's... Why did you get this ring? Is that where you went earlier?"

"Yeah. Rhett knew about it. I'd wanted him to help pick it out, but he chose to stay with you. For what it's worth, I couldn't get anything like the ones he showed me on the phone, but the amethyst stone was of his choosing, and so is the cut." I pressed my forehead to hers. "I wanted him to feel like part of the family. He's my son, and now he's yours as well. I'd planned to have this elaborate dinner or something, but... I had Wire marry us, Lina. You're officially my wife if anyone were to go digging in the vital records. I'm sure Wire can get us a copy of the marriage certificate if you want one."

Her lower lip trembled. "We're really married? He wasn't just saying that to Dima?"

"Wait, Rhett already said we're married? That little snot." I smiled. "I wanted to be the one to share the news."

"I'd thought he was just saying it to either protect me or because it's what he really wanted. I didn't think we were actually married." She gave me a slight smile. "Are you sure about this, Dylan? After today... I'd understand if you didn't want to be married to me, or if you wanted me to leave."

I cupped her cheek, my heart shattering at her words. "Hey. None of this was your fault, Lina. That asshole was a sadistic fuck who thought he owned you. He didn't have a soul, or a heart. I saw the pure evil in his eyes, even as he was dying. He's the one to blame for everything. So no, I don't want you to leave, and I'm not changing my mind. We'll get through this together, as a family."

She started crying again, and I held her against my chest. I didn't know what else to say or do. I'd give her anything she needed or wanted. We'd only been together a short time, and she already had my heart. Maybe what she really needed was to hear the words from me.

"When you first came here, you caught my attention. I thought you were beautiful, and probably a fuck ton of trouble. I wanted you gone because the last thing I thought I needed was someone as tempting as you right under my nose. But the joke's on me because you're precisely what was missing from my life."

"You really think so?" she asked.

"I know so. Lina, I fought so hard because I didn't think I deserved to be happy. I'd failed Jenny and Rhett, and I thought I'd lost them both. It wasn't until Wire and Lavender found my son that I realized everything I thought I knew had been wrong. And if I was wrong about that, then it meant I wasn't right about anything else. Well, not relationship stuff anyway."

I wasn't good with words. There was so much more I needed to say, and I worried it wouldn't come out right. Giving her a ring and saying she was my wife was one thing. Explaining why I actually *wanted* her was another matter.

"I didn't want to ruin your life. You saved me the night you brought me home from the clubhouse and sent Penny on her way. Waking up next to you that next morning wasn't as awful feeling as I'd thought it would be. In fact, I kind of liked it. Scared the shit out of me, then the club burst in and everything went to hell. I know I hurt you with my words and actions, and I'm sorry."

"I understood why you were pushing me away," she said. "Especially after you told me about Jenny. It wasn't your fault I had feelings for you. If my heart got broken, that was my own choice. I'm the one who put myself into a position where it could get battered and bruised."

"There hasn't been a day I didn't want you. I just couldn't admit it, not even to myself. Then once I finally owned up to the fact I wanted you and needed you in my life, I wanted us to have a real chance."

"What exactly are you trying to say?" she asked.

"I love you, Lina. I think I fell for you the night you saved me. If not then, definitely the next morning."

"I love you too," she said "And Rhett. I know he's not my biological son, but I don't care. I love him so much."

"He feels the same about you. He never got to meet Jenny, and doesn't know anything about her, other than the little bits I've shared with him recently. For him, you *are* his mother and always will be. You're the only one he's known. Blood doesn't always determine our families, Lina. Take this club for example."

"Does this mean I'm getting one of those property cuts like Lavender was wearing?" she asked.

"Yeah, you will. To be clear, it doesn't mean I think I own you in the way Dima thought you were his possession. We're equal partners in this family, all right?"

"What happened to Dima?"

"Are you sure you want to know? He's dead, I can promise you that. Is it important how he died?"

"A little," she said. "He hurt me, terrified me, and the things he said he would do to me and Rhett... I threw up after I heard some of it."

I drew back and stared down at her. "What the fuck did he say he would do to Rhett?"

She glanced away, apparently unable to hold to my gaze. "He said if I refused to let him do whatever he wanted to me, then he'd force me to watch as he did them to Rhett instead. He mentioned a boy like Rhett earning a lot of money for him."

Now I wished I hadn't let the bastard off so easy. No, even if I'd heard this beforehand, I still wouldn't have dragged things out. Lina had been hurt and I knew I needed to get her home. I'd done the right thing.

"I cut him open and removed some of his organs," I admitted. "I only stayed long enough to see the light in his eyes go out. If I'd had more time, I'd have made him suffer for a while. You and Rhett were more important than my revenge."

"As long as he can't hurt anyone else, that's what

counts," she said.

"Turn around and let me see how much damage he did," I said. "I promise I'll be gentle."

She hesitated only for a moment. Slowly, she turned and bent over a little. The welts on her ass had broken open and bled. The water might have washed away the dried blood, but I still saw the raw areas that would eventually scab over.

"I'm going to get out for just a minute. I have some antibacterial soap under the sink. I keep it on hand for whenever I have wounds. I'll use it to wash you today. It doesn't smell awesome, but it will keep these from getting infected."

She waited while I got out and back in as quickly as I could. I lathered my hands and gently washed her ass cheeks, trying to keep my touch as light as possible as I cleansed the welts. I should have taken his belt and beaten him with it before I killed him.

"You're sure he didn't... I mean, he only came on you, right?" I asked. "You can tell me the truth, Lina. If he did more than that, I can go with you to the doctor. Make sure he didn't give you any diseases or hurt you inside."

She faced me and reached up to cup my cheek. "I promise he didn't get that far. I told you that you came in time to stop him, and I meant it. I wasn't just saying it to make you feel better. He wanted to breed me, then give me to his men once I'd served my purpose. But you killed him, and he'll never get the chance to do those things now."

"I want to touch you, but I'm worried I'd only hurt you more. You can't even lie on your back right now."

"You said you'd bought some other types of toys. Is there anything we could use in here where I wouldn't have to lie on the bed?"

I shook my head. "No, Lina. We're not doing that right now. You need to rest."

"What I need is to feel complete," she said, her voice breaking as more tears slipped down her cheeks. "He took so much from me, Dylan. When he told me to pull down my pants and bend over, I thought he was going to rape me. Then he handcuffed me to the bed. I couldn't escape. Whatever he wanted to do, I had no choice but to lie there and take it. He could have murdered me and I'd not have been able to fight back."

"What do you need, Lina? Tell me and I'll make it happen."

She gave me a tremulous smile. "Make me feel good like before. Show me that you don't see me differently because of what happened."

"The toys are waterproof, but what if we moved to the bed and you were on your hands and knees? Or..." I swallowed hard hoping I wasn't about to fuck up. "What if you leaned over the bathroom counter? You'd be able to see us in the mirror, so you'd know it was me behind you. Putting you in the same position Dima forced you into might help ease some of your fear."

"Okay. We can try that, but can we start in here? This is our space. It's where we were intimate for the first time, and again after Rhett came to live with us. I feel safe in here with you, and while it's just a shower, it still holds good memories for me."

"Then wait here. I'll bring everything to the bathroom."

I got out and went to retrieve the bag of toys. I opened it and looked inside, thinking of the one item we hadn't used yet. An extremely small vibrator. Well, tiny compared to my dick at any rate. I'd planned to use it on her a few times before taking her virginity, knowing I was large enough to hurt her if she wasn't used to having anything inside her.

I didn't know when she'd be ready for us to take things all the way, but I would give her as much time as she needed. The fact she still wanted me to share this much with her was a miracle as far as I was concerned.

I got into the shower again, with the toy we'd used before. The shower was pretty big, and I had an idea I wanted to try. Taking her by the hand, I kneeled down and brought her with me, then leaned against the shower wall, stretching my legs out, then patted my thighs.

"Straddle me, then lean forward." She did as I said, bracing her hands on my shoulders. I turned on the toy and teased her clit with it. "Let's get you warmed up."

Her nipples hardened and her eyes darkened. I slid the toy along the lips of her pussy several times before fitting it into place. Once I had the piece over her clit in place, I pressed the heel of my hand to it. She gasped, then moaned.

My cock grew so damn hard it hurt. She rocked against my hand, and I wished like fuck I was inside her while she moved like that. I'd be willing to bet it would feel amazing. "That's it, Lina. Get yourself off. Come all over my hand."

She tipped her head back and thrust her breasts out. Her nipples dragged across me as she kept rocking. Fuck, but she was driving me crazy! I pressed the heel of my hand tighter against the toy, then eased the tip of one finger inside her pussy. Pushing the inside piece against her G-spot, she came instantly, screaming out her release. As she twitched and moaned with every pulse of pleasure, I worked my finger in and out of her. Feeling how tight her pussy was nearly made me come.

Her orgasm seemed never-ending. I continued to tease and torment her, feeling her cream coat my finger. She squirted twice as she peaked and I thought I might die before she decided she'd had enough.

"More," she murmured. "I want to do more."

Jesus fucking Christ. I'd give her whatever she wanted and more... but I might end up with the worst case of blue balls ever before we were finished.

Chapter Fifteen

Lina

I felt like the wanton whore Dima had thought me to be. I didn't know what it was about Python, but his touch was addicting. Despite the pain in my ass cheeks, I didn't want him to stop. In fact... I wanted all of him. I didn't want to be a virgin anymore. We were husband and wife, so I wanted to feel like I truly belonged to him.

"He came on me to mark me as his," I said. Python stiffened under me.

"Excuse me?"

"He said he was marking me as his. He asked if I'd ever had a cock in my mouth, my cunt, or my ass." My cheeks burned when I said the C word. "I'd had you in my mouth, so... he punished me for the betrayal, then said he'd fill me full of his cum."

"Why are you telling me this?" he asked.

I squirmed and pressed against his hand. "I want everything from you, Dylan. He tried to make me his. I need you to prove to everyone I belong to you and only you."

He closed his eyes and groaned. "Lina, I'm not fucking your ass. I'm too damn big."

"Then improvise. I want to do everything. Don't hold back anymore."

"You'll get hurt. We need to wait until you've healed."

I shook my head. "No. Now, Dylan. Please. I need this, and I think you do too."

"Then we're getting out."

He helped me stand, but I noticed he didn't

remove the toy. He didn't even bother to dry either of us. After he turned off the shower, he led me to the bathroom counter, and had me lean over it. I braced my hands and stared at him in the mirror. He looked around the bathroom and retrieved two footstools from the corner. I'd wondered why he had more than one. He lifted first one of my feet, then the other, placing a stool under each. The rubber tops kept me from slipping, which I appreciated. I noticed the height put my pussy in full view of the mirror. Had that been his intention?

"You're too short." He grinned so I knew he didn't mean it in a bad way. He took another toy from the bag and showed me the slender vibrator. Python twisted the end, and I heard it turn on. "You ready for all kinds of firsts?"

"Yes."

"Watch." He slid the toy between my thighs. I saw it peek out from between my legs, then he eased it back and slowly pushed it inside me. It pressed against the other toy, and I sucked in a breath at how much fuller I felt. Twice as wide as his finger had been, it felt both good and a bit intense. "Don't look away."

He pulled the toy out to the tip before pushing it back in. As he fucked me with it, I found myself mesmerized by the sight. He removed the toy and eased it between my ass cheeks. I tensed for a moment as I felt it press against me. Python thrust his cock between my legs, letting it slide against the toy inside my pussy.

"Focus on my cock. The asshole said he'd take your ass? Then I'll claim you there, just like you wanted. I'm going to fuck you with the toy, make you come and beg for more. Only then will I give you my cum."

"How? You said you were too big," I said.

"It's going to be tight, and it's going to hurt." He leaned in, placing his lips near my ear right as he eased the toy into my ass, slick from where it had been inside me. "I'll push the head in and make you come again. You won't be able to help but to fuck yourself on my dick. I'll fill your ass with my cum, and when you're ready for more, I'll fuck your pussy too."

My heart felt like it was going to beat out of my chest it was pounding so hard. My body felt hot and achy just from hearing his words alone. How could such a thing turn me on like this?

Every time he drew his hips back, he pulled the toy nearly all the way out of my ass. When he thrust forward, he plunged the toy inside me again. I stared at his cock, watching as it seemed to swell and the head became darker.

"Fuck, Lina. I'm so close to coming," he said. "Come for me. Please come. I need to be inside you so bad."

I reached down and felt his cock sliding against me. As I touched him, I pressed the toy tighter against my clit, and I came, screaming his name. He abruptly removed the one in my ass and pressed his cock there instead. I heard a popping sound and realized he'd grabbed a bottle of lube from somewhere, and the ice-cold liquid slid down the crack of my ass. He worked his cock into me, and I thought I might die it burned so much. Despite the pain, knowing it was Python had me holding still and taking whatever he gave me.

He pressed his hand between my legs once more. I rocked against him, shallow movements, until my clit was aching. When I couldn't hold back, my hips seemed to move without my permission, taking his cock inside me as I also got myself off using the toy. As

I came, I felt him thrusting inside me, then the heat of his release.

"Fuck, baby! You only have two inches of my dick in you, but it's a beautiful sight." He pulled free and I felt the trickle of his cum sliding out of me. "Don't move."

He cleaned himself up in the sink, then took my hand and led me to the bedroom. Python stretched out on the bed and helped me straddle his waist. Even though he'd just come, his cock still seemed hard to me.

"Do whatever you want to make yourself come. When you're ready, take my cock and slide down on as much of it as you can take. I'm going to let you have control so I don't hurt you."

"But..." I touched the toy between my legs. He flashed me a smile. Shit. So he wanted it to remain inside me. I wondered if I could handle him.

Python reached up and cupped my breasts in his hands, running a thumb over one of my nipples. He twisted the peak and pinched down. A shudder of pleasure went through me, and I found myself moving before I'd consciously thought about it. When I was close to coming, I lifted up and reached between us, gripping his cock. I placed it against my pussy and braced myself as I tried to take him inside me. I couldn't hold back the whimper of pain as he stretched me. I didn't think I'd taken very much. The pressure against the toy increased and I straddled a fine line between pleasure and pain.

"That's it, beautiful. Show me how much you want this. Only way you're getting my cum is if you fuck me."

Leaning forward, I placed my hands on either side of his head and felt my nipples scrape against his chest. The friction felt so incredibly good. I realized the more of him I took inside me, the easier it was to rub my pussy against his body. The pressure against the toy gave me enough stimulation I had a small orgasm, and he slid in a little farther.

"Come for me, Lina."

I rode him, pushing both of us closer to the breaking point. The next time I came, I felt his cock swell inside me. He gripped my hips and thrust into me twice before he came. His release spilled from around his cock and ran down my thighs.

"When you're all healed, we're going to explore a bit more. I want to know everything you like to do in the bedroom," he said. "And I may have to visit that adult store again. I think we need a few more things."

I collapsed on top of him, completely exhausted. Every part of me ached, and all I wanted to do was sleep. He'd been right about me needing rest, but this had been important too.

* * *

Python

As much as I'd enjoyed what we'd done, I still thought we should have waited. But I'd promised to give her what she wanted and needed, so I'd given in. Now she slept soundly in the bed beside me. I called Saint to see how Rhett was doing, keeping my voice low so I wouldn't wake up Lina.

"Hello," Saint said as the call connected.

"Just checking on Rhett. He doing okay?"

"Yeah. Sofia gave him a bath, fed him, then he and Tate played for a bit. They're both asleep in the living room. The boys wanted to camp out and watch TV."

"Whenever he wants to come home in the

morning, I'd appreciate it if one of you could drop him off. I don't want to leave Lina alone, and I don't think she'll be walking around much for a day or two. Fucker used a belt on her ass and she has welts."

"He's dead, right?" Saint asked.

"I gutted him. Someone Wire sent to help said they'd take care of the cleanup."

"Good. If y'all need anything, give any of us a shout. The entire club is aware of what happened, to some extent. No one expects you to do a damn thing right now except take care of your family. And if Rhett gets to be too much for Lina while she's healing, he's welcome here any time. I know he liked playing with Theo too. I'm sure Sarge would be okay with a sleepover at his place as well."

"Thanks, Saint. I appreciate it." I wanted to see my son and hold him. Much like I'd done with Lina, I'd try to give him whatever he needed. At eleven, he'd most likely do his best to act tough. I'd have to watch for signs he wasn't doing as okay as he pretended.

"I'm going to probably ask Lina to stay in bed tomorrow. It's not like she can sit down anywhere at the moment. Probably going to be a few days. Do you think Doctor Myron would make a house call and bring his partner with him?"

"You know he would," Saint said. "I'll give him a call in the morning and send the two of them your way. Even if Rhett wants to go home, I'll try to stall him until the doctor is leaving or nearly ready to go. I'm sure Lina would prefer some privacy during the visit."

"If he wants to call when he wakes up, I'm sure Lina would like to hear his voice. We both would, actually."

"Consider it done. Take care of your woman.

Don't worry about anything else."

I ended the call and got up to get a drink. While I was in the kitchen, I found the bottle of naproxen and carried it to the bedroom with a bottle of water. Whenever Lina woke up, I'd get her to take them. I also fetched the triple antibiotic from the bathroom, and doing my best to not wake her up, I slathered the wounds in the ointment. She whimpered in her sleep, but otherwise it didn't seem to bother her.

I stretched out beside her and read on my phone, glancing her way every few minutes. I wasn't sure I'd want her out of my sight anytime soon. Even knowing the men responsible were dead, I still felt an anxiousness over knowing she'd been taken from me so easily. What if someone else in the Bratva decided to come for her? I couldn't think of anyone else who would, but... it didn't stop me from worrying.

I shot off a quick text to Wire, hoping he could find out if the Bratva planned to retaliate in any way. It only took him a few minutes to respond.

We received a message from them before you even got home. You're in the clear.

What the fuck? Why hadn't he said something before now? *You're an asshole for not telling me sooner.*

Wire called and I answered before the ringing could wake up Lina. "You're a dick."

He snorted. "Fuck you, too. I didn't realize you'd be thinking about the Bratva right this minute. Galina and Rhett both doing okay?"

"Rhett is with Saint. I've been assured he's fine and is currently asleep. Lina seems okay, but she's been injured. Saint was going to send Doctor Myron and his partner over tomorrow morning."

"Listen, Dima wasn't very high up in the Bratva, but he was significantly more important than Galina's

father. That being said, the Vor transferred half of
Dima's money to us. I've placed it into a holding
account for now. When Lina is in a better frame of
mind, we can either give it to her, or she can tell us
what she'd like done with it. The Bratva is, of course,
keeping all his properties, the other half of the money,
and whatever other assets he had."

"I don't think any of us give a shit," I said. "What
about her dad's assets?"

"It's a quarter million dollars. That's more than
enough to send Rhett to college, if he decides to go.
You can buy a new car for Lina, get one for Rhett when
he's old enough, and still have money in the bank for
emergencies. So like I said. Take some time to think
about it. And honestly, it's Lina's decision, not yours."
He paused. "As for her father, the Bratva already took
over anything he owned. It wasn't nearly as much as
Dima."

"Fine. Just don't tell her for a few days. Let her
have some time to find her footing again."

"Consider it done. Lavender said to let her know
when Lina is up for some company. She wants to drop
by and visit for a bit. I'm sure Ridley and the others
will be dropping off food for you. It's not like Lina will
be up for cooking, and if you feed your family they
may die."

"Hey! Asshole, I'm not that bad of a cook."

"Keep telling yourself that," Wire said.

I hung up on him and kept watch over Lina until
the sun rose. She'd quickly become my everything, and
I didn't want to even contemplate life without her. If
I'd gotten there too late, or found her body because the
insane bastard decided to kill her, I'd have completely
lost myself. Not only would I have slaughtered Dima,
but I'd most likely have taken my own life. I wasn't

even sure Rhett would have been enough to keep me sane enough to leave that place if Lina hadn't made it.

"You have my heart, Lina. I've never given it to anyone before. Knowing it's you, I'm not scared. I know you'll take care of it." I lifted her hand and kissed it.

When I finally managed to fall asleep, I did so with our fingers entwined.

Epilogue

Lina

It had been four months since the kidnapping, and I felt whole again. Thanks to Saint sending over Doctor Myron and Doctor Sykes, I'd not only been physically healed, but I'd also been going to therapy once a week. I hadn't realized how much I needed to unpack from both my childhood and the incident with Dima. Rhett had been seeing Doctor Sykes as well, and I could tell he was a much better adjusted little boy than before. He smiled freely, but he also cried when he felt the need. Our son didn't put on a show and pretend he was fine when he wasn't. He now felt safe enough to truly be himself.

I stared at the stick in my hand. Python mentioned wanting a child with me. A boy or girl who was half of each of us. I hoped this news was going to make him happy. Of course, I'd need to set an appointment with Doctor Myron to make sure it wasn't a false positive, but I didn't think that was the case. I'd noticed my breasts were more tender, my moods were... well, Jekyll and Hyde had nothing on me these days. From what I'd been reading online, all signs pointed to me being pregnant.

Rhett was currently off with Tate and Theo. They liked to ride their bikes all over the compound, and only go to one of their houses when one of them was thirsty, hungry, or needed a bathroom. Since they'd been here an hour ago, I figured we had a little time before Rhett came home again. I leaned against the doorway to the living room and watched Python. He'd put on a movie and was doing his best to relax. It had taken a lot for me to get him to sit still ever since he'd come to rescue me and Rhett. If I wasn't right beside him, insisting he stay with me, then he was on the phone, in the kitchen, or trying to find some item or other to make our lives easier. Much like the small SUV in our driveway that he'd bought me a month ago. Wire had insisted he keep the Challenger he'd used to drive into Bratva territory, so we now had those two vehicles plus his motorcycle.

"Dylan, can I talk to you for a minute?" I asked.

He looked up and smiled. "You need something? I can make lemonade if we're out. Or do I need to head to the bakery for those cookies you like?"

I shook my head. "All I need you to do is stay right there and listen to what I have to say."

His brow furrowed. "Not if it's bad news."

"Well… I guess that depends on you."

He leaned forward. "What's that supposed to mean?"

"How do you feel about shopping and spending tons of money, and renovating one of the rooms in the house?" I asked.

"Do you want a craft room or library or something?"

"No. I was thinking more along the lines of… a nursery." I showed him the stick I'd hidden behind my back. "It's positive."

He sat completely still for a minute or more. When he stood and came over, I saw the tears in his eyes. Gently, he wrapped his arms around me and hugged me. "I'm so fucking happy, Lina. I have everything I never thought I wanted. A beautiful wife, a smart son, and now another baby on the way. I can't think of anything else I could ever want or need."

"Think Rhett will be happy about this?" I asked.

"Yeah, especially if we give him a little sister who looks just like his mom."

"If someone asked me five months ago if I thought we'd ever be together, I'd have told them no. I'm glad I've been proven wrong. I love you so much, Dylan. You and Rhett both. Coming to the Dixie Reapers was the best thing that ever happened to me. I might have been running from my father and an unwanted marriage, but by coming here I gained everything I never had. Love, acceptance, and family."

He kissed me, slow and deep. My toes curled and I clung to him. For such a big brute, he could be incredibly gentle at times. And sexy as hell. I was lucky to have him in my life, and I knew it.

"Let's go tell everyone," he said.

"Shouldn't we talk to Rhett first?"

"Fine. We'll tell Rhett, and then we'll tell everyone else. I want the entire world to know we're having a baby."

I rolled my eyes. "In a few months I'll start showing. Then the entire world will know because they'll see me coming. My stomach will arrive in a room several seconds before the rest of me."

"You're going to be cute with a baby belly." He kissed me again. "Thank you for being mine, Lina... for saving me that night, and not giving up on me. There's no one in this world more perfect for me than you."

"That's because we're meant to be." I smiled and hugged him. "Come on, my big, sexy biker. Let's find our son before you burst from not being able to tell everyone we're having a baby. God forbid you have to wait an hour or three."

"Nope. Two seconds is too long, much less two hours."

I really did love the man, and by some miracle, he loved me too.

Joker (Dixie Reapers MC 19)
A Dixie Reapers Bad Boys Romance
Harley Wylde

Cleo -- My family put me through hell, and I escaped the only way possible... by marrying a biker locked up in prison. Joker gave me his name and a way to hide from my family. Until the day they find me... Now it's time I return to the husband who doesn't want me and hope he doesn't find out all my secrets -- because if he does, I have a feeling he's going to make me leave.

Joker -- She seemed sweet and innocent. Marrying her wasn't a big deal. Then I managed to obtain my freedom, and with it, I decided to set her free as well. Only one problem. She doesn't want a divorce. Now Cleo is living with me, and my club has accepted her as part of our family. None of us realized she was hiding something that could destroy us, but at the end of the day, she's mine and I'll do whatever it takes to keep her safe.

Prologue

Joker

The clanging of metal bars and shouting inmates jolted me awake. Another day in this hellhole. I blinked against the harsh fluorescent lights as the guard banged his baton against my cell, barking at me to get up. My joints creaked in protest as I slid off the thin mattress onto the cold concrete floor. I'd wasted away in this cage for over a decade, my youth fading with each endless day.

"Mail," the guard said, thrusting a letter into my cell.

Only one person wrote to me. Someone I'd never met in person, though she'd sent me a picture one time. Out of boredom, I'd signed up for a pen pal program, not expecting much. To my surprise, I'd received dozens of letters -- all from women. One had stood out. A teen girl named Cleo.

I'd been hesitant to respond. At forty-eight, I'd felt like it was wrong to reply to her. My morals might be questionable, but I still had a line I wouldn't cross. In the end, I'd answered her, and we'd been writing to each other ever since. She'd needed a sympathetic ear, and I'd needed a distraction.

I opened Cleo's latest letter, her looping cursive filling the page. My light in this darkness. She saw the man beneath the cut, the heart behind the grim façade. Her letters were a glimpse of the world outside these walls. She shared her dreams, her troubles, her very soul. And I confessed things to her I'd never uttered aloud. The abandoned boy who turned to the club for family, the gnawing loneliness beneath the swagger.

She understood. We were both fighting our own demons.

The guard slammed the bars again. "Chow time, Joker! Look alive!"

I tucked Cleo's letter into my pocket, close to my heart. I'd survive another day in this concrete tomb just to read her words again tonight. And someday, somehow, I'd be free. I wasn't sure what would happen then. We were worlds apart in a lot of ways. Once I left this place, Cleo would come to be a part of my past. It would be dangerous for us to keep in touch.

I shuffled into the cafeteria, the din of inmates engulfing me. I kept my head down as I grabbed my tray of slop and found an empty table. Solitude was survival in this jungle. Placing my arm around my tray, I shoveled food into my mouth. In this place, you had to protect what was yours.

My thoughts drifted to Cleo as I forced down the cold mush. She hadn't written in weeks. Her family was poison. From what I'd gathered they were all rotten to the core. She only hinted at the horrors she'd seen, but I sensed the fear beneath her brave words. At seventeen, she shouldn't be worried about surviving. She should be having fun with her friends, enjoying her high school years, and figuring out where she wanted to go in life. I hated not being able to do anything for her, except listen.

My fists clenched, rage simmering through my veins. If they touched one hair on her head, I'd kill them. She was too pure for this world, an angel who deserved so much more. I had to protect her, no matter the cost. Except... the shackles binding me went deeper than this prison. I owed my club my life and my loyalty. I couldn't do anything without talking to them first, and I hadn't heard from any of them in a long-ass time. I'd fucked up, and it had felt like they all turned their backs on me.

The guards herded us to the yard, the sun blinding after days under flickering fluorescent lights. I found a shady corner and waited. Breathing in the fresh air meant nothing without freedom. I'd only traded an interior cage for an exterior one.

A hush fell over the inmates. The warden stormed across the yard, his face like thunder. He stopped in front of me, his eyes hard. Well, shit. Had I done something wrong again? It wasn't often he came in person. Then again, I wasn't always nice to the guards. Maybe he was simply protecting his men.

"You've got a visitor, Joker."

My pulse quickened. No one had come to see me in years. What the fuck was going on?

The warden didn't like me. In fact, we'd frequently butted heads during my incarceration. It had to piss him off that I had a visitor. The man would do anything to keep me from even one moment of happiness. I knew if he could, he'd keep me locked up for the rest of my life.

I followed the warden through the maze of fences and gates until we reached the visitation room. My breath caught when I saw her. Even though I'd only seen one picture of her, I recognized her right away.

Cleo.

She looked small and fragile in the plastic chair, her fingers twisting a tissue. Bruises shadowed under her eyes, barely hidden by makeup. My heart clenched.

I sat down, picking up the phone. Her eyes flooded with tears as she did the same.

"Joker," she whispered. "I'm so sorry…"

"What happened?"

She glanced around quickly before answering. "My brother found out about the letters. He was furious. Said no one in the family should associate with your kind."

My jaw tightened, fury rising. My kind, huh? Seemed like her brother wasn't any better. "Did he hurt you?"

"It doesn't matter --"

"The hell it doesn't!" I snarled. "You listen to me. I'm getting you out of there, you hear me? We'll leave town, start over somewhere new."

"How?" Her voice trembled. "You still have years left of your sentence."

I placed my hand against the glass. "Marry me."

Her eyes widened. "What?"

"Marry me," I repeated. "You just turned eighteen, right? So you don't need your family's permission. I know the warden hates me, but... I'll convince him somehow. He'll do the ceremony right here. Then when I get out, we can start over -- together, if that's what you want."

Tears spilled down her cheeks. She put her hand against mine, even though the glass separated us. "Yes. I'll marry you, Joker."

"I'll find a way to get word to you. If your brother is angry about us talking, then I can't send it to your house. Find someone willing to help you and send me their address. I'll correspond with you through them."

She nodded and wiped away more tears. We talked for another minute, then our time was up. I watched her walk away and hoped I'd made the right choice. If this came back to bite me in the ass, it might end up harming her too.

* * *

It took two weeks to convince the warden. In the end, he only agreed in order to help Cleo. I stood in a dingy room, still cuffed and wearing my prison-issued jumpsuit. It wouldn't be the wedding of her dreams, but hopefully it kept her safe.

Cleo entered the room in a simple white dress, holding a small bouquet of daisies. Her smile nearly blinded me. I didn't know why she looked so happy. It made me wonder what she thought about this marriage. I had to admit, she looked beautiful.

We exchanged brief vows. No kiss or embrace could seal our union. It ended nearly as soon as it had begun. The guards escorted her from the room and sent me back to my cell. I could only hope changing her name from Cleo Lathem to Cleo Clemons would help her in some way.

My heart ached, knowing she had to return to that abusive household. I felt powerless, stuck in this damn cell while she suffered. I slammed my fist against the concrete in frustration. They couldn't legally force her to do anything, but people like that didn't care about the law. She'd have to disappear to avoid the danger of living with her family. At least with her name changed, she'd have a chance to get away. Hopefully, it would take them a while to figure out she'd gotten married. I only wished I had some money to give her too.

The next visiting day, her eyes were puffy from crying as she picked up the phone. "It's time. I'm leaving this week. Today will be my last visit with you."

I hadn't expected her to ever come here again. Seeing her one last time was more than enough. I nodded, letting her know I understood.

"Go as far as you can and don't look back," I

said.

"Will you be okay?" she asked.

"Don't worry about me. I've survived this place this long. I'll be fine. Protect yourself, Cleo, whatever it takes."

I hung up the phone, forcing her to leave. This was for the best. She needed a clean break. As much as I'd enjoyed her letters, I hoped she didn't write anymore. It was time for her to start living. I'd miss her like hell. She'd been a bright light in this dismal place. Without her words to carry me through, I wasn't sure what would happen to me. Didn't matter. I'd possibly die in this place. Even if I got out, my life was probably halfway over. Assuming I didn't get shot, stabbed, or die in some other fun way long before I became an old man. Cleo was just getting started. There was so much of the world for her to explore, and I hope she got the chance to see it all.

For me, days passed. Then weeks. Months. I didn't hear from Cleo again. Time blurred. I lived one monotonous day after another. Wake up, work out, eat, work, eat again, sleep. Wash, rinse, repeat.

My thoughts constantly drifted to Cleo when I wasn't occupied. Was she eating enough? Getting any sleep? Staying safe from her family's crooked dealings?

I wondered where she was now. How far had she gone? Was it a big enough distance her family couldn't find her? Part of me wondered if we'd ever bump into each other again in the future, once I put this place behind me. It ate at me, not knowing if she was safe or not. Had the plan worked? Or had I married her for no reason?

I lashed out in my frustration, getting in fights, mouthing off to the guards. I couldn't help her, so I took it out on anyone available. The more trouble I caused, the longer my sentence became. The warden loved adding time to my stay. At the rate I was going, I'd never be set free.

The isolation wore on me almost as much as the helplessness. Cut off from my club, my brothers, my wife. I didn't exactly have friends in this place. Stripped of the bonds that defined me there were days I felt lost. Here I was just another prisoner.

Some days I thought I'd lose my mind. Other days I wished I could. Anything to escape this torturous limbo.

When I got out of here, I knew I should try to find Cleo. Make sure she was safe. If she wanted to date, or had fallen in love with someone, then I'd give her a divorce and let her move on with her life. I'd only married her as a way to help her hide from her family. There wouldn't be a happily ever after for us. We didn't have that sort of relationship.

I'd return to my club and do my best to acclimate to life on the outside. I'd been locked up for so long, I wasn't sure I knew how to live beyond these bars. Was it even possible for me to do normal things like have a beer with my brothers, and watch a game on TV? Even when I left this place, would I feel truly free? Or would these bars stay with me for the rest of my life?

Chapter One

The prison gates clanked open, assaulting my ears with the harsh sound of freedom. My heart pounded as I stepped across the threshold. I was free. Breathing in, even the air seemed different out here. It had been nearly two decades since I'd been on this side of the bars.

I strode quickly to the parking lot, desperate to put distance between myself and this godforsaken place. My ride was waiting -- a gleaming Harley Fat Boy, all sleek lines and rumbling power a gift from my club. At least, according to the note I'd been given with the key. The guard had seemed reluctant to hand it over. I'd thought the club had turned away from me, but maybe I'd been wrong. I swung my leg over the leather seat, gripping the handlebars with white knuckles. The engine roared to life beneath me, drowning out the chaos in my head.

I peeled out of the lot, the wind whipping against my face. Miles of open road stretched before me as I gunned the throttle, the Harley eating up the asphalt. I flew past trees and fields, the prison shrinking away in my rearview. Out here, I was untethered, unconfined. A man with no walls or bars to hold me back. No more guards. No schedules. I could do whatever the fuck I wanted.

My mind turned to the clubhouse. I wondered if the brothers would welcome me back with open arms or closed fists. I'd find out soon enough. The Dixie Reapers were my blood. As the clubhouse came into view, I steeled myself. I was back, and I had no idea what to expect.

I rolled the Harley to a stop outside the compound gates. A Prospect came closer, one I'd never met before. He eyed me, then saw the cut over my shoulders and he froze. Without a word, he threw open the gate and let me through. Even if no one had told him I was arriving today, it seemed he knew my name.

Home, sweet home.

I scanned the parking lot, taking in the line of choppers. It looked like quite a few of my brothers were inside. I pulled up to the clubhouse and parked, killing the engine. I'd barely had a chance to get off the bike when the doors flew open and Tank stormed out, his hulking frame rippling with tension. Neither of us were young anymore, but he still looked like he could break a man in half.

"Well, look who finally decided to show his face," he growled. Behind him, Venom, Bull, and a few others gathered on the porch, watching me with narrowed eyes.

I met Tank's glare and held it. I wouldn't be intimidated, not on my home turf. If they hadn't wanted me here, then they shouldn't have left the Harley for me at the prison. Or at least included a note that said to never darken their doorstep again.

"Time away gives a man perspective," I said evenly.

Tank's lip curled in a sneer. "Yeah? You here to make amends?"

I stepped forward until we were nose-to-nose. "I'm here to grab a beer with my brothers."

The tension hung thick between us. Then Tank cracked a smile and pulled me into a bone-crushing hug. "Just fucking with you. Welcome back, brother. It's been too damn long."

The others descended, clapping me on the back and crushing my hand in firm handshakes. I saw relief, curiosity, and caution in equal measure on each of their faces. But above all -- brotherhood. I was home.

I nodded at my brothers, accepting their cautious welcome. Inside, my thoughts churned.

Should I tell them about Cleo? We married in secret, without the club's blessing. Technically, she was my old lady, or would have been if the club had voted. Since we hadn't done things the proper way, she wasn't an old lady -- wasn't part of this world. I noticed Tank's cut no longer had an officer patch. Same for Venom and Torch. How much had changed while I'd been locked up?

Now I was torn. The Reapers were my family. But Cleo... she needed me. Or at least, she had. I hadn't heard from her since the day she'd come for that last visit. But bringing her into the club's orbit could put her in danger. I knew I should at least send a letter. I'd written one a month since her last visit, but I hadn't received a response. I had no way of knowing whether she'd received any of the letters I'd sent. If I didn't hear from her this time, I'd know she'd either moved on or wasn't getting the mail I sent. Either way, I wouldn't write again.

Tank clapped me on the shoulder, jolting me from my thoughts. "Come on, brother. Club meeting's about to start."

I took a deep breath. I had to make a choice -- reveal my secret marriage and risk Cleo's safety, or keep silent and live a lie. For now, I'd play it close to the vest. Protect Cleo and assess where things stood with the club. I had to be smart. Strategic. There would be a right time to reveal the truth. But not today. It seemed like a lot had changed, and I needed to figure out where I stood now.

I nodded and followed Tank inside. The clubhouse enveloped me in its gritty familiarity -- the tang of booze and rumble of laughter. Music pounded from the speakers. I didn't see a single club whore, which made me a bit uneasy. They'd always been around before I'd been locked up. Only this time they weren't, it was as if we were expecting trouble, or something was about to happen they shouldn't see.

All eyes turned to me. A man with the President's patch stood a few feet away. *Savior.* I hadn't met him before. He came closer, holding out his hand. I shook it.

"Welcome home, brother," he rasped, his face unreadable.

I met his stare and gave a nod. "Good to be back."

Why had Torch, Tank, and Venom stepped down? Had it been voluntary or had they been forced to give up their positions? So many new faces. I wasn't sure what to feel at the moment. Unease churned inside me.

"I know lockup wasn't easy," he said. "You kept your mouth shut and did your time. Club appreciates that loyalty. I know I'm a stranger to you, as well as a lot of other brothers in the room. We all joined after you were locked up, and I'm sure this is a bit overwhelming. You need anything, you let me know. You're family, whether we know one another or not."

A murmur of assent went around the room. I relaxed slightly. Drinks were poured, joints passed around. The club's boisterous welcome washed over me. I grabbed a cold beer and took a swallow, trying to remember the last time I'd had one. It had most likely been in this very room.

In the corner, Tank watched me, his brow furrowed. I could tell he sensed something off. We'd been tight before I'd been locked up. Little got past him. I avoided his gaze. Wasn't ready to spill my secret. Not here. Not yet.

The party raged late into the night. Finally I slipped outside for some air. Tank followed.

"All right, brother, what's going on?" he asked, crossing his arms, his gaze boring into me.

I hesitated. Swore under my breath. My first night back and I was already caught. The club apparently wasn't the only thing that had changed over the years. This never would have happened before. Then again, I wouldn't have tried keeping a secret in the past either.

"There's something I've got to tell you," I began. "But you have to swear it stays between us for now."

Tank considered me. Then nodded.

I steeled myself. No turning back now. "While I was locked up, I got married... Her name's Cleo. We met through the prison pen pal program. At first, I was just a person she could vent to, someone who would listen without judgment. Then things changed. I could tell she was in trouble and needed my help. Married her so she could take my name and get away from her family. I couldn't think of another way to help while I was behind bars."

I trailed off, shaking my head. Tank just stared, waiting for me to go on.

"She's a good woman. Innocent. Doesn't know anything about the life. Only that I got locked up for some trouble. Nobody can know, Tank. It's too dangerous for her if word got out I have an old lady.

The kind of heat that could bring... She has enough on her plate already."

Tank was silent for a beat. Then he clapped my shoulder. "Your secret's safe with me. But you know you can't keep this quiet forever, brother. Secrets have a way of coming out."

I nodded grimly. It was only a matter of time. I didn't like the idea of lying to my brothers. Not even by omission, but in this instance, I thought it might be better. "For now, she doesn't need me, or any more trouble, in her life. I'm going to end it, clean and quiet. Sending her a letter to let her know she's free to fall in love."

My throat tightened. It wouldn't be easy to pen those words. Even if I didn't know whether she'd receive the letter or not, it still felt like I was betraying her in a way. I wouldn't ask for a divorce. She could keep my name. Until she didn't need it anymore.

Tank eyed me with sympathy. "You're doing right by her. Even if it kills you. Something tells me you care more than you realize, or are willing to admit."

I could only nod, not trusting my voice. We stood in silence for a few moments. Finally I cleared my throat, clapped his arm. "Appreciate you having my back."

"Always, brother."

We headed inside to rejoin the chaos. My secret still safe, for now. I needed time to find my place here again. Watching my brothers drink and carry on made my heart feel a little lighter. They'd accepted me back, when I'd worried they'd forgotten me. Even though I hadn't seen some of them in about two decades, they acted as if I'd only been gone a short while.

I scanned the room, taking in the familiar faces --

and those of the family I hadn't met yet. They were playing pool, drinking, laughing. For a moment, it was like I'd never left. Although, the pool table hadn't been there before, and the absence of women still seemed strange.

Venom spotted me, his weathered face breaking into a grin. We hadn't really had a chance to talk yet. "How's it feel to be a free man?"

"Honestly, a little scary. Not sure of my place now, and it's been so long since I've been on this side of the bars, it feels... I don't know. It's almost like my skin is crawling and I feel like I'm breaking a rule or something. Not sure if that makes any sense. My head's a bit of a mess right now."

Torch joined us. "Good to have you home, brother."

He gave me a rough hug. I clapped his back, managing a smile despite the turmoil churning inside me.

"Thanks, Torch. Good to be back."

More back slaps and handshakes followed as I made the rounds. I kept up a stoic front, laughing at the crude jokes, giving the expected answers about prison life. But my thoughts strayed to the letter I needed to write.

This was my family. I owed the Dixie Reapers my loyalty and brotherhood. But as much as it felt wrong to hide Cleo from them, I wasn't sure I could trust everyone here. Too much had changed, and there was a lot I needed to figure out. I'd act as normal as I could and learn the ropes again. With all the changes, I doubted things were done the same as before.

"What happened to the club pussy?" I asked Venom.

He rocked back on his heels and folded his arms.

"Well, about that... I'm sure you noticed things weren't quite the same as when you left. Most of us have settled down, started families. My two daughters are married into the Devil's Fury, and Torch's oldest is with the president of the Reckless Kings. Our women got tired of the drama from the whores, and honestly, those bitches have caused nothing but trouble. Savior decided it would be best to not allow them access to the compound."

I glanced at Torch. "Why aren't you president anymore?"

"Wanted more time with my family. Besides, I'm getting old. All the officers stepped down the same day, handing everything over to our successors. Things are different now, Joker. Calmer. More peaceful. This place isn't the wild club you once knew, and we try to keep things legal these days. Our priorities changed."

If what he said was true, then if Cleo did show up, maybe there would be a spot for her after all. "Do I still have a room here?"

"No. You have a house. Not a big one, but the structure is sound. Two bedrooms, two bathrooms. When you're ready to call it a night, one of us will take you there," Venom said. "Our women took the time to stock a few necessities. Kitchen should have everything you need, as well as some basic food and drink items. They bought new bedding and set up the master bedroom for you. None of us had any idea what size clothes you wore. I'm afraid you'll have to take care of that yourself."

Torch pointed to someone across the room. "That's Wire. He's our club hacker. If you need access to cash, ask him. There's more than likely an account with your name on it. Savior would have made sure you had some funds for whatever you needed while you find your footing around here."

"I'm not sure what to say." I really wasn't. They didn't have to do so much for someone they hadn't seen in a lifetime. I'd been a youngster when I'd gone inside. Now I was an old man. Of course, if I hadn't caused so much trouble, I would have gotten out sooner.

"You're family, Joker. You always have a place here," Torch said. "As long as you follow the rules."

I breathed a little easier and felt some of the tension melt away. I had no idea what the upcoming days would bring, but with these men beside me, I knew I could handle anything.

Chapter Two

Cleo
Ten months later

My heart pounded and felt like it might burst from my chest as I sat in the sterile doctor's office. The fluorescent lights seemed to flicker and buzz louder than usual as Dr. Stevens adjusted his glasses and cleared his throat. The fact I'd been called into his office and not an exam room filled me with unease. Then again, if he'd had good news he'd have told me over the phone.

"I'm afraid the test results show your heart is failing rapidly, Cleo," he said, not making eye contact. "Given the severity, you likely only have a few months left without proper treatment. That's obviously not an exact number. I have no way of knowing when your heart will give out. It could be a month, it could be in half a year. There are some options available, but a full reversal isn't possible. A transplant would give you the longest lifespan, but there are some things we can try for now."

His words were like a wrecking ball slamming into my world. Months. Only months to live. I gripped the padded armrests until my knuckles turned white, trying to ground myself against the tidal wave of shock and fear crashing over me.

This couldn't be real. I was only twenty-two, nearly twenty-three. My life was just getting started. Was I even going to live long enough to see my next birthday? I blinked back hot tears as the weight of Dr. Stevens' diagnosis sank in. No more lazy Sundays or girls' nights out. No falling in love or starting a family.

My time was now limited, each grain of sand falling too quickly through the hourglass.

I thought of the plans I'd made -- goals, dreams, a whole future stretching out ahead of me. But now my life had been reduced to mere months. The room started spinning as I struggled to breathe. I was dimly aware of Dr. Stevens droning on about medications and treatment options, but his voice sounded far away, drowned out by the pounding of my heart.

This was it. My life was ending. I was dying.

Dr. Stevens cleared his throat. "Cleo, it's not over. We can start the medication today. Right now, your heart is functioning at thirty percent. In my opinion, a transplant is your best option. Adding more prescriptions to your already lengthy list is about like putting a bandage on a severed limb."

I winced. I could have done without the analogy. It wasn't like I hadn't known something was wrong. It just never occurred to me it would be this bad. After all the time it had taken to get the tests approved, for them to come back with this result was like a slap in the face.

What had been the point of running from my family? Poor Joker married me so I'd be safe. Neither of us counted on my body being my worst enemy.

I barely heard anything else the doctor said. Somehow, I made it outside to my car. I stared at my phone, wondering who I should tell.

Since moving here, I'd made two friends -- Nicole and Rhona. I wouldn't say I was particularly close with either of them. More like acquaintances who occasionally hung out or went to movies together. What would I even tell them? I already had so many secrets. They had no idea who I truly was, or about my husband. Could I consider him a husband? He'd given me his name, and legally we were married. As far as our relationship went, I'd have called us friends more than anything else.

The letters in my backseat caught my attention. I'd read them. Countless times, including the most recent. Joker wasn't in prison any longer and was back with the Dixie Reapers. He'd been freed, and insisted I live my life how I wanted. The tone of his words told me plenty. He'd let me have his name, but he didn't want anything else from me. Reading the words giving me permission to fall in love and request a divorce whenever I wanted had felt like someone tore through my chest and ripped out my heart. It was the only time he'd made me feel like an inconvenience.

I gulped a lungful of the crisp autumn air, but it did little to clear the panic flooding my mind. I fumbled for my keys with trembling hands. I needed to leave. Go home. Then what? If this was truly the end, there was only one person I wanted to see. The man who wanted nothing to do with me. Joker. I didn't think my presence in his life would be welcome, regardless of my recent news.

He was the only person I could think of now. The man I had married in a whirlwind prison ceremony nearly five years ago. The man who was now living with the Dixie Reapers motorcycle club. He was my last hope, my only chance at feeling like I belonged somewhere during the final chapters of my life. Going to him was a gamble. He could refuse to see me, even tell me to leave. But I wouldn't know if I didn't try.

With shaking fingers, I typed out a message to the phone number he'd included in his last letter:

It's Cleo. I need to see you. It's urgent.

My heart pounded as I hit send. Would he even respond? I knew the club life kept him busy, on the road. It was something we'd talked about in previous letters while he'd been locked up. And despite our impromptu marriage, we weren't really anything to each other. Or rather, I didn't mean anything to him. He'd saved me. Been the only person I could confide in. I wondered if it wasn't partially my fault. I hadn't answered his letters in years. Not because I hadn't wanted to, but I'd worried I wasn't good enough to stand by his side once he was free again.

My message remained unread. I only lived two hours from him, even though he didn't know it. At first, I'd traveled more than a day from Alabama, needing distance from my past. But as time ticked by, I'd wanted to be closer to Joker and I'd returned to this area once I heard he was being released from prison. Not close enough my family could find me, but near enough I could go see Joker right now. It would be so easy to just drop by and see him in person, assuming he didn't run me off.

I was running out of time. I needed to see Joker soon, before my body gave out. This was my last shot at human connection, at being part of something real. I refused to die alone. Sure, the medication might help, and there were probably other things that could give me better odds. Maybe either or both would buy enough time for the doctor to find me a heart. Regardless, it felt like I was only borrowing time. I'd never been the religious sort, but if my time was up, then would anything really prolong my days here on earth?

With new determination, I jumped in my car. I'd go home and regroup, come up with a plan. One thing I knew for certain, I wasn't giving up yet.

The phone buzzed beside me as I sped down the highway, weaving between cars. My heart leaped when I saw his name flash across the screen. He'd called! How long had it been since I'd last heard his voice?

"Joker?" I answered, my voice trembling.

"Yeah, it's me," his gruff voice responded. "What's going on?"

I let out a shaky breath, gripping the steering wheel tightly. "I need to see you. It's important. Are you still with the Dixie Reapers?"

There was a pause on the other end. "Maybe. What's this about, Cleo?"

I bit my lip, hesitating. Should I tell him about my diagnosis over the phone? No, I needed to do this in person.

"I just really need to talk to you. Face-to-face. It's... life or death." I cringed at my own word choice.

Another pause. "All right. I'm in Louisiana now, outside Baton Rouge. I'm on a job for another two days, then I'm going home."

"Can I meet with you when you're back?" The line remained quiet for so long I worried he'd hung up. Glancing at the screen, I saw the call was still connected. "Joker?"

"I'm here. Look, Cleo, I think it's best if we keep things the way they've been. My club doesn't know about you, and I'm not sure they'd understand."

He'd kept me a secret? Why? I didn't know what to say to him. After I hung up, I pulled off the highway and stopped in a parking lot. Tears blurred my vision, and my chest ached. He was the only person I had in my life, and he didn't want me around. Was I really going to end my life in misery? I'd fought so hard to live this long, and now...

Once I had my emotions under control again. I continued on to my apartment. Everything began to feel numb. Until now I had hoped Joker hadn't meant the words in his letter. Speaking to him changed things. Now I had to wonder if he'd been counting on me requesting a divorce. Had he found someone? Was I holding him back?

I parked in my assigned spot and walked up to my door. Three feet away, I froze. Why wasn't it closed all the way? I knew I'd locked it. Not once had I ever forgotten.

Swallowing hard I crept closer and nudged the door open wider with my foot. I stifled my gasp. Everything inside had been completely destroyed. Who would do such a thing? Bracing myself, I went inside. A note on the fridge caught my attention. The words, and the unmistakable handwriting, sent a chill down my spine.

Come home.

My brother had found me. Staying was no longer an option. I quickly searched the apartment for anything I could salvage. A few changes of clothes and some bathroom items were the only things worth keeping. I tossed them into a bag and went back to my car.

The few choices I'd had were now gone. My only chance to survive even the short time I had left was to get to Joker. I'd head to his town and get a motel room. Once he was back, I'd go see him, no matter how furious it made him.

* * *

The Dixie Reapers' compound was exactly what I expected -- a fenced-in area with the club's logo emblazoned on the front gate. I pulled up and eyed the man standing guard. He approached and I steeled myself. Would he be nice? Or was I about to get the third degree?

The motel I'd found wasn't the nicest, and the area seemed a bit shady. I really didn't want to be sent back there without even having a chance to speak with Joker. One night had been enough. I knew it was a gamble he wasn't back yet, but I had to hope he was here. If he truly wanted me gone, then I'd have to figure something out. I didn't have enough money to start over somewhere, much less hide from my brother for whatever time I had left.

"You lost?" he asked.

"Um, I'm here to see Joker," I said.

His eyebrows arched. "Joker? He didn't say anything about a guest."

"He isn't aware I'm here. Please, it's really important."

"If I let you, I need to check you, your bag, and your car for weapons or drugs. We typically don't let people in without a background check," he said.

Damn. I hadn't realized security would be so tight. I wasn't sure how to respond to him. Was I okay with it? Not really. The thought of him putting his hands on me made me want to turn around and run. Instead of answering, I got out of the car and held my arms out so he could frisk me. Once he'd checked me, my car, and my belongings. I pulled through the gate and parked in front of the building ahead. As I got out of the car, I could feel people watching. Several bikers were nearby, each with their gazes locked on me.

A muscular, tattooed man strode up. "Who the hell are you?"

I shrank back, intimidated. "My name's Cleo. I'm Joker's…"

"Old lady?" he cut in. "Funny, he never mentioned you. Unless he knocked up someone before he was locked up. Are you his daughter? Don't look anything like him."

"I'm not his daughter."

Just then, the clubhouse door swung open. Joker stepped out, his face unreadable.

"She's with me."

The man looked skeptical but stood aside. The rest of the Reapers in the vicinity continued staring suspiciously as I followed Joker. He led me to a picnic table nearby. My heart pounded, knowing I still had to reveal my secret to him. But at least now, I was here, and he hadn't thrown me out.

Once we were alone, he spoke. "What are you doing here, Cleo?"

His voice was flat, emotionless. I searched his face, looking for any sign of the man who'd saved me. But his expression remained closed off. The warm gaze he'd given me years ago was nowhere to be found.

"Joker, I... I needed to find you," I began hesitantly.

He crossed his arms. "Why? Did you need a biker husband to show off to your friends?"

I flinched at the bitterness in his tone. Had things changed so much between us because I hadn't written him back? "No, that's not it at all. How could you say such a thing to me? You were my only friend. My confidant. I've thought about you every day."

"You don't know anything about my life now. About the club, what it means to be an old lady. This..." He gestured around. "This isn't your world."

"I know. But it could be, if you just give me a chance. Please, Joker." I took a breath before my voice broke. "I don't have anywhere else to go. My brother found me."

His brow furrowed slightly. I could see his inner struggle, the battle between his loyalty to the Reapers and his need to protect me. Would he let me stay? Or was he going to push me away?

I'd never confided everything in him. He knew my family was bad news, but I hadn't told him the worst of it. Saying anything now would likely drive an even bigger wedge between us. I waited, hoping he'd relent and give me the help I needed, just like he had five years ago.

Chapter Three

Joker

What the hell did she mean? She'd left her family years ago. I'd married her and given her my last name. I knew that wasn't a foolproof way of fooling them, but unless they had a way to get access to our marriage certificate, they'd never know her new name. How had they managed to track her down? Had they been searching for her all this time? Even though she'd been scared back then, I'd thought once she was out of their reach, they'd move on. Something told me there was more to the story than I knew, but I could tell now wasn't the time to ask a lot of questions.

"How did they find you?" I asked.

"How am I supposed to know? When I got home, the door to the apartment was open. I knew I'd closed and locked it. The inside had been trashed. Nearly everything I owned couldn't be salvaged, and I found a note on the fridge in my brother's handwriting, telling me to come home." She bowed her head, placing her hands over her face. "I didn't know what else to do. I came straight here, got a motel room for the night, then drove to the compound this morning. I wasn't even sure anyone would listen to me."

"Came home one day early. Which motel?" I asked. The one she named made me wince. It amazed me she'd gotten out of there unscathed. "You can't stay there anymore. It's not safe."

She snorted. "Apparently my apartment wasn't either."

"I'll have to tell the club something. They don't

know about you, and I'm not sure how to go about explaining you're my wife. Until I talk to them, I can't do much."

"It's fine. I wasn't even sure you'd speak to me." She smiled sadly. "Your last letter made it clear you didn't want anything to do with me."

I wanted to tell her she was wrong. At the same time, I didn't feel like I had the right to say anything. I could have tracked her down, especially once I understood what Wire and Lavender were capable of doing. The truth was that I was scared shitless. Cleo was so much younger than me, and she had her entire life ahead of her. What the hell did I have to offer? Nothing. I was just an ex-con who was old enough to be her father.

"I'm going to text my club President and ask him to call Church. It's like calling a meeting for a business. I can talk to everyone then." I pulled out my phone and sent a text to Savior. *Can you call Church? There's something I need to tell everyone.*

He responded almost immediately. *Does it have to do with the woman?*

Jesus. How many of my brothers ran tattling the moment Cleo arrived? I told him he was right, and not a minute later my phone went off, along with several others in the area, with a text notification to be in Church in ten minutes.

I wasn't sure what to do with Cleo. I didn't like the idea of her sitting out here by herself, and the clubhouse wasn't a good place for her either. Was it all right to let her stay at my house while I got this sorted?

"Follow me in your car," I said. "I'm going to take you to my place, then I need to meet with my brothers and tell them who you are."

"You won't get into trouble?" she asked.

"They're going to be pissed I didn't tell them about you, but it will get worked out one way or another. It wasn't like the club was in contact with me back then."

I helped her into her car, then got on my bike. My house was farther back in the compound, and I hoped I wasn't going to be late getting to Church. I didn't know what she'd think of my small house. I had a carport and pulled up under it, pointing to the spot beside me. She parked her car and held my gaze through the window. The way her hands gripped the steering wheel told me how nervous she was right now.

I killed the engine and got off the bike, then helped her out of the car. I noticed a bag in the backseat and reached in to grab it. While it didn't weigh a lot, I had a feeling it contained all the items she'd said she'd managed to save at the apartment. I led her inside. The carport door opened to a small laundry area, which I'd turned into a pantry as well. Shelves lined one wall. Towels and bedding on the top two shelves, and canned goods on the bottom two, with bottled water stashed underneath on the floor.

"If you need to wash anything, as you can see the dryer sheets, detergent, and fabric softener are all on top of the dryer. Machines are simple enough. I didn't get the fancy ones that had too many damn functions." We stepped out of the laundry room and into the kitchen. I showed her the living room and pointed to the door on the back wall. "That's the master bedroom and bathroom. I don't have much in the guest bath except hand soap and a hand towel. If you need a fully functioning bathroom, then use mine."

"Where's the guest bath?" she asked.

I pointed to the hall on the opposite side of the

room. "Guest bath and bedroom are over there, but the bedroom doesn't have much. I don't really have company that stays over, so there's just a futon in there for an emergency."

"You're going to be late," she said.

"You have my number. Text me if something comes up, or if you get scared." I hesitated a moment, then leaned in and kissed the top of her head. Before I could second-guess myself, or do anything else, I decided it was best for me to leave. Not to mention, Savior might have my ass if I was late.

By the time I got back to the clubhouse, it looked like everyone was there. I went inside and back to the doors for Church. The moment I stepped into the room, everyone went silent and stared.

"Sorry if I'm late. I had to handle something before coming here."

"You were already at the clubhouse," Tank said. "Where'd the woman go?"

"My house." I cleared my throat and took my seat. Savior glared at me, and I wasn't sure what the hell he wanted. Was I supposed to say more right now? "So... everyone knows I was locked up for a long-ass time. Long enough for just about everyone I knew to start families and have kids who are now grown. Would have gotten out sooner if I'd behaved myself, I guess."

"The point?" Savior asked.

"While I was locked up, the club forgot about me. A few visited in the beginning, then after a few years, I didn't hear anything from anyone. No visitors, calls, letters. Radio silence." A few of my brothers shifted uncomfortably in their seats. Guess the guilt was getting to them. "I joined the prison pen pal program for the hell of it, not thinking anyone would actually write. Mostly I got letters from women who wanted bragging rights to being with someone in prison. Not sure how that's something to be proud of, but whatever. To each their own. I met Cleo through those letters. At the time, she was a teenager who just needed someone to listen. Her life at home was hard, and she felt like she didn't have anyone."

"And you felt the same way, so the two of you bonded," Venom said. "Sorry we ghosted you. It wasn't intentional. The club had a lot of shit going on back then. By the time we caught a break, so much time had passed I guess none of us felt right approaching you. We should have checked in. Behind bars or not, you're still our brother."

"Cleo is my wife," I said. "She needed a way to escape her family, so we had a prison wedding in order for her to take my name. I only saw her one time after that and told her to leave town and never come back. And she listened to me until now. Her brother found her. Scared the shit out of her, and she came looking for me."

"You're married?" Savior asked. "And you didn't think to bring this up before now? You've been out nearly a year."

"I honestly thought we'd end up divorced at some point. It wasn't like we had a real marriage. We've never shared a kiss or slept together. At best, I'd say we were friends. After Cleo left, I didn't hear from her again until yesterday morning. I'd thought she was off living her life, making happy memories and new friends, maybe even falling in love. I was fine with it all, even wrote her one last time to give her permission to do whatever she wanted."

Savior pinched the bridge of his nose. "Joker, I know you're still acclimating to the club and all the changes. Hell, we still had women at the clubhouse until about a month before you were released. But you've been here long enough to know how we feel about marriage. It's a forever thing for us. If you felt like taking responsibility for her, enough to marry her, then she's yours."

"So, you're saying she's not just my wife but my old lady and needs a property cut? And you're all fine with her staying here?" I asked. I wasn't sure how *I* felt about it. Or Cleo for that matter. She came here for help. Not to play house indefinitely.

"We'll order one for her. Explain how club life works," Savior said.

"I could send Ridley over," Venom offered. "She'll be happy to answer any of Cleo's questions and can give her a woman's view of what it's like to live here. Wouldn't be bad to give her a few people to talk to other than Joker."

"I'd send Dessa, but Joker's house isn't wheelchair accessible," Savior said.

"Isabella typically goes everywhere with Ridley," Torch said. "Think those two are joined at the hip."

"And Darian sticks close too," Bull said. "No reason all three can't go welcome her."

"Fine, but can I have at least twenty minutes to tell her she's here to stay? It's going to be a shock for her, and I'm not sure how she'll handle it. This is the first time I've seen her in about five years." I leaned back in my seat. "Definitely not on my list of things to do this week. I should have known when I got her call."

"You said she called you, but then showed up out of the blue today." Savior's gaze narrowed. "Why did she call after being out of touch for so long? Did she know then about her brother?"

"First, I actually called her after I got a text from her. As for her brother, I don't think she knew at the time. She made it sound like that happened afterward." My brow furrowed. Now that I thought about it, it had sounded like she was close to crying that day, and she'd said she had something urgent to tell me. "I'm not sure why she called."

"No offense, but you suck at being a husband," Tank said. "She's going to need a support system other than you. At least until you pull your head out of your ass."

I flipped him off, but the fucker only grinned at me.

"All right. Joker will speak with his wife, and Ridley, Isabella, and Darian will stop by in about a half hour to welcome her to the club." Savior sighed and shook his head. "When I became President, this wasn't the sort of stuff I thought we'd be discussing during Church, but I have to say it's far better than dealing with murderers and rapists."

"And now that the Pres has jinxed us, are we free to go?" Tank asked.

Savior waved his hand, setting all of us free. I stood and went out to my bike. The sooner I spoke with Cleo, the better.

When I got to the house, it seemed far too quiet. I found Cleo asleep on the couch. I had to wonder if she'd been awake since she'd discovered her brother had found her. She'd been scared enough of her family to marry me, so I could only imagine how terrified she must have been. I ran my fingers through her hair. Cleo murmured my name in her sleep and pressed her cheek against my hand.

How the fuck did I tell this sweet girl she was now stuck with me forever? Her eyes fluttered and slowly opened.

"You're back," she said, sitting up.

"Yeah. I have some good news and not so good news," I said. "You're allowed to stay. Or more accurately, you have to."

"Which was that? The good or not so good?"

"Both." I smiled faintly. "Since we're married, you're now stuck with me forever, and have to live here. President's rules. Or apparently the club's rules these days. I didn't know a damn thing about it when I married you."

"I'm sorry. I should have never agreed to let you help me in that way. You spent all that time in prison, and now I've ruined your life."

I cupped her cheek. "No, you didn't."

"I won't stand in your way," she murmured, looking away.

"What the fuck is that supposed to mean?"

"It's not like I think you've been celibate this entire time, Joker. You've been out of prison for nearly a year. Are you telling me you haven't been with a woman in all that time?" she asked.

"I haven't." I stood straighter and folded my arms over my chest. "Our marriage may not have been the real deal, but it didn't mean I was going to cheat on you. I spent almost half my life in prison. Hell, I'm not sure my dick even knows how to work properly anymore."

She pressed her lips together, but the look she gave me was full of mirth. "Really? Did you think I didn't notice you got hard during our wedding ceremony? I think it works just fine."

"Smart ass," I muttered. "Whatever relief I've needed, my hand has been perfectly fine. From the horror stories I've heard since I've come back, not sure

I want to deal with the drama of sleeping with random women."

"What about your wife?" she asked. "Do you want to sleep with her?"

I shook my head and backed up a step. "You have no idea what you're asking for, Cleo. I think it's best if we keep our distance."

"So which of us is sleeping on the futon? Because you said there's only one bed."

Fuck. How had I forgotten that? It wasn't like I fit well on the damn futon, and I should know because I'd tested it. But I also wasn't going to make her sleep on it either. The damn thing wasn't the least bit comfortable.

"Then we can sleep together, and by that I mean *only* sleep," I said. "No reason we can't share a bed."

"Whatever you say… husband."

Shit. I had a feeling my life was about to become very fucking difficult.

Chapter Four

Cleo

Someone knocked on the front door and Joker went to answer it. I heard women's voices and a moment later, he stepped back to let three ladies into the house. They each wore cuts like Joker's, but as one of them turned, I saw the back said *Property of Bull*. So not quite the same. Did that mean they belonged with one of Joker's club brothers? I still didn't understand how any of this worked.

"Cleo, these ladies came to visit with you and answer any questions you might have." Joker shoved his hands into his pockets. "They can tell you more than I can about being an old lady in the club, as well as the current rules everyone is following. Things changed a lot while I was locked up. Ridley is with Venom, Darian is with Bull, and Isabella belongs to Torch. I'll be in the kitchen if anyone needs me."

He walked off and left me with three strangers. I motioned to the empty spots on the couch and the loveseat. "Want to sit down?"

"We were all surprised to hear Joker had a wife. I'm Ridley, by the way. This one is Darian," she said nudging the woman next to her. "She's my stepmom."

Darian rolled her eyes. "Would you knock it off with that shit. Although, technically, she's right. It's just weird."

I wasn't sure how to process that. I stared at them for a moment, and then realized it meant Darian was in the same position as me and was married to a much older man. "And everyone's okay with your relationship?"

Ridley snickered. "Honey, everyone here is with an older man. Hell, I don't think there's a single woman in this club who hooked up with anyone near their age. So, you're in good company as far as that goes."

"Did you really get married while he was in prison?" Darian asked. "How did you even meet?"

"We were pen pals," I said. I told them about the letters I'd shared with Joker and how we'd gotten to know one another, then how he'd found a way to save me from my family. All three women wore knowing expressions.

"Yeah, he's a Dixie Reaper all right," Isabella said. "They all have hero complexes. Torch married me because it was the only way my father would agree to save Ridley. And she claimed Venom while she was on the run from her mom and stepdad."

Darian shrugged. "Bull saved me too. I found this place by accident after I ran from a party where my boyfriend planned to offer me up to anyone who wanted a turn."

My heart felt like it might give out right then and there. If they'd all been saved from those situations, then how would everyone react when they found out about my family? I may have told Joker I needed help escaping from them, but I'd never outright told him what sort of monsters I lived with.

"Does everyone have a story like that?" I asked.

"Some are even worse," Ridley said. "I was lucky and so was Darian. We both escaped before anything could happen to us. There are quite a few women here who suffered horribly at the hands of men."

Yeah, I didn't need these people to ever find out about my family. It wouldn't end well for me. I'd always worried what Joker would think, and now I had to be concerned about an entire club of people turning their backs on me. Some secrets were better left buried.

Ridley tugged on her leather vest. "This is a property cut, and I've heard you'll be getting one. Except yours will say *Property of Joker* on the back. It doesn't mean we're actual property, but it does send a clear message to other bikers that we're not only taken but protected."

"The clubhouse has changed a lot, especially recently," Isabella said. "It used to have a bunch of naked women running around. Those willing to get on their knees for any guy wearing a Dixie Reapers cut. They caused a lot of trouble, and while Wire and Lavender were running background checks on them for a short while, about a month ago the President kicked all the women out and said they weren't allowed back in."

"Did something happen to make him do that?" I asked.

"Not really sure, except he knows none of us liked them being around," Ridley said. "His wife probably had a lot to do with it."

"If you see a woman in a wheelchair, that's Dessa. She's Savior's wife, and he's the club President. She's such a sweetheart," Darian said.

"A lot of our kids are older now and all grown up. You're probably around the age of my babies." Ridley smiled. "So you'll see people your age here too. Ares is a bit younger than you. She's Savior's daughter."

"How old are you?" Darian asked. "We're all just assuming you're in your early twenties, but you could age well and be older."

"I'm going to be twenty-three soon," I said.

"Ah, the years before everything snapped, crackled, and popped when I went to get out bed in the morning," Ridley said with a bittersweet smile. "I miss those days."

"I do too, but for other reasons." Darian sighed. "Your dad doesn't give me much of a break."

Ridley's nose wrinkled. "That's disgusting and not something I ever want to hear again. Keep that shit to yourself."

"The two of you seem really close," I said.

"They are. Don't let their bickering get to you. Sometimes I think it's their version of foreplay," Isabella said.

"Now *that* is gross," Ridley said. "Not because she's a woman but because she's with my dad. Like I want his leftovers."

Darian gasped. "Did you just call me a leftover? What am I, freakin' meatloaf?"

These two were hilarious. I found myself smiling and relaxing. If the other women here were anything like them, then I was going to enjoy getting to know everyone. Even Isabella set me at ease. I'd never met anyone like these three before.

"Is there anything you need?" Isabella asked. "I'm not sure how prepared you were to stay for good. Do you need to go back up your place or something?"

The smile slipped from my face. "They didn't tell you anything about me, did they?"

"Not really. What's going on?" Ridley asked.

"Joker married me to protect me from my family, but somehow my brother found me. He broke into my apartment, trashed the place, and left a note for me to return home. I'd been free of them for almost five years. I don't know how they found me."

"Shit. Did he ruin everything you had?" Darian

asked.

"Pretty much. I have a few changes of clothes, some bathroom items, and that's it. I'll eventually need more things, but I'm fine for right now."

Ridley started shaking her head. "Nope. Hell, no. If you need shit, then we're going shopping. My half-brother, Foster, is twenty-four but he's huge. We can take him as a bodyguard."

"Did you just volunteer my troublemaking son?" Darian asked.

"Well, would you prefer we take Dawson? I love my boy, but he's not exactly fierce," Ridley said.

"Hadrian is only fourteen," Isabella said. "Not sure he'd be of any help if something were to happen."

"You know, if your son didn't cause all that trouble, he'd probably be patched in by now. I think he's the reason Owen is still stuck as a Prospect too. I have a feeling they'll be patched together, or Owen will have to wait until Foster screws up so bad he's booted," Ridley said. "Not that I'm hoping that happens. It would be nice if he'd pull his head out of his ass and straighten up."

"I don't know who all these people are that you're mentioning, but do we really need to take anyone with us?" I asked.

"Yes, you fucking do," Joker yelled from the other room. "Don't even think of wandering around on your own. What if your brother is lurking nearby?"

He made a good point. If he'd found me before, there was a good chance he could have followed me here. What if he was waiting to catch me alone? Although, I'd have thought if he wanted to snatch me and force me back home, he'd have done it the night I stayed at the motel. I doubted anyone in the area would have filed a report if he'd kidnapped me.

"Then who do you recommend?" Ridley yelled back.

I heard his booted steps. He stopped in the doorway and leaned against the frame. "Anyone over thirty but younger than me. You don't need a bunch of hotheaded youngsters."

I hadn't met anyone yet, so I wasn't any help. They discussed it a little while longer, and decided on two men called Slayer and Warden. By the time they arrived, we'd piled into Ridley's SUV. Darian rode up front with her and I sat in back with Isabella. Slayer and Warden rode their motorcycles, one in front and one behind. It seemed like overkill to me, but if Joker was worried about my safety, then I'd listen to him.

"Where do you want to shop? The mall?" Ridley asked.

"Um. I don't have a lot of money, so… anywhere inexpensive is fine."

Ridley stopped the SUV in the middle of the road and turned to look at me. "You're married to Joker, but you don't have access to his money?"

"We never lived together," I said. "It was only a marriage in name. Why would he have added me to his bank account?"

"Well, fuck. Hang on." She took out her phone and called someone. Ringing filled the car and a woman answered a moment later.

"Hello? Ridley?"

"Hey, Lavender. Need a favor," Ridley said. "Isabella and Darian are with me, and so is Joker's wife. She needs clothes, shoes, and pretty much everything else. But she's not on his account and said she doesn't have much in the bank. Can you help us out?"

"Give me twenty minutes at a computer and I'll

have some money transferred to her account. She's technically been part of our family for years and hasn't received any help from the club. I'll run it by Grimm, but I'm sure he'll be fine with me putting a few thousand in there."

I choked on air and started coughing. "I'm sorry. Did you say a *few* thousand?"

"Hi, Cleo! My name is Lavender, and you heard me right. Can you check your bank from your phone?"

"Yeah, but why?" I asked.

"When you get to the first store, see if the transfer went through. If it didn't, get Ridley to cover the expense and I'll get the money back to her today. Welcome to the Dixie Reapers family!"

"Thanks, Lavender! We owe you one," Ridley said.

She ended the call and I tried not to hyperventilate. What kind of people had I fallen in with? Who moved thousands of dollars as easily as loaning five bucks to someone? I hadn't ever had so much in my account at one time. In fact, I didn't even bring home two thousand a month.

Ridley took me to the mall, despite my request for a cheaper place. I also had to hope none of my symptoms presented in a noticeable way while I was with these women. I hadn't told Joker about my heart problem, and I wasn't even sure where to begin, or if I should. Everything was moving too fast.

When we got inside the mall, Slayer and Warden trailed us, giving us enough space to not feel crowded, yet close enough they could protect us.

"Is it always like this?" I asked.

"Um, no. I go out all the time without guards," Ridley said. "But until we know you're out of danger, this is the best option."

"Unless Joker is like Rocky," Isabella said. "We hardly ever see his wife, Mara. At first, I thought she just stayed home because she was shy or something. Now I think it's more that Rocky likes having her glued to him, or knowing she's there waiting when he gets home from a job."

Sounded like he was overbearing. Would Joker be like that with me? It was too soon to tell. My mind was still spinning over the fact we wouldn't be getting a divorce, and I'd be living with him forever.

We spent the next few hours shopping, until I literally thought I'd drop. I'd had several dizzy spells and begged for a spot to sit. Of course, I'd had to come up with another reason. The ladies didn't seem suspicious, and neither did the two bikers with us. It seemed my secret was still safe for now. Slayer and Warden had taken turns carrying the bags to Ridley's SUV. When we got back to the parking lot, I wasn't sure I could take another step. I managed to get to the vehicle and pulled myself inside.

"Anywhere else you need to go?" Ridley asked.

"Home. I'm exhausted and my legs and feet are killing me," I said. In reality, if we stayed out any longer, I worried I'd end up on the floor, or in the emergency room. "How can you shop this much?"

Ridley laughed. "This is nothing. You should see us when we hit up the fun stores."

I wasn't sure I could handle seeing it, much less experiencing it. *Note to self, next time Ridley says the word shopping, run!*

Chapter Five

Joker

The sun streaming through the window woke me. I really needed to buy better blinds, ones that would block more of the light. I scrubbed a hand over my face and shifted, only to realize a small body had curled against me. For a moment, I'd forgotten Cleo and I were now sharing a bed. It seemed a bit surreal. There had been nights I'd been wide awake, staring at the ceiling as I wondered where she was and how she was doing. Now I had her next to me.

She murmured something in her sleep and buried her face against my side. I curled my arm around her, pulling her closer to me. Not once had I ever thought this would be possible. As much as I wanted to have her with me, I also worried this wasn't fair to her. She'd come to me for help, and instead I'd put a leash on her. It made me feel like an asshole. I should have done a better job pushing her away, but when I'd spoken to her on the phone, my resolve started to crumble. I'd known damn well she'd been in tears by the time I ended the call.

I watched her sleep, wondering why she'd still come running to me, even though I'd been an absolute ass to her. She'd said she had nowhere else to go. After all these years, had she not made any friends she could rely on in a bad situation? Or had she been too scared her family might hurt them?

We needed to talk. There was a lot I didn't know, and even more we needed to figure out about our future. The fact she'd had a good time with Isabella, Ridley, and Darian had relieved some of my worries about her settling in here. Although, she'd been so exhausted when she came back that she'd slept for an hour. I'd had to wake her for dinner, and not long after eating, she'd gone back to sleep again.

I had to admit the first night in our house hadn't gone quite the way I'd planned. Something seemed off about Cleo. Almost as if she were hiding something from me. I couldn't imagine what it would be. Had there been more to her brother breaking into her apartment? She'd said she didn't know how he found her. Had she been telling the truth? It seemed odd he'd tracked her down after so many years. The way she'd talked about her life at home, I'd thought once she changed her name and moved, they'd wash their hands of her. Why work so hard to locate her?

She whimpered a little, shifting in her sleep. I got out of bed and tugged the covers up over her. Lightly, I brushed her hair back from her face. In sleep, she looked even more innocent than when she was awake. I'd never met anyone like Cleo before. Even the women here at the compound seemed jaded compared to her, and most of them were sweethearts. A few were a bit frightening, and entirely too boisterous. Like Ridley. I didn't know how Venom handled that woman.

Cleo's eyes fluttered open. "Morning."

"You can sleep longer," I said. "You seem tired."

She shook her head and sat up, then placed a hand against her head. Was she all right? She seemed paler than yesterday. I'd even go so far as to say gaunt. I could only imagine how stressed she must have been since finding her apartment trashed.

"I'll be fine," she said. "Do you want me to make breakfast?"

"I can have something delivered to the house. I'll call one of the Prospects and get them to pick up some food. Any requests?"

"No. I try not to eat anything salty, though."

In the south, pretty much everything was either drowned in salt or fried -- sometimes both. I did recall the diner having a heart-healthy option of plain scrambled eggs, wheat toast, and plain grits. I texted Sam and asked him to pick up an order of that for Cleo, then told him what I wanted.

I'll knock and leave it on the porch.

Sounded good to me. "Food will be here probably within a half hour. Want to soak in the tub or take a shower before it gets here?"

"The tub would be nice," she said.

"I'll go fill it for you. Did you get any bubbles or anything while you were out yesterday? Or do you just want hot water and nothing extra?"

She smiled a little. "I can't remember the last time someone ran a bath for me. It was probably my mom. Ridley talked me into some lavender bath salts. I put them in the bathroom last night."

"I'll take care of it. Just wait here."

I stepped into the bathroom and rinsed out the tub before filling it. Once it got about half full, I added the bath salts. Steam rose from the water, and I shut off the tap when I thought it was the right level for her to enjoy a good soak. Calling Cleo into the bathroom, I placed a towel on the counter, then walked out, giving her some privacy.

For some reason, I lingered in the bedroom. I couldn't explain it, but something told me to remain close. I'd never felt this way about anyone before. Cleo was the only person I'd ever truly worried about. The same was true even before I'd married her. The minutes ticked by and I eventually heard the knock at the front door. I got our food and placed it in the kitchen.

"Cleo, breakfast is here," I called out. I strained to listen for her response, but I didn't hear anything. My brow furrowed and I wondered if I should check on her. Would she be offended if I went in there? Technically, we were married. Although, I'd never thought it would be a real marriage.

A few minutes went by and still no answer, and no Cleo. I decided to incur her wrath if I overstepped and went back to the bathroom. When I went inside, my heart nearly stopped.

"Cleo?" She didn't answer, nor did she open her eyes. I kneeled down beside the tub and reached out to check her pulse. I felt it, but it seemed a little weak to me. "Honey, I need you to wake up."

She moaned and slowly opened her eyes. "Sorry. Did I fall asleep again?"

"Yeah."

Her cheeks flushed when she became alert enough to realize she was in the tub naked while I leaned over her. I'd been good and hadn't looked. Well, I hadn't done more than peek. It had been hard to ignore the slender curves under the water. I held out my hand to help her out of the tub, then drained the water. She wrapped a towel around herself, and nearly fell. As she reached out to brace herself against the counter, I put my arm around her.

"I think the hot water made you lightheaded," I said. "Why don't you put on clean pajamas and spend the day resting? After we eat, you can watch a movie in the living room or sleep a little longer."

"All right." She couldn't meet my gaze as I led her into the bedroom and helped her dress. The fact she didn't seem steady on her feet worried me. While it was true the hot water could have fucked with her head a little, I wondered if that was really all there was to it. I'd keep an eye on her and see what happened. I also knew stress would make her more susceptible to illness. It was possible she was coming down with something.

I held onto her as we walked into the kitchen, and I pulled out a chair for her. "Do you want juice, milk, or coffee? Or there's water."

"Juice would be nice," she murmured.

I placed the back of my hand against her forehead, wondering if she had a fever. She didn't feel overly hot. "If you start feeling bad, let me know. You may have caught a bug or something."

She smiled faintly. "Are you worried about me?"

"Yeah, I am. Is there a reason I shouldn't be concerned about my wife?"

She sobered immediately, her face going blank. I could have kicked my own ass just then, recalling the phone conversation we'd had, and the letter I'd sent. Her surprise was understandable. I'd made it sound like I wanted nothing to do with her. In truth, I'd thought she might not fit in with the club, or that I'd be placing her in danger by bringing her here. Then her asshole brother had to go and find her, ruining the life she'd created for herself.

"Tell me what you've been up to the last few years," I said. "Where were you living before you came here?"

"About two hours away, but that's not where I went after we got married. I moved out of state and only came back after you were released from prison. Since the warden knew we were married, he told me when your release date was coming up, assuming you didn't do anything to add to your sentence. I'd wanted to be close by on the off chance I ever got to see you again," she said.

"You said you had an apartment, so I'm assuming you had a job. What about friends? Any boyfriends?"

She glared at me. "I'm a married woman, Joker. Of course, I didn't have boyfriends. It may have been in name only, but it didn't feel right going on dates with other men."

I lifted my hands in surrender. "Sorry. I won't mention it again."

She sighed. "I had two friends. Sort of. We'd go to movies together and sometimes meet for a girls' night. I wasn't really close to them, though."

"When you texted me, you said it was urgent. Why did you need me that day?" I asked. "You said you hadn't known about your brother at that point. What else happened?"

"Nothing. It's not important."

She wouldn't look at me, which told me she was lying. I wanted to press the issue, and yet, I didn't feel like I should. I'd broken her trust by pushing her away, and now I needed to earn it back.

"Tell me about your life. What I've missed," I said.

"I'm sorry for not writing," she said. "I didn't get your letters for quite a while. The person who was collecting them for me got sick, then had to go to rehab before they could move back to their house. By the time they forwarded everything to me, six months had passed. As much as I wanted to write to you, I thought..."

"What?"

"I thought you might have given up on me. The letters came in batches, so all the months in between, I always thought you'd stop writing and move on.

Except you didn't, and as more time passed, the harder it became to write to you."

"It's fine, Cleo. I did worry that something may have happened to you, but I also hoped you were busy living a happy life and didn't need me anymore."

She sighed and stared at the table. "I think I'll always need you. Until the very end."

Why did she sound so sad when she said that? It seemed like she thought that time would come sooner rather than later. I started to question her about it and stopped. The last thing I wanted was for her to feel like this was an interrogation.

"As for my job, it wasn't anything glamorous," she said. "I worked two part-time jobs before moving back to Alabama. When I got here, I found a job as part of the cleaning crew at a four-story office building."

"What kind of part-time jobs did you have?" I asked.

"I worked at the register for a small store and stocked shelves at a grocery store. None of them paid well. The cleaning job was the best I've had. The work wasn't easy, but I was able to work full-time and had benefits."

"Did you even tell them you were leaving? What about your apartment?" I asked.

"No to both. I need to get the keys back to the manager. I didn't even call the police when my brother broke in. I didn't know what to tell them, or if he might be watching me. The entire way here, I worried every car that lingered behind me might be him."

"I'll get the club to handle the apartment for you. But I'm afraid you'll have to call your boss. Tell him a family emergency came up and you won't be able to return." I reached for her hand, closing my fingers around hers. "You don't need to work anymore, Cleo. I can take care of both of us."

"Someone named Lavender put several thousand dollars into my bank account yesterday. I'm still having trouble processing that. I spent over one thousand, but there's still so much left. What do I even do with it all?" she asked.

"Whatever you want. It's the club's way of taking care of you. When you feel up to it, we can go to the bank, and I'll have you added to my account."

"I don't think I can eat any more." She shoved her half-full plate away. Standing, she swayed for a moment, and I nearly jumped up to catch her, but she balanced herself. "I think I need to sleep a little more if that's all right."

"Sure. I'll come check on you in a little bit."

Cleo left the room and I stared at her plate. Had she always been a light eater? Even at dinner last night, she hadn't finished her food. As tiny as she was, it seemed like she should be eating more. She'd felt entirely too light in the bathroom.

I dumped the leftovers into the trash and cleaned off the table. While Cleo slept, I watched TV and tried to figure out what I should do about her. I'd planned to live my life alone. Giving her my name had been one thing. Living with her day in and day out was entirely different.

As for her brother... I wasn't sure what to do about him. I needed to know if he was in town, or why he wanted Cleo. Picking up the phone, I called Wire.

"Shouldn't you be busy getting reacquainted with your wife?" he asked the second the call connected.

"She's sleeping. Listen, I'm going to text you a name and I'd like you to look into him. It's Cleo's brother. The one who broke into her apartment. She's terrified of him finding her, but it feels like she's holding something back. I need to know more about her family."

"Not a problem. Get me the info and I'll see what I can dig up."

"Thanks, Wire. I'll send it now." I ended the call and texted it to him. I didn't know how long it would take, or what he'd find. But I couldn't protect her if I didn't know what dangers she might be facing.

I only hoped she wasn't hiding anything that would cause a problem for the club.

Chapter Six

Cleo

In the month I'd been at the compound, not much had changed between me and Joker. I still hadn't told him about my heart condition, or come clean about my family. We slept in the same bed, and we'd often held hands. Our marriage felt more like friendship than anything else.

Things needed to be different.

While I enjoyed my time with him, I felt like I was wasting the precious months I had left. I wasn't sure how he hadn't noticed something was wrong. Or maybe he had. The fact he hadn't said anything told me where I stood. Would he even miss me once I was gone? I'd called my doctor last week, hoping there might have been an update. I couldn't very well drive two hours to go see him without Joker finding out. For that matter, if I hadn't managed to get my prescriptions filled the night I first arrived here, I wouldn't have had them.

They'd run out, and I needed refills. Except someone went with me every time I left the house. I didn't know what to do. A dull ache settled in my bones, too heavy to shake off. I could almost hear the whispers of vitality fleeing my body, leaving me hollow. I needed to get my shit together. There wasn't time to wallow.

Joker came in from the carport, where he'd been tinkering with his bike. Grease smeared across his hands, on his shirt, and even his face.

"Want me to start the shower for you?" I asked.

"If you don't mind, that would be great."

I nodded and then decided it was now or never. "I could... join you."

He froze, every muscle going tense. His gaze lifted to mine, and I nearly stumbled back a step. Had my words angered him? Offended him? I couldn't tell, but everything in me screamed at me to run. I'd never felt more like prey in front of a predator, and not in a sexy way.

"I'll just go... start the water." I rushed from the room. My heart pounded when I reached the bathroom, and the world spun for a moment. I gripped the edge of the sink, hoping I'd remain upright.

"Thought you were starting the shower," Joker said, coming up behind me.

"Sorry. I think I moved too fast. It made me lightheaded, but I'll be fine in a minute."

He moved in closer, placing his hands on my hips. The grease smeared on my clothes, and I nearly groaned. These hadn't been cheap, and I knew the stains wouldn't come out.

"What's wrong?" he asked.

"Nothing. Really. Just give me a minute and I..."

"Did you mean it? About showering with me?"

My breath froze in my lungs, and I met his gaze in the mirror. "Yeah."

"If we go down this road, it changes everything. You realize that, right?"

"We're married, Joker, but I feel more like a roommate."

"Then why don't you start by using my real name? At least when we're alone. Around the club, I'm still Joker."

I smiled faintly. Was he serious about this? I still remembered his name from our marriage certificate. Sadly, it wasn't one of the things that survived my brother's attack on my apartment. I'd need to order a new one in case I ever needed it for something.

"All right. Travis."

"Give me a minute in the shower to get this grease off me. Why don't you sit if you're dizzy?" He nodded toward the closed toilet lid. I took a seat and watched as he started the water and stripped out of his clothes.

I felt my jaw go slack as I stared. For an older man, he'd kept in shape. He might not have an eight pack, but he'd stayed toned. The ink on his body mesmerized me. I wondered if they all had a meaning behind them, or just things he liked. Except the tattoo covering most of his back. That one I recognized as his club colors. It looked old and faded. Had he gotten it when he'd first joined the club?

It made me realize there was still a lot we didn't know about each other. Had he been keeping secrets, same as me?

He crooked his finger at me, and I stood. After I undressed, I joined him in the shower. My cheeks felt hot. No one had ever seen this much of my body before, except the doctors, and I didn't count them. He lightly took my hand, linking our fingers together.

"You can still change your mind," he said.

"No. I want this."

"You a virgin still?" he asked.

"Yeah." I cleared my throat. "I told you I'd been faithful to you."

"Then I'm not taking you in here. Doesn't mean we can't have some fun, though. Just remember I haven't been with a woman in over twenty years. Not sure I'm going to last long once this gets started."

I reached up to cup his cheek. "Are you worried you'll disappoint me?"

"Something like that."

"Impossible. You're the man who saved me. The one who gave a lifeline to a tormented teen who felt incredibly alone. My one and only husband. It doesn't matter how long it lasts. Getting to share something like that with you is the only important part of the equation."

His lips kicked up on one corner. "Sometimes you sound so much older than you are. It's part of why I wrote back that first time. Even though you were just a kid, you came across as an adult who'd already experienced too much in the world."

"You're the first man I've seen naked," I said. "For someone who calls himself an old man, you're awfully sexy."

He chuckled and pressed his forehead to mine. "You're good for my ego."

"You keep asking if I'm sure about this. Are you? Because if you change your mind after we take this step, I think it will break my heart."

"I pushed you away as much as I could, then my club decided you were here to stay. Even still, I didn't want you to feel forced into accepting this relationship. When I asked you to marry me, I never thought we'd end up living together. I only wanted to save you."

"And you did." I went up on my tiptoes to kiss him. My lips lightly brushed against his. "Because of the sacrifice you made, I was able to escape my family for almost five years. If I hadn't, there's no telling what would have happened to me."

"Let's clean up and take this to the bedroom. Your first time is going to be on the bed and not in here. At least let me do that much right."

My heart warmed at the tender look in his eyes. Had I finally broken down the wall he'd built to keep me out? I was skeptical, and yet, I really hoped it was true. I was tired of being alone. Of feeling as if I'd never experience love. He may not have said the words, but if he wanted me as his wife in more than just name, surely those emotions would follow.

I'd tell him about my health tomorrow. Tonight, I wanted to be treated like a normal woman, and not someone staring death in the face. But once I divulged my heart issue, then maybe I could convince him to go to the doctor's office with me. I really did need to see Dr. Stevens again. If there was any chance of a transplant, then I needed to move quickly. Now that I had a reason to live, I wasn't ready to die quietly. I'd go down fighting.

We washed ourselves then got out and dried off. Joker lifted me into his arms and carried me to the bed, where he gently laid me down.

"Have I ever told you how beautiful you are?" he asked. "I've thought it since the first moment I saw you. It was like an angel had walked into hell that day. I wanted to chase you out of there, keep you away from the filthy men locked up and the leering guards, and at the same time, I wanted to pull you closer."

"You don't have to hold back anymore. I'm all yours," I murmured.

His lips devoured mine, as the weight of his body settled over me. I cradled his hips with my thighs and wound my arms around his neck. I'd never felt so excited and scared at the same time before.

He trailed his lips down the column of my neck, between my breasts, and then they closed over my nipple. I sucked in a breath as his teeth grazed me. It didn't hurt exactly, but it stung just enough that it felt good. I'd never imagined I'd like such a thing.

"Look how responsive you are," he said, his

voice low and husky. "Your nipples are already hard."

His words set me on fire. I'd thought I'd find something like this embarrassing. Instead, it seemed to be turning me on. He shifted his hips, his cock brushing against me.

"And your pussy is already wet. If this weren't your first time, I'd slide right in and fill you up. Tell me your desires, Cleo. What fantasies have lurked in your mind all these years? Whatever it is, I'll make it come true if I can... as long as it doesn't require me to share you in any way."

Oh God. I closed my eyes and swallowed hard. Was I brave enough to tell him? I'd read a lot of dirty books, and there was so much I'd been curious about. My favorite heroes were the possessive alpha men with a dark side, the twisted psychos who'd slaughter everyone without hesitation, but would do anything for the woman they desired.

"What does my sweet, innocent wife want?" he asked, rubbing his beard against my breasts. "What naughty things do you want me to do to you?"

"Travis, I..." I stopped, licking my lips. "I like reading romances with twisted men, forced seduction, and bondage."

"Oh really." A gleam entered his eyes. "Put your hands over your head."

I did as he said. He slid his palm up my arms and closed his fingers around my wrists, holding me in place. My pulse quickened and I knew I was getting even wetter. What else was he going to do to me?

He placed his lips near my ear. "I'm going to fill you up, claim what's mine, and make sure you never forget who you belong to."

A shiver raced down my spine, and my nipples got even harder. He must have noticed because I felt him smile.

"You're going to do everything I tell you. If you don't, you'll be punished."

"How?" I asked, feeling breathless.

"What's a good threat for you, Cleo? A spanking?" I whimpered and squirmed under him. "Hmm. Clearly not. Then how about I push you to the edge again and again, and never let you come?"

My eyes went wide. "You wouldn't, would you? I've never even had an orgasm before."

"Then I guess we better start with fixing that." He released me and kissed his way down my body. I moved my hands and he stopped, glaring at me. I quickly placed them over my head again, and he continued. The moment he spread my thighs wide and blew on my pussy, I thought I was going to die from pleasure. His tongue flicked out, giving me quick, hard licks. My toes curled and I fought hard not to reach for him. "That's it. Come for me, Cleo. Show me how pretty you are when you let go."

The pleasure was right *there* yet remained out of reach. I shifted and twisted. Joker growled and pinned me in place. He attacked my pussy with his lips and tongue, driving me crazy with need. Something was building inside me. It felt so intense it frightened me.

"Travis, wait... I... I..."

"Uh-uh. You don't call the shots in bed, Cleo. Now be a good girl and come."

His words seemed to trigger something, and I felt the tension in my body crest and then explode. I screamed out his name as I thrashed under him, the feelings almost more than I could handle. I whimpered and tried to pull away as he continued to use his wicked tongue on me. Joker made me come twice more before he rose up over me again.

"You ready?" he asked. I nodded and spread my thighs wider. I felt his cock push against me, felt the burn as he forced his way inside. My body gave a little at a time, and I was torn between lifting my hips to take in more of him and wanting to retreat. How could it both hurt and feel good at the same time? "That's it. Let me in."

"I can't take much more," I whispered. "Please… it's too much."

"Brace yourself." That was the only warning I had before he started thrusting. Long and slow. Every drag of his cock made those intense sensations begin to build again. Just when I thought I'd lose my mind if he kept going, I came once more. It seemed to be the only thing holding him back. "So fucking beautiful. And mine."

He took me hard and fast, every stroke of his cock driving in deeper than the last. When he came, the heat of his release filled me. I felt overwhelmed, a little relieved. My pussy felt sore, and like I'd been rubbed raw. The small twinges of pain became more pronounced as he pulled out.

"Fuck." He stared down between us. "I didn't use protection. Please tell me you're on the pill or something?"

"No." Was it even possible for me to get pregnant right now? I didn't know what all the medication had done to my body since I'd first met with Dr. Stevens. My period wasn't exactly regular. I hadn't discussed it with Dr. Stevens since there hadn't been a point. Now I wanted to know. If there was the slightest chance we'd just created a baby, then I had even more of a reason to live.

"I'm sorry. I should have done a better job protecting you. We haven't even discussed the possibility of kids yet."

"Do you want them?" I asked.

"Honestly, I'm kind of old to be chasing little ones around. But you're not. If you want a family, then we'll have one. I just know I'm not as young as I used to be. I don't like the idea of me dying and leaving you behind with a bunch of kids."

I felt my face pale a little. Right. Except he wasn't the one dying. I was. My chest ached, and I realized I'd probably overdone it. I'd been meaning to get some sort of fitness tracker, not for the actual fitness part, but something that would monitor my heart rate. I had a feeling it was pounding out of control right now.

"Maybe I'm not pregnant."

"Yeah." He fell to his side next to me. "But if you are, then I'll do everything I can for our child."

"I know because that's just the kind of man you are. I hope you realize how amazing you are."

He kissed me softly. "No, Cleo. I'm just a stubborn ex-con who got lucky enough to find a sweet woman like you. Let's get some rest, then we can shower again and figure out food."

I closed my eyes and snuggled into his side. I'd tell him about my heart later. The last thing I wanted to do right now was ruin the mood.

I think I've fallen for you, Joker. Please don't break my heart. It's doing a good enough job of that all on its own.

Chapter Seven

Cleo

"Jesus, Cleo, you look like hell," Ridley said, as she entered the house. Joker was off to Church, and I had the house to myself. She sat down beside me, her eyes scanning my face with that unnerving intensity that seemed to see right through me.

I managed a weak smile, one that didn't reach my eyes. "Just tired, Ridley. You know how it is."

"Too tired because your man can't keep his hands off you? Or is something else going on? You're pale as fuck and look like you might pass out at any moment."

She wasn't entirely wrong. Since our first time together, Joker had taken full advantage of us being husband and wife. Now, five days later, I felt like I might break. "It's fine."

Ridley sighed and grabbed my hand. "Look at me, Cleo."

It wasn't a request. It was an order, and despite myself, I obeyed.

"Something's eating at you, and it's more than just Joker making up for lost time. This club is your family. If there's something wrong, let us help."

"Family," I echoed, the word tasting bitter. If only she knew the darkness lurking behind that term for me. But I couldn't burden her with my ghosts -- not when they were liable to tear everything apart, including this fragile sense of belonging I found here.

"Damn it, Cleo!" Ridley's grip tightened, her nails digging into my skin. "Tell me what's wrong! I know you're hiding something."

"Some secrets are best left buried," I said. And some I needed to confess before it was too late. But I was scared. Things were going well with Joker. I didn't want to wreck it, even though I knew my time was running out. He'd treat me differently once he knew I was sick.

"Ridley," I started, then stopped. How could I explain without dragging her into the abyss with me? She'd faced her own demons. I didn't want to burden her with mine.

"Talk to me, Cleo. Whatever it is, we'll tackle it. Together." Her voice softened, but the edge of steel lingered. I had a feeling she wouldn't let this go. "Don't shut us out. Don't shut *me* out."

She'd been so nice to me since the first day we'd met. Out of all the women here, she'd dropped by the most often. Since I was close to the age of her kids, I had to wonder if she saw me as another daughter. Whatever the case, I owed her a lot.

A single tear escaped, trailing down my cheek. Ridley caught it with her thumb, her touch gentle. In that moment, I felt the weight of a thousand unspoken words pressing on my chest, each one screaming for release.

"Please, Ridley. Just… let it be." I pulled my hand free and stood up, every muscle protesting. The room spun, a carousel of blurred colors, and I stumbled.

"Whoa there, kiddo," Ridley was by my side in an instant, her arm around my waist, steadying me. "You need to take care of yourself. You hear me?"

I nodded, not trusting my voice. Her concern made me feel terrible. I'd essentially lied to her, and everyone else. Would they ever forgive me?

"Promise me you'll try," she said, her gaze

holding mine, demanding an answer.

"Promise," I lied, and the word tasted like ashes.

With Ridley's help, I made it to my room. I stretched out on the bed and closed my eyes, praying this was just another episode like all the others. It would pass in a moment or two, right?

"Tomorrow," I whispered. I'd tell them about my illness in the morning. For today, I wanted Joker to treat me the same as any other day.

I couldn't sleep, and my mind kept spinning, creating problems that hadn't even happened yet. Giving up on getting any rest, I pulled out the tablet Joker had bought for me and opened one of the apps for my web comics. I'd found it accidentally, and discovered I really enjoyed reading them. The artwork was always so beautiful, and the storylines intrigued me. I lost myself in one about a woman who'd died of an incurable disease only to wake up in a fictional world as a duke's daughter.

If there really was a life after death, I could think of worse places to go. The woman had once been a villainess, but the transmigrated soul decided to live a different life. I devoured the scenes, and soon ran out of episodes. The hiatus notification at the top left me feeling aggravated. Would I even be alive when the next season became available?

Glancing at the time, I realized Joker had been gone for quite a while. Just as I was going to text him, I heard the front door open and shut. Then I heard multiple sets of footsteps. Had Joker brought someone with him? I struggled out of bed and made my way to the kitchen. He sat at the table with Wire, Lavender, and Ridley. What was going on?

"I didn't realize we had company," I said, forcing a smile.

"We need to talk," Joker said.

I swallowed hard, looking at the folders, papers, and laptop Wire and Lavender had brought with them. I hadn't spent much time with the two of them, but I heard about their skills. Had they gone digging into my past? Was that why Joker had such a fierce expression on his face?

"Here," Wire grunted, handing me an old, dog-eared photograph. "Recognize them?"

In the image, a younger version of myself stood flanked by two menacing figures -- my dad and brother, masked by civility. But behind their eyes lurked the familiar specters of cruelty and greed.

"Where did you get this?" I asked, my voice barely audible.

"Old police records," Lavender replied, her face drawn with concern. "Cleo, there's something you need to know."

My gut twisted as they unfolded tales of my family's sins -- tales I had heard whispered in the dead of night, tales I had silenced with denial. Until they talked about the things I'd witnessed. They spoke of human lives traded like currency, of innocence sold to the highest bidder, and my blood ran cold with the memory of close calls and narrow escapes.

"From what Joker had said about saving you, I had a feeling they were bad people," Wire spat. "But this... this is... They're pure evil."

"Your folks were deep in it," Lavender added, solemnity etched into every word. "Leveraging you as... bait. We know almost everything, Cleo. Only thing we aren't sure about is how much you remember or have been trying to hide."

I flinched as if struck. Each syllable was a nail in my coffin. The life I'd tried to build here was fading fast. They wouldn't want someone like me to stick around. Even if they didn't like the idea of Joker divorcing me, I didn't think they'd force him to remain married to me after this. Once they told the others, it would all be over for me.

"Is that why you left?" Wire's eyes drilled into me, searching for confirmation.

"Partly." The admission clawed its way up my throat. "I couldn't be part of it. Couldn't let them use me anymore. And… I worried I might be next."

Lavender frowned for a moment, then nodded. "We won't let them touch you again. You're one of us now."

"Us" felt like a sanctuary, a promise of something resembling a family -- albeit forged not by blood but by shared scars. I glanced at Joker, trying to determine how he felt about everything. His jaw was so tight I worried he might crack his teeth.

"Ridley came to us to help you, not to dredge up nightmares," Wire said, his hand briefly squeezing mine. "But knowing this changes everything. Whether it was by force or not, you were still a part of what they did."

"Changes what?" My voice trembled, betraying the dread that knotted my insides. "What happens now?"

"That's not something we can answer," Wire said. "It's between you and Joker first, then the two of you and the President. But we can't keep this hidden. You should have told us from the beginning. When you said you were running from your brother, none of us had any idea this is what you meant."

"And if you'd looked into it when I asked you to, we'd have known sooner," Joker said.

"You asked them to do this?" I stared at him.

Had he not trusted me from the very beginning? The others left. Even Ridley wouldn't look at me or say a word. It felt like my entire world was crumbling.

"Your old man's been involved in some nasty business. Trafficking. And your name came up more than once." Joker sighed. "What am I supposed to think of all this, Cleo?"

A cold dread settled in my gut, snaking up to coil around my heart. The memories of shadowed figures and hushed threats played in my mind. "They never saw me as family, just another asset. An obedient doll."

"People protect their assets," Joker said.

"Or use them as bait." I sighed and sat on the chair Wire had vacated moments before.

"Nobody's using you, Cleo -- not anymore," Joker said. "A lot of people here care about you. Including me. There's a lot of ways this can play out."

"Like what?" I asked.

"We have the evidence we need to either have them locked up, or…"

"Or what?"

"You can let the club handle this. Me, specifically. I'll make sure your father and brother can't hurt anyone ever again."

I swallowed hard. Was he saying what I thought he was? "You're going to kill them?"

He shrugged. "Won't be the first time I've taken a life. Doubt it will be the last."

I wasn't sure how to process his words. The man I'd come to know wouldn't hurt an innocent person. Had he killed bad people like my family before?

"What does this mean for us?" I asked.

"Well, I guess that depends on you. Are you going to keep any more secrets from me?"

Shit. There was still one hell of a secret I hadn't

shared. Now didn't seem like the right time. It *never* seemed like the right time.

"There's one more, but..."

"We'll talk about it tomorrow. Or after we have a plan for tackling your family. At least you've admitted there's something else you need to share with me. That will be enough for now," Joker said.

Maybe it was, but what if I ran out of time before I had the chance to tell him what was wrong?

"I have an appointment I need to go to. It's where I lived before coming here," I said. "Will you go with me?"

"Just tell me when." He stood and leaned over to kiss the top of my head.

After he left, I called Dr. Stevens' office and scheduled a visit to discuss my options. I'd need to tell Joker before then, but at least I'd bought myself a few more days. I'd use that time to figure out the best way to tell him I was dying.

Someone knocked on the door and I went to answer it. Ridley stood on the other side, arms crossed.

"Um, did you forget something?" I asked.

"Yeah. You're a dumbass," she said. "Why didn't you tell anyone?"

"Because I worried I'd be chased out of here, or that you'd all look at me differently." I pressed my lips together and motioned for her to come in. "I'm sorry for lying to everyone."

"Did you not trust us?" she asked. "Have I done something to make you think I'd hate you because of what your family forced you to do?"

I sighed and sat down on the couch. "Honestly, Ridley, I didn't know what anyone would think or believe. I didn't have proof of what happened. It was just my word against theirs. What if you found my father or brother and they said I'd been a willing participant in everything?"

"I'd have called them liars," she said. "Anyone who's met you couldn't ever believe you'd do something so awful. You're a sweetheart, Cleo."

"I'm sorry, Ridley."

She came closer, sitting beside me, then pulled me in for a hug. "You're one of us, which means you need to tell us when something is wrong. You don't have to fight on your own anymore. If you're scared, then we'll listen. Please don't push us away."

"Why do you care so much?" I asked. "I'm just some random woman who showed up one day. None of you knew Joker was married."

"I wish my girls were a little more like you," she said. "They're both mouthy little shits and get themselves into trouble. Farrah is the worst of the two. You're a little like a female version of my son, Dawson. The two of you tend to be quiet and reserved."

"So, I'm… what exactly?"

"Family. You're my family, Cleo. I don't know what happened to your mom, and I'd never go so far as to say I want you to consider me as a mother figure, but I'd hoped we were at least friends."

"We are. I'm really sorry I didn't tell you." I sighed. "And there's something else no one knows. I'm supposed to tell Joker soon."

"What? Do you want to share it with me now?" she asked, leaning back a little.

"I'm dying, Ridley."

Her face paled and she shook her head. "That's not funny."

"I'm aware." I closed my eyes. "It's why I tried to reach Joker. I got the news, spoke to him on the phone, where he did his best to make me feel unwanted, and then got home to discover my brother had found me. Maybe I should have just gone home to them. It's not like I'd have lasted longer than six months. In fact, I could have stopped taking all my meds and maybe I'd have been gone within a month."

"Six months?" she asked, her voice shrieking. "What the fuck?"

"Give or take a few. The doctor said he couldn't give me an exact timeframe. My heart is failing. I promise I'm going to talk to Joker about it. Just... not today. I think he's angry with me right now."

"Fine. I'll keep quiet, but not for long. If you need anything, tell me. I'm only a phone call away."

"Thanks, Ridley. I really appreciate it."

She hugged me again and then let herself out. Well, at least it wasn't entirely a secret anymore.

Chapter Eight

Joker

I'd waited until after dinner, but I couldn't hold back anymore. The revelation from today weighed on me.

"Everything's changed," I muttered, my voice a hoarse whisper against the pounding in my ears. I felt like I had been split open, raw and bleeding with the festering secrets that lay exposed.

How could she have kept something like this from me? On the one hand, I'd known she was hiding something. It had been clear many times during the past month. If I'd simply asked what was weighing on her, would she have told me? On the other... she had to have known what this would do to our relationship.

"Nothing's changed about how I feel about you!" Cleo's voice cracked with desperation. "It's why I..."

"Hasn't it?" The question hung heavy in the air. She'd lied to me. It felt like a betrayal, even if she hadn't meant it as such. Could I forgive her for this? Could the club? I didn't know what would happen once Savior found out.

She crumpled before me, her knees hitting the floor with a dull thud, her cries slicing through the tension. I stood there, watching the woman I'd come to care for as she fell apart. I could have been nicer about it, but... she'd hurt me. Deeply. Why hadn't she trusted me?

"Cleo, what am I supposed to do with this? You lied to me. To the club. It's not as simple of a matter as you seem to think." I stared down at her. How had we gotten here? I'd thought things were going well for us.

"Your family is responsible for the one thing this club won't abide -- human trafficking. Not only that, but they targeted women and children."

"I know they're monsters," she said, her voice hoarse. "It's why I needed to run from them. I didn't tell you back then because I didn't want you to look at me differently. Your letters had always been so kind and warm. If you knew the type of people I came from, you'd have turned your back on me."

"Damn you," I growled, not sure if I was cursing her or myself. Even now, she made me want to comfort her. I couldn't tell her she was wrong. There was a good chance I'd have stopped answering her letters, and I damn sure wouldn't have helped her run from them. Not if I had even a hint of doubt as to how involved she'd been in it all.

"Joker," she reached out, a frail hand seeking mine. But before our fingers could brush, her eyes rolled back, a gasp escaping her lips as she crumpled to the ground.

"Cleo!" I dropped to my knees. I lifted her body into my arms, holding her close. All thoughts of betrayal evaporated, replaced by a singular, piercing focus. Had the stress been too much? I didn't know why she'd collapsed. "Stay with me."

My scarred hands shook as they brushed hair from her forehead. Why wasn't she waking up? My hold on her tightened. Had I done this to her? Was it because I'd verbally attacked her and tried to distance myself again?

"Please. Open your eyes, Cleo. Don't do this to me."

"Joker..." It was barely a breath, her voice a ghost in the room, before her body went slack in my arms. Panic, raw and savage, tore through my chest.

This wasn't a mere collapse. It felt more like a fall into an abyss from which there might be no return.

"Damnit, Cleo," I cursed. I needed help -- I couldn't lose her, not like this, not when there were questions unanswered and feelings unexplored. I had to save her. Whatever it took, whoever I had to confront or challenge, I would do it. Because in that moment, with Cleo's fragile life in my hands, nothing else mattered.

Time seemed to fracture, each second splintering into shards of eternity as I knelt beside her, my calloused fingers trembling against the pallor of Cleo's cheek.

"Stay with me," I urged, desperation threading my words. I fumbled for a pulse, the usually steady thump of life now an elusive whisper under her skin. "Come on, baby, fight."

I slapped her cheeks gently, hoping to coax her back from whatever edge she teetered upon. Her chest rose and fell in shallow, ragged breaths. My hands danced over, seeking a response. Any sign that she'd heard me, felt me. There was nothing -- just my own panicked breaths filling the air.

I snatched up my phone and before I could second-guess myself, I dialed 911.

"911. What's your emergency?" the operator asked as the call connected.

"Send help! My wife is unconscious. I think... I think it's bad."

"Sir, can you tell me your location?" The question anchored me, tugged me back from the precipice of terror.

"The Dixie Reapers compound." I rattled off the address and gave her my name. "The person at the gate can tell the ambulance how to reach my house.

Please hurry!"

"An ambulance is on its way. Stay on the line with me." The dispatcher's instruction was a command, but my gaze never wavered from Cleo's still form.

"Keep breathing, Cleo. Fight!" I whispered. "You can't leave me."

"Sir, I need you to check if she's breathing." The dispatcher's tone was steady, a counterpoint to the cacophony of dread that roared in my ears. I placed my finger under her nose and felt the warmth of her breath.

"Yes, but I couldn't find a pulse earlier. I think it's faint."

"Can you do CPR if necessary?" the voice asked, clinical yet not unkind.

"Y-yes," I stuttered, my hands balling into fists, then unfurling, ready to pump life back into her if it came to that. At least prison had been good for something. Out of sheer boredom, I'd taken a CPR class. One of the few things that had caught my attention while I'd been locked up.

The sirens in the distance grew louder as the ambulance drew near. I knew the club would have questions, and Savior might kick my ass for not giving anyone a heads-up. Panic clawed at my chest as I watched the rise and fall of Cleo's chest -- shallow, too shallow. My hand trembled as it hovered over her heart, feeling the erratic stutter of its beat. Fear gripped me with icy fingers. This couldn't be happening -- not to Cleo, not the woman who'd become my everything amidst the chaos of our lives.

And yeah, I'd been too fucking stubborn to even admit it to myself, but I'd fallen for her. In the last month, she'd become my entire world.

"Come on, baby, stay with me," I urged. Every second was an eternity.

"Help is on the way," the dispatcher assured me, but the room spun with a vertigo that had nothing to do with movement. It was the terror of loss, the dread of a future torn away before it had the chance to unfold. I knew I could be overreacting. She could have simply passed out from stress, but in my gut, I knew something was wrong. She'd said she had one more secret. Did it have to do with her collapse just now?

A thousand thoughts raced through my head. The sirens were close now, a wail that pierced through the thick fog of fear enveloping me. Red and blue lights flashed outside, casting dancing shadows across the walls.

"Sir, are you still with me?" The dispatcher's voice was a lifeline in the tempest threatening to swallow me whole.

"I'm here." My voice sounded distant, even to my own ears. "They're here."

"Okay, go let them in. We'll stay on the line until they take over."

I nodded, then realized the dispatcher couldn't see me. "Yeah, going."

My legs moved stiffly, as if I was wading through molasses. Opening the door, I was met with faces etched with concern and professionalism -- the paramedics.

"Over here," I managed to say, pointing toward Cleo's fragile form on the floor.

As they rushed past me, I turned back to Cleo, a silent plea in my eyes. *Don't you dare give up!*

The paramedics swarmed around her, their actions efficient and practiced. I stood there, feeling utterly helpless as I watched them work to save the woman who held my heart.

"Sir, you can hang up the phone now," one of them said without looking up from where they were administering CPR.

"Right." I ended the call and shoved the phone into my pocket. My hands were still shaking, but now there was nothing left to do with them. Nothing except hope and wait.

"We're losing her," one of them said.

It felt like my heart stopped right along with hers. As they lost her pulse, they began chest compressions.

"You said her name is Cleo?" one of them asked.

"Yeah. She's my wife."

To his credit, he didn't bat an eye at our age difference. Hell, I'd often thought our roles would be reversed in this sort of situation. She'd be the one praying for me to open my eyes, and I'd pass on to the afterlife.

"Come on, Cleo, stay with us," one paramedic muttered, his words more command than plea. "Got her! Pulse is back."

The other worked to secure an oxygen mask over her face, his brows furrowed in concentration.

"Can you tell me what happened?" The man's voice pulled at the edges of my focus, bringing me back from the darkness filling my mind.

"Uh…" My thoughts tangled like barbed wire. "She just… collapsed. We were talking and she…"

Guilt clawed at my throat, choking the rest of the words. It was my confrontation that had pushed her over the edge, wasn't it? I'd done this to my sweet wife. All because I'd felt hurt at her secrecy.

"Sir, we need to get her to the hospital now." The urgency in the paramedic's tone snapped me back to the present. They loaded Cleo onto a stretcher, her body limp and vulnerable, a stark contrast to the vibrant woman I knew.

"Can I come with you?" I asked.

"It's best if you follow," he said.

I scrambled to grab my keys and started my bike. As the ambulance drove through the compound to the front gates, I stayed right behind them. I heard the sound of pipes and knew some of my brothers were joining me. I'd need their support while I waited for news on Cleo, and I felt grateful they were in my life.

Who did Cleo have other than me and the Dixie Reapers? No one. Only a brother and father who'd most likely sell her to the highest bidder. Whatever happened, I'd apologize for the way I acted. She had to be okay! I wouldn't accept any other possible outcome.

At the hospital, I quickly parked my motorcycle and rushed to the ER entrance, where the ambulance was unloading Cleo.

"Stay strong for her," one of the paramedics said. "She needs you."

"Is she… Is she stable?"

"We've done everything we can, and now it's up to the hospital staff and doctors. She's in good hands. I'll pray she makes a full recovery."

I went to the ER triage desk, desperate to find out what I needed to do next. My brothers came in and I felt their presence behind me. Would they see me fall apart? If Cleo didn't make it…

"Hey," a deep voice interrupted my spiraling thoughts. It was Venom. I hadn't realized he'd been one of the men to follow me. "We're here for you, Joker. Whatever you need."

"Thanks," I managed to say, though what I needed was beyond anyone's power to grant.

"Let's sit down," Venom suggested. "Savior's here too. Let him handle the paperwork."

Sitting felt like giving up, like letting go. And I wasn't ready to do either -- not yet. Not ever. I stubbornly stood, staring at the doors where Cleo had vanished.

"Joker, you can't help her if you fall apart."

I barely registered the truth in Venom's words, my mind a maelstrom of guilt and fear. Images of Cleo's pale face, her body crumpling, played on a loop in my head.

"She needs you strong," Venom said.

"Strong? What use is strength when I couldn't..."

"Stop." Venom sighed. "This isn't your fault. Ridley told me something when she saw the ambulance. It's about Cleo. She's been hiding a health condition from all of us. Whatever happens, she has you. And you have us. We're family."

Family. The word echoed hollowly in my skull. Was I about to lose the only person who'd made that word mean something again? Sure, I had my brothers, and they *were* family, but not in the same sense. The thought was a blade twisting deep in my gut.

"Stay with me, Cleo," I whispered, a silent prayer to whatever gods might be listening.

And so I waited, a broken man clinging to hope. The clock on the wall was a relentless tick, each one a hammer blow to my chest. I paced the sterile linoleum of the hospital waiting room, my boots scuffing the floor in time with the pendulum of dread swinging through my mind. The sickly fluorescent lights above cast a pallor over everything, as if the very air we breathed was tainted by the shadow of death.

"Joker, man, you've got to sit down," Tank urged from behind me. "Getting worked up isn't going to help either of you."

"Can't," I muttered, my voice barely above a rasp.

"Joker?" A voice cut through the fog of my thoughts, sharp and clinical. I turned to see a doctor clad in blue scrubs, a stethoscope draped around his neck like some harbinger of fate. His face was drawn, eyes weary but kind -- the kind that had seen too much yet still held onto compassion.

"Tell me she's going to be okay," I said. The words clawed their way up my throat, desperation lacing every syllable.

"We've stabilized your wife for now, but her condition is precarious." The doctor's gaze locked onto mine, unwilling or unable to look away from the train wreck of emotions that must have been written all over my face.

"Talk to me straight, Doc. What are we looking at here?" My hands clenched into fists at my sides, knuckles white and straining against the skin.

"Her heart -- it's failing. The stress of her condition, compounded by external factors, has taken a significant toll. She needs a transplant, and soon." The words hit like a shotgun blast, each one splintering into my soul with brutal force.

"A transplant..." I repeated dumbly, the concept too vast and treacherous to fully comprehend. It felt like being told to catch a star from the sky -- impossible, unreachable.

"Without it, her chances --" The doctor didn't finish, but he didn't have to. The unsaid hung between us, a silent verdict passed down by an unseen judge. "I spoke with her cardiologist. Your wife has been aware of her condition for about a month now. She's already on the list, but as to when there will be a match... Well, that's up to God."

"Damnit!" I exploded, the word tearing from my lips before I could reel it back in. "Is she conscious? Can I see her?"

"Only for a moment," the doctor conceded, nodding toward the restricted area beyond. "She's very weak, and we need to keep her rested."

"Thanks, Doc."

"Joker, you're not alone in this." Tank smiled. "We'll be here waiting."

I followed the doctor toward Cleo's room, each step a march toward an uncertain future, my heart echoing the same refrain: survive, fight, endure. Because if Cleo was going down, I'd be damned if I wasn't going down with her. No point in living if she wasn't part of this world anymore.

The sterile scent of the hospital clawed at my senses, a stark reminder that her life hung by a thread -- a damn fragile one. My boots were loud against the linoleum floor, each step syncing with the hammering of my heart as I made my way back to the waiting room after seeing Cleo. She was a ghost of herself, pale and barely hanging on. The beeping of her heart monitor was still drumming in my ears, a morbid metronome counting down the seconds of her life.

"Joker," the doctor's voice broke through the fog of my thoughts, "I think it goes without saying, but given her condition, it's imperative we find a donor soon."

"Find one," I spat out, desperation creeping into my tone. "Whatever it takes, Doc."

He nodded solemnly, his eyes not quite meeting mine. "It's not that simple I'm afraid. We're doing everything we can, but these things... they're unpredictable."

Unpredictable. Like the road that had led us here -- the twists, the turns, the cliff edges we'd skidded around. I dug my nails into my palms. Cleo couldn't be another casualty of fate, not when she'd fought so hard to escape the darkness of her past.

"Isn't there anything else?" I demanded. "Anything at all?"

"We just have to wait," he replied. His voice held a note of finality that made me want to grab him, shake him -- anything to stir him into action.

"Waiting isn't something I'm good at." My voice trembled with the strain of holding back a torrent of emotions.

"Understood," he said before turning to leave, his white coat disappearing down the hallway.

I stood alone, the weight of the situation pressing down on me like the heat from a thousand suns. If only anger could fix this -- if only sheer willpower could repair a failing heart. But this wasn't a bike that I could wrench back to life or a rival I could intimidate into submission. This was Cleo's life, her heart, and it was slipping through my fingers like grains of sand.

"Damn it," I muttered under my breath. Not knowing what else to do, I texted Wire.

Cleo is on a transplant list for a heart. Find one for her! Whatever it takes. She won't last long without one.

He responded almost immediately. *Already on it. Got word from Savior. You need anything, tell someone. We're all behind you one hundred percent.*

Yeah. I didn't have to do this alone.

Chapter Nine

Cleo

Finding myself in the hospital wasn't the greatest start to my day. Now Joker and the others knew about my heart condition. The way he'd gripped my hand told me plenty. It must have terrified him when I passed out. Especially since he hadn't known why it happened. Had he blamed himself? If so, he hadn't said anything to me. I barely remembered him being here. By the time I was thinking clearly, he'd left and I was alone.

"Cleo, how are you feeling this morning?" Dr. Perkins asked.

"I'm alive. That's about as much as I can say."

He nodded. "I've been in touch with Dr. Stevens. We've tried to move you up the donor list for a heart, but as you're aware, it's not easy receiving one."

"How bad is it?" I asked.

"You need to take it easy. Dr. Stevens agrees that the time he'd estimated is wrong. You have, at most, three months left if you can't get a new heart."

"By take it easy…"

"I know you're married, and I can understand you'd want to spend as much time with your husband as possible. Try not to exert yourself too much, and you certainly don't need to worry about a pregnancy right now. When you were admitted, we ran bloodwork. You aren't pregnant as of this moment, however, we can't give you birth control. If you're up for having sex, be sure to use a condom. And above all, tell him to be gentle, and watch for any signs your heart can't handle it."

"Have you spoken to Joker yet? Does he understand everything that's going on?" I asked.

"I didn't. However, a friend of mine is close with the club members. He treats all their women. Dr. Myron offered to speak with Joker and the others. While he's not a cardiovascular specialist, he knows enough about your condition to answer the sorts of questions they may have."

"Thank you, Dr. Perkins."

He left and I was alone once more. I'd heard Joker had been with me all night, not even closing his eyes for a few minutes. If he got sick because he wasn't taking care of himself, it wouldn't do either of us any good. I hoped being with his club would help him cope with everything he'd recently learned. And hopefully, he'd get some sleep while he was at home. I didn't think I'd be leaving until tonight or possibly tomorrow. No one had mentioned discharging me yet.

The upside of being here? My family couldn't get to me. Even if they stopped by, I could decline their visit. I had a feeling once they knew I was dying, they wouldn't be interested anymore. Knowing the Dixie Reapers had so many women and children did make me ill at ease. If my brother found out about them, I could only imagine what he'd do. His twisted mind would probably feel like they owed him.

I stared at the TV mounted on the wall, not really paying attention to the movie playing. I wondered what would happen to me now. Like the doctor said, there was no guarantee they'd find a transplant in time. If I really did only have a short time left, then I wanted to make the most of it.

There were so many things I'd wanted to do. I'd already fallen in love, so I could cross that off, even if I hadn't exactly confessed to him. I'd tried to show him through actions, but it felt like I hadn't done a good enough job. And of course, having a family wasn't in the cards right now. Aside from that, I'd wanted to travel. It wasn't something I'd be able to do on my own, and if there was the chance of a transplant surgery, I needed to stay close enough to the hospital to get there quickly.

Someone knocked on the door, and Lavender poked her head inside the room. "Are you up for company?"

"Is it just you?" I asked.

"Um, what if it isn't?"

"It's fine. It's better than staring at the TV. I'm not even sure what's on right now," I said.

She stepped into the room, followed by Ridley and Darian. Ridley gave me a sheepish look. "Sorry about before. I felt a little blindsided."

"I shouldn't have kept it from everyone. I was just..."

"Scared?" Darian asked.

"Yeah. Joker is the only person I've ever trusted, but after he kept pushing me away, I didn't feel comfortable telling him about my family or my heart condition. Although, I'd decided to talk to him about my medical issues the next day, after he'd had time to cool down. Except I ended up in the hospital."

"Is there anything you need?" Ridley asked.

"I want to go home." I sighed. "I have no idea when I'll get released from this place."

"Wire is going to keep an eye on the cameras around town and make sure your family isn't lurking. If they are, the club will handle it." Lavender came closer. "I'm sorry if it felt like we attacked you. It wasn't my intention for that to happen, but the things we found..."

"I get it. The picture it painted was far from pretty. For what it's worth, my part happened while I was still a minor. I didn't have a choice but to go along with them. The few times I refused, they beat me and starved me."

"Did you talk to Joker about it?" Ridley asked.

"Not exactly. He was really angry about it and came after me once everyone left. He was in the middle of yelling at me when my heart gave out," I said.

"That explains a lot," Darian muttered.

"What do you mean?" I asked.

She sat down in the chair next to the bed. "Well, he kept blaming himself for what happened. He thought he'd caused you too much stress. Although, from what I've heard, it probably did contribute to what happened."

"I'm not supposed to get stressed out," I said. "Not sure how they expect anyone in this day and age to live a stress-free life. Even millionaires have their issues."

"Not something I'll ever have to worry about," Darian said.

"Oh, please. Like my dad doesn't make enough to take care of you." Ridley rolled her eyes. "He goes on more jobs than Venom does, and we're comfortable enough."

"Speaking of money, don't worry about the hospital bill," Lavender said. "While we were waiting on news about you, I decided to hack into a few accounts. All criminals who earned their money illegally, or by doing horrible things. I created a medical account for the club and funneled about half a million into it."

"Um, won't they go looking for their money?" I asked.

"Nope. They'll be too busy running from the police. I took a copy of all the incriminating files I found and sent it anonymously to the authorities."

I didn't even know what to say. The fact she'd said it was for the entire club made me feel better. The last thing I wanted was for her to do something like that only for me.

"We also brought you a few things," Ridley said, lifting a bag I hadn't noticed. "There's a book in here, a magazine, a puzzle book with pencils and pens, and a few other odds and ends."

"Thanks." I smiled and took the bag from her. "Too bad you couldn't smuggle in some decent food."

Everyone laughed, but seriously, hospital food was the worst. At least, the food they served the patients. The ladies stayed a while longer. I enjoyed their company. After they left, I napped off and on. It wasn't until night fell that I finally got up the courage to ask when I could go home. The nurse came in to take my vitals and see if I needed anything.

"Did the doctor say when I could go home?" I asked.

"You seem stable. As long as nothing happens overnight, you'll probably go home sometime tomorrow."

"Sounds good to me. I want to sleep in my own bed."

She patted my leg. "I hear that often. Push the call button if you need anything."

"Thanks. Um, are visiting hours over for the day?"

"I'm afraid so, but if your husband comes by, the nurse at the desk will let him through."

Which meant Joker hadn't been back all day, and probably wouldn't come at all. Now that he knew I was all right, and he'd had time to think things through, maybe he'd decided I was too much trouble. The club apparently still felt like I was family since the ladies had stopped by. But what about my husband?

Needing to get my mind off things, I took out the puzzle book and grabbed a pencil. Better to stay occupied than think of all the *what ifs*.

* * *

Joker

Since we no longer had club whores, even the married brothers frequented the clubhouse these days. It had been a great place to enjoy a beer and catch up with everyone. Even now, I saw Venom, Bull, Tank, and Torch at a table in the corner. Saint and Savior were at another one, and a handful of other brothers were scattered about the place.

I made my way to the bar and grabbed a beer before walking through the room. I stopped next to Venom's table, drawing their attention right away.

"You doing okay, Joker?" Tank asked.

"Best I can. Got a minute?"

Venom peered up at me, his eyes sharp as ever. "Joker, sit down. You look like you're carrying the weight of the world. Can't say I'm surprised what with everything going on."

I pulled a chair over and sat down, the wood creaking under my bulk. The ink on my arms seemed to pulse with a life of its own under the flickering light. "It's Cleo's family -- I don't think they're the type to go away quietly. I think they're plotting something, and I doubt it's a family reunion. At least, it won't be once they find out she's dying."

Even saying the words felt like I'd swallowed hot ashes. My wife could die. Within a few months, I could very well be burying her. It didn't seem real.

"Mike and Jared?" Venom asked. "We haven't seen or heard from them the entire time Cleo has been here. You sure they know where she is?"

"The brother tore up her apartment and told her to go home. It's only a matter of time before he finds her again if he hasn't already. Just because we haven't heard anything, doesn't mean he isn't watching her."

"Joker," Torch began, his tone solemn, "you know as well as I do that blood calls to blood. They won't stop until they've dragged Cleo back into their mess. If they do discover her medical issues, I'm not sure what they'll do next. They don't seem like the type to walk away empty-handed."

"You thinking we need to put our women and kids on lockdown?" Tank asked. "Should we bring Tempest in on this?"

Venom and Torch shared a look. Yeah, they were thinking exactly that. I didn't blame them. I wanted to protect Cleo as much as they wanted to protect their women and kids. Especially Tank since he had three daughters.

"That's why I'm here. Shouldn't we come up with a plan or something? Savior hasn't called Church to discuss the issue, and I'm worried something is going to happen," I said.

"Keep your eyes open. Stay one step ahead of them. I doubt they'll stroll up to the gates and ask nicely for us to hand over Cleo. They'll strike when we aren't expecting it," Venom said.

"Then we'll be ready for them," I vowed, the determination settling like steel in my belly. "I won't let them near her, or any of our women and children."

"Protect Cleo, but don't underestimate those bastards." Bull's gaze held mine, unflinching. "And,

Joker, remember this -- sometimes the best defense is a good offense. I'm willing to bet Wire is already looking into those two, trying to figure out where they're hiding."

"Thanks." I rose, feeling the coiled tension in my muscles. "I'll keep that in mind. Maybe I should stop by Wire's place on my way home."

"Anytime," Torch said as I walked away.

The clubhouse door slammed shut behind me. My skin prickled with the sensation of someone's gaze, sharp and searching. I scanned the lot and saw Ridley in the shadows. "Everything okay?"

"Went to visit your wife today." She came closer. "Are you ready for her to come home?"

"What kind of question is that?"

"A serious one. Knowing she may not be here in a few months, are you going to be able to stand by her side and give her the things she needs?" Ridley asked. "Or are you still angry and hurt over the secrets she kept?"

"No. I get it. Well, I don't understand why she didn't tell me her heart was failing, but the rest..." I shrugged. Honestly, it hurt like hell, knowing she hadn't trusted me. Until I reflected on the way I'd acted once I did find out about her family. I'd only proven her right.

"Where are you going?" she asked. "Hospital?"

"No. I heard Wire might be trying to locate Cleo's family. Thought I'd stop by his place and see what he knows."

"Because Savior hasn't called Church so everyone is in the dark," she said. "I'm not sure what the holdup is. I mean, at first, he was waiting for Cleo to wake up. Now it's anyone's guess what's going through his mind. Doubt even Dessa knows."

"Thanks for being a friend to Cleo," I said. "I'm glad she has people to rely on other than me. That way when I let her down, she has someone else to stand beside her."

Ridley punched me in the arm. "Jackass! How about you just not let her down anymore? That sounds like a much better plan."

I smiled faintly. "Yeah, guess it does. Your man is inside, if you were looking for him."

I headed over to my bike and swung my leg over the seat. Once I had the engine going, I walked it back out of the space, then started off down the road. I pulled up to Wire's house and saw the living room lights were still on. At least I wouldn't be disturbing them.

I parked and shut off the bike, then went up to knock on the door. Lavender opened it and motioned for me to step inside.

"I'm assuming you're here for Wire," she said. "He's in the garage on his laptop."

"Thanks." When I entered the kitchen, he didn't bother looking up from his screen, but he did kick a chair out from the table. I took a seat and waited while his fingers pounded on the keyboard. A stack of papers caught my attention, and I sifted through it, noticing it was a trail of evidence against Cleo's family starting back a few years. Not far enough in the past to have Cleo's name pop up, though, for which I was grateful. I had no idea what he was going to do with the info.

Whatever it took, I needed to protect her -- even if it was from my own club.

Chapter Ten

Joker

"Any new dirt on Cleo's family?" I asked, my voice gravelly with the exhaustion of the past twenty-four hours.

Wire shook his head, his eyes not leaving the mess of papers and photographs spread before him. I'd stayed with him for hours last night as he tried to locate them. Finally, Lavender had forced me to go home and sleep. I'd mostly tossed and turned. The moment the sky turned gray with the rays of early morning light, I'd come right back to Wire's place, hoping for good news. The pungent smell of oil and leather clung to the air in the dimly lit garage where I'd found Wire hunched over a cluttered workbench. His fingers, stained with grease, were wrapped around a mug of coffee that had long since gone cold. The night felt somber, as if a weight had settled over all of us.

"It's like they've vanished into thin air," he muttered. "But they're sloppy -- left a trail of attempted kidnappings in their wake. Thankfully, the girls got away each time."

"Sounds like desperation," I noted, stepping closer, my boots scraping against the concrete. The recent crimes seemed too erratic, too risky for an outfit that had kept itself hidden for so long. Not having Cleo return to them must have royally fucked with their most recent plans. It made me wonder if they specifically needed her for something.

"Exactly," Wire said, picking up a grainy photo. "They're running out of options, out of money. We need to think like them, get into their heads. Although,

I honestly don't care to know how these twisted fucks think."

I leaned over the bench, focusing on the map, letting the gears in my mind grind away. "They need a hideout, off the grid. Somewhere secluded, somewhere they can regroup."

More than that, if they did succeed in kidnapping someone, they'd want to take them someplace the woman's screams wouldn't be heard. It didn't leave a lot of options in town. From what I saw of the evidence Wire gathered, if they weren't here, then they were nearby.

My finger stopped on the northern edge of town, tapping on a cluster of abandoned industrial sites. "What about here?"

"Could be," Wire admitted, squinting at the location. "Near enough to keep tabs on their interests but far enough to avoid heat from the law. Not to mention people in that area tend to keep to themselves."

"Let's scout it out come first light tomorrow," I proposed. My heart pounded a staccato rhythm against my ribs. We were close, I could feel it in my bones. I wanted these fuckers off the streets before they could hurt someone I loved.

"Agreed," Wire replied, his voice steely with resolve.

Ending the conversation there, I turned and walked out, the image of the map burned into my mind. I couldn't shake the gnawing feeling in the pit of my stomach. Was Cleo in more danger than any of us realized?

The early morning air slapped me awake as I stepped outside, the sun slowly rising in the sky. I needed to prepare, to plan. But first, I had to steady the shaking in my hands, the rage that threatened to consume me whole. For Cleo. For my club. For the countless women and children these assholes had already harmed.

Instead of going straight home, I decided to ride for a little bit. After everything that had happened, I needed to clear my head. Nothing better for that than cruising the streets on my bike.

The phone vibrated and I pulled over, answering it the moment I saw Wire's name flashing across the screen. "Talk to me."

"Joker, it's worse than we thought," Wire's voice crackled with urgency over the line. "I kept digging and got my hands on some intel."

My hand tightened around the phone, knuckles whitening. "What kind of intel?"

"Shipping manifests and encrypted messages. They're holding a live auction, and I'm sure you only need one guess as to what they're selling."

A cold shiver ran down my spine, as if a shadow had passed over the sun. "Are you certain?"

"Wouldn't be ringing you if I wasn't. Found two profiles they're actively circulating. Young females. They're shopping them like they're nothing more than merchandise." He cleared his throat. "Worst part is they're claiming there will be two surprise auctions. I'm wondering if Cleo pissed them off to the point they planned to make her one of the surprise auctions. Half the shit they're doing doesn't make any sense. There's no way to know what they're thinking or planning."

"Damn it," I cursed under my breath. "Got anything else on these girls? Any identifiers? As much as I don't want to talk to Cleo about this, maybe she'll recognize them."

Then again, she hadn't been home in so long. The

girls being auctioned had only been young kids when she'd still lived with her family. Better to keep this from her for now. There was a chance they'd been reported missing, so maybe we'd catch a break by getting more info off the news outlets.

"Names, photos. It's all here," Wire confirmed grimly. "Sending it your way, and I'm going to alert Savior."

"Good." I disconnected the call and stared at the device in my hand for a moment, flipping through the info Wire texted. Fury boiled in my veins. The image of Ares flashed in my mind -- a girl so close to those victims' age, and my brother's child. And Cleo... Part of me shattered at the mere thought of her being caught up in this hell. Not to mention Tank's daughters and countless others these sick fucks could get their hands on.

Shoving the phone into the pocket of my jeans, I started my bike again and headed home. According to Ridley, Cleo might be coming home today. I needed to make sure we'd have everything she'd need.

I got home and pulled into the carport, then shut off the bike. Once I got inside, I ran a hand through my hair and tried to figure out what I needed to do first. Probably talk to the Pres.

I dialed Savior's number. It rang once, twice, then his deep voice came through.

"Joker, something wrong?"

"Did Wire contact you yet?" I asked. "He's got more proof Cleo's family is deep into trafficking and found a lead on their current plans."

"Yeah, I'm still going through everything he sent me," Savior said. "Have you seen it?"

"I glanced at it. They have a list of potential buyers for two young girls. Wire also said there was mention of two secret auctions. We think they intend for Cleo to be one of them."

He let out a muffled curse. I knew this wasn't the news he wanted, especially right now. With Cleo's heart issue, we had enough on our plates already.

"I'll put out the call for Church."

"I need to check on Cleo. Ridley said she thought they were sending her home today." And I couldn't very well be in two places at once.

"Then get to the hospital. Let me know when you'll be back. Church can wait until then. I'll go ahead and clue in Tempest, Saint, and the rest of the officers," Savior said. "We can start formulating a plan."

"Thanks, Pres. I'm sorry my woman brought this shit to our doorstep, but I'm damn grateful everyone has her back."

"She's family, and so are you," he said. "We take care of our own. Besides, what woman hasn't brought us trouble?"

After I ended the call, I double-checked the contents in the kitchen and pantry, then got one of the club trucks so I could go to the hospital. On the off chance Cleo was coming home with me, I knew it wouldn't be possible for her to ride on the back of my bike.

I parked and made my way up to her room. When I got there, the doctor was on his way out. He paused in the hallway.

"You're Cleo's husband, right?" he asked.

"Yeah. She going home today?" I asked.

"I'm putting in her discharge papers now. I've already told her she needs to limit the stress in her life, make sure she takes her medication, and be ready to get here in a hurry if we find a heart for her. Any questions, you're more than welcome to call my office.

The information will be in her paperwork." He paused. "There will also be a procedure scheduled in the near future. She needs a ventricular assistance device. It will help buy more time while we wait for the transplant. She's also going to be sent home with a pager. When it goes off, it means a heart has been found and you need to get her here immediately. I went over everything with Cleo, but it's always good for the caregiver to hear it too."

"Thanks, Doc." I shook his hand and went into Cleo's room. She gave me a hesitant smile, and it made me want to kick my own ass. I'd caused her to doubt not only me but our relationship.

"I'm sorry I didn't come back last night. I had to talk to a few club members, got a little sleep, then went back to Wire's house this morning. The club is going to handle your family, so I just need you to focus on staying as healthy as possible."

She reached out a hand to me. "I missed you, and I'm sorry I didn't tell you everything."

"I'm not mad. If anyone should apologize, it's me. I didn't handle things as well as I should have. If I'd known about your heart, I probably would have kept my mouth shut. No matter who tells me this isn't my fault, it still feels like it is."

I tightened my hold on her fingers and lifted her hand, kissing the back of it. I saw the items stacked on the rolling tray and knew the club ladies had to have brought them to her. It should have been me. I was failing at being a good husband.

"I was so scared. It's the only reason I didn't tell you."

"That's my fault too. I should have made you feel more welcome and made sure you knew your place was by my side. If I'd done that, you wouldn't have been worried about the club turning their backs on you."

"I guess neither one of us are entirely blameless."

I sat in the chair beside her bed, still holding her hand. Knowing what I did now, she was even more remarkable. She'd faced so much at a young age. Even though I'd known her home life wasn't ideal, it never occurred to me her family had used her in such a way. I wondered if it haunted her, knowing she'd helped them lure in innocent girls and women. Probably. She had a softness and innocence most people didn't have these days.

"The doctor talked to me in the hall," I said. "He mentioned a procedure being scheduled for a device that's supposed to buy you some more time."

"Yeah. I think the information will either be in my discharge papers, or they'll call with a day and time. Since I collapsed, he wants to give me a few days to get my strength back, but I've made it clear I don't want to stay in the hospital."

We watched TV in silence while we waited for the nurse to come in and tell us we could leave. Cleo seemed more relaxed than she had when I'd first arrived today. It would take some work, but the club and I would make sure Cleo knew she had a place with the Dixie Reapers. I'd done a shit job of it so far.

It was another two hours before we got to leave. I'd barely gotten Cleo situated at home before I got the text alert from Savior. *Church in thirty*.

"I have to go somewhere for a little bit. I'll keep my phone within sight. You text or call if you need something. Everyone will understand."

"Are you going to discuss my family?" she asked.

"Yeah, we are. Nothing for you to worry about."

I kissed her forehead. "Get some rest. I'll see you shortly."

* * *

"We've got a situation that hits too damn close to home," Savior said, once he had everyone's attention.

Tempest's knuckles whitened against the tabletop, his jaw set, looking ready for war. Venom sat back, eyes hooded but alert. Torch's gaze fixed on Savior, steady and unflinching. Every brother at the table seemed prepared to do whatever it took to keep our club safe, including our women and children.

My stomach tightened as I thought about what was to come.

"Wire's brought evidence to light regarding Cleo's family -- they're neck deep in human trafficking," Savior continued, "and they've brought this shit to our turf. There's an auction coming soon. They already have two girls and a list of buyers."

"Those sick fucks," Tempest said with a growl to his tone, his fist slamming into the table.

"Plan?" Torch's gaze was laser sharp as he stared at Savior. "Because I have a feeling you already have one, or at least part of one."

"Here's what we know," Wire said. "It looks like they may be using some warehouses outside of town. Rundown buildings that haven't been used in a decade or more. There's only one way into the area, but there are multiple buildings and we haven't been able to narrow down which one they'll use. The camera footage in that general area shows an unusually high amount of traffic."

"We're going to let them hold the auction," Savior said. "It's the only way to know for certain where they'll be. Once the buyers are inside, as well as the girls, then we'll strike."

Tempest held up his hand. "Not to rain on anyone's parade, but we can't go in guns blazing or those girls might get hurt. We need this to be a stealth mission."

"Agreed." I nodded, my mind racing with strategies. "We get in, get the girls, signal the cavalry. That's when we let hell loose."

"Risky," Venom said, his voice a low rumble. "But it's a risk worth taking. We end this, then and there, or we don't rest easy again."

"We know there are two girls already selected," Savior said. "It's the two unknowns that bother me. We'll need at least two men to extract them. Preferably ones who look the least scary out of all of us."

"I say we send in Sticks and Warden," Prophet said. "I think they're the most approachable out of all of us."

"I'm fine with that," Sticks said.

"We can't leave the compound empty. We need brothers here to protect our families," Savior said. "I'll hang back. Any volunteers to stay behind?"

Torch, Venom, Rocky, and a half dozen others raised their hands. Which left Prophet, Tank, Wraith, Royal, and quite a few more ready to go fuck up these assholes. I hadn't raised my hand because I wanted a shot at Cleo's family.

"What are you thinking, Joker?" Savior asked.

"I want some time with Cleo's father and brother. I don't care if I'm in on the rest of it, but they used her, hurt her, and I need to make them pay."

Savior nodded. "Done."

He dismissed Church, while we waited for those assholes to make their move. Once the auction was a go, and we had a time, then things would move quickly. For now, I was going home to spend time with my wife.

Chapter Eleven

Cleo

I trailed my fingers over the polished chrome of Joker's bike, which sat like a sleeping beast in the carport. He'd enclosed one side and set up shelves for his tools and miscellaneous items. A rolling cart with a wood top sat in the corner.

"Careful there, darlin'," Joker's voice rumbled behind me, his presence a comforting shadow. "She bites."

I turned, leaning back against the cool metal, watching him tinker with a set of tools. The rhythmic clinking of metal on metal was oddly soothing, almost like a heartbeat.

"Wouldn't be the first thing around here that does," I quipped, a smirk playing on my lips. He hadn't touched me intimately since I'd collapsed, and I understood why. It terrified him to think I could die at any moment. Still, I wished things would go back to normal between us. Even when he held me, it still felt like there was a distance between us now.

Joker straightened up, wiping grease-stained hands on a rag before tossing it aside. He took a few steps closer, the intensity of his gaze holding me captive. "Nothing's going to bite you while I'm around, Cleo. You've got my word on that."

His protection felt like a tangible thing, wrapping around me. For a moment, I allowed myself the fantasy that this sense of safety could be my reality. But fantasies were dangerous things. All this could disappear in the blink of an eye.

"Your word is worth a lot to me," I said, meaning

every syllable.

The rough pad of his thumb brushed against my cheek, and for a heartbeat, the perilous life we led seemed a distant concern. But the serenity shattered as my phone buzzed insistently from the pocket of my jeans. I flinched, not ready for the intrusion.

"Go ahead," Joker encouraged with a nod, the crease in his brow betraying his concern.

I pulled out the device, the cold screen lighting up to display an unknown number. My heart clenched, each ring a hammer against my chest. Swiping to answer, I brought the phone to my ear.

"Hello?"

"Is this Ms. Cleo Clemons?" The voice on the other end was clinical, detached.

"Speaking," I replied, my throat tight.

"This is St. Mary's Hospital calling to confirm your appointment for the ventricular assistance device procedure. It's been scheduled for two days from now, at ten o'clock. It's crucial you don't miss this, Ms. Clemons."

The words hit me like a freight train. Two days. The reality of my condition, always lurking in the shadows of my thoughts, now stood glaringly in front of me. This wasn't a fix, but more of a bandage on a gaping wound. It wouldn't cure me, but I had to hope it would buy enough time for them to locate a heart for me.

"Thank you," I murmured, struggling to keep my voice steady. "I'll be there."

As I ended the call, Joker's hand found mine, squeezing gently. I looked up into his eyes, searching for strength in their depths.

"Two days, huh?" His voice was soft, but it carried the weight of unspoken fears. At least he'd heard the woman so I didn't have to repeat everything. I hadn't realized she'd been speaking so loud.

"Two days," I echoed, my mind racing.

"Then let's make them count," he said, resolve hardening his features.

I nodded, not trusting my voice. In the silence, my thoughts churned -- a tempest of what-ifs and maybes. But for now, I was here, with Joker, and that would have to be enough. He led me inside the house, not letting go of my hand.

The afternoon sun filtered through the curtains, casting a lattice of light and shadow across the living room floor. I traced the patterns with the toe of my shoe. Outside, the rumble of an engine broke the silence. Joker's hand tensed on my shoulder.

"Company," he muttered, his gaze shifting toward the window as an SUV pulled up outside.

The front door creaked open, and Ridley yelled out my name as she let herself in. "Cleo!"

"Ridley, keep it down," came Isabella's chiding tone, softer but no less commanding. Their figures filled the doorway, with Ares trailing behind them -- a contrast in her youthful uncertainty.

"Hey, Cleo," Ares said, her voice threading through the air like a hesitant melody. Her eyes flickered to me and then away. I wondered if her father had told her about my family and their dirty dealings. Since I'd heard Ares had been trafficked in the past, I knew it had to be hard for her to be around me right now.

"Good to see you guys." My voice sounded hollow, even to my own ears. I forced a smile, though it felt brittle on my lips. I'd been enjoying my time with Joker and didn't feel up to entertaining guests. At the same time, I didn't want to be rude.

Isabella approached first, her presence warm and enveloping as she wrapped me in a tight hug. "How are you holding up?"

"Counting down the minutes," I replied, managing to keep the tremor out of my voice.

Ridley clapped her hands together, the sound sharp in the quiet room. "We're here to take your mind off things. Right, Ares?"

Ares nodded, her hands fidgeting at her sides. "Yeah, we brought some board games. Thought we could all use a distraction."

The fact she'd volunteered to come here warmed my heart and made me realize how strong she was. If our roles were reversed, I wouldn't want anything to do with me right now. It didn't matter that I wasn't part of what my brother and father were doing. I'd taken part in the past, even though it had been forced on me.

"Thanks," I murmured, feeling grateful.

As we settled around the kitchen table, a knock sounded at the front door. Joker rose, a silent sentinel, and moved to answer it. The others didn't seem to notice, caught up in setting up the game.

Probably just one of the Prospects. I tried to brush off the unease that had settled over me like a second skin.

Joker returned, an envelope held loosely between his fingers. His expression was unreadable as he handed it to me. "For you."

"Who's it from?" I asked, but the lack of return address answered my question before I tore it open. Inside, a single piece of paper, a line of typed text so cold it felt like ice against my fingertips.

We know where you are.

Joker had to know something was up with this

letter, but he'd given it to me anyway. Since we had company, I wasn't going to ask any questions. There wasn't a stamp, which meant it had been hand delivered. I didn't think a Prospect would have accepted it from anyone who appeared suspicious. Had they convinced a woman to bring it? I knew my brother could be charismatic when he needed to be.

"Everything all right?" Isabella's voice cut through the fog of fear that was creeping over me.

"Fine," I lied smoothly, shoving the note into my pocket. "Just a reminder for my appointment."

"Ah, can't forget that," Ridley said, oblivious to the tremors that had started in my hands.

"Let's focus on the game," I suggested, desperate for any kind of normalcy. I'd discuss the note with Joker after everyone left.

"All right!" Ares exclaimed, her enthusiasm genuine as she rolled the dice.

Sitting there, surrounded by laughter and the clatter of game pieces, I felt a chasm open within me. Fear and dread coiled in my gut like a living thing, ready to strike. My family -- my past -- it seemed no matter how far I ran, it always found a way to reel me back in. Would they ever leave me alone?

"Your move, Cleo," Ridley prompted, pulling me back to the present.

"Right," I mumbled, forcing my hand to stay steady as I reached for a game piece. But my thoughts were elsewhere, racing ahead to what this ominous message meant. And behind my façade, I was already planning, plotting, readying myself for whatever storm was headed my way. This time I wasn't going to run.

We played for two hours before they finally left. Normally, I'd have been exhausted, but the note in my pocket felt like it weighed a ton. There was no way I would fall asleep until I'd told Joker about it.

After locking up the house, Joker led me to the bedroom. I brushed my teeth, washed my face, and changed into pajamas. He'd removed his cut and boots but remained dressed otherwise. He'd stretched out on the bed and I joined him.

The house was silent, a stark contrast to the laughter that had filled it just minutes before. I curled up against Joker, my head resting against his chest. His heartbeat, steady and strong, was a soothing counterpoint to the racing thoughts in my mind.

"Joker," I murmured, my voice barely above a whisper.

"Mmm?" He tilted his chin down, his eyes searching mine with that intense gaze that could either comfort or interrogate.

"I need you to be careful," I said, the words tumbling out in a rush. "It's my brother -- he's... he's not someone to underestimate. He's far worse than my father."

Joker's arm tightened around me, his other hand tracing idle patterns on my back. "Talk to me, Cleo. What's got you spooked?"

"The letter earlier..." I hesitated, then forced myself to continue. "It was just one line, but it's enough to know they've found me."

"Who has?" His voice was steel wrapped in velvet, protective anger simmering beneath the surface. "Your family?"

"Yeah. I know you wondered if they were in the area, but this confirms it. If my brother is involved... He's dangerous, Joker. He's the kind who leaves a trail of blood in his wake." My heart pounded against my ribs.

"I'll pass the word along. We'll keep our eyes

peeled, tighten security. Nobody is going to touch you, Cleo. Not while I'm breathing."

"Promise me," I insisted, clutching at him like a lifeline. "Promise me you'll all watch your backs. I'm not worried only for myself. Everyone here is in danger."

"I promise." His lips pressed to my forehead in a kiss that was both tender and fierce. "There's something you should know."

"What?" I asked.

"My time in prison... I wasn't in there for some petty crime. I beat several men nearly to death. It was club business, and if someone hadn't called the cops, I'd have most likely killed them. The club was different back then. Just the same, it won't be easy for someone to take me out."

"You're sure that sort of thing won't happen again?" I asked.

"The club isn't into that shit anymore. I'm perfectly safe when I go out on a job. It's nothing illegal."

As the tension bled from my body, exhaustion crept in. My eyelids grew heavy, the adrenaline that had fueled me now giving way to a bone-deep weariness. I burrowed closer into Joker's warmth, allowing myself to succumb to the pull of sleep.

"Rest now," Joker whispered, his voice a low rumble that vibrated against my cheek. "I've got you."

In the sanctuary of his arms, I let go of the terror that had been gnawing at my insides. For a moment, there was no fear of what might come, no dread of the demons lurking in my past -- just the rise and fall of Joker's chest, the comforting scent of his soap and cologne, and the silent vow that hung between us like a shield.

My breaths evened out, matching the rhythm of his, and I drifted off, lulled by the illusion of safety that only his presence could provide. As I slipped into dreams, the real world -- with its threats and shadows -- faded away, leaving only the quiet certainty of his embrace.

* * *

Joker

The rhythmic hum of Cleo's breathing was a siren song, tempting me to close my eyes and join her in oblivion. But duty clawed at my conscience, an unrelenting beast that refused to be ignored. Gently extricating myself from the tangle of limbs and sheets, I replaced my warmth with a pillow hugged close to her side. She stirred but didn't wake, and for a heartbeat, envy lanced through me -- she could escape into sleep, while I had to face the nightmares head-on.

"Stay safe," I murmured into the dark room, the words more prayer than statement. The moonlight slanted through the blinds, casting ghostly stripes across her peaceful face -- a stark contrast to the storm brewing within me.

Boots silent on the floorboards, I left our sanctuary behind and moved through the house with purpose. The night air slapped me awake as I stepped out onto the porch, the familiar scent of the compound wrapping around me like a second skin. It was late… the perfect time for secrets to crawl out of the shadows. I got on my bike and rode over to the clubhouse.

The place was alive with low murmurs and the clink of bottles. Inside, Wire, Savior, and Tempest were huddled over a table strewn with maps and photographs, their faces grim. Tempest gripped a beer bottle, his jaw set in a hard line.

"Joker," Wire acknowledged with a nod, eyes flicking over me.

"Talk to me," I said, cutting straight to the chase. My fingers itched for action, my skin feeling too tight.

"Got word on the auction," Tempest growled, the words grating like gravel. "It's going down in two days."

Two days. The same as Cleo's procedure. A bitter laugh almost escaped me, but I trapped it behind clenched teeth. Of course, fate would play its hand like this -- dealing a blow meant to scatter our focus and divide our forces.

"Time?" I asked, already calculating the impossible logistics in my head.

"Noon," Savior replied, his voice eerily calm. He tapped a finger on one of the photos, circling a warehouse on the docks. "No idea why they're brave enough to do it in broad daylight. Makes me think they've bought off the police or something. It's being held here. Or at least we've detected a lot of movement in this area."

I leaned over the table, my mind racing. Noon -- Cleo would be lying in a hospital bed, her heart in the hands of surgeons and machines. And I'd be... what? Taking down her family?

"Shit," I cursed under my breath. The club had to come first, always. That was the code we lived by -- the creed that bound us together. But Cleo... she was the one thing I hadn't known I needed until she turned my world upside down.

"Joker?" Wire prodded, his eyes sharp.

"Right," I managed. "We'll need eyes on every exit. Can't let anything -- or anyone -- slip through."

"Already on it," Tempest said, his temper a living thing that crackled in the air. "They'll have to go through me first."

"Good." I nodded. "Let's plan on fortifying the perimeter, make sure we're watertight. No surprises. Cleo had a letter delivered. It was from her brother. Only one line, but they know she's living here. Which means they have eyes on this place."

I knew it wasn't my place to say anything. But damn... in a way, I felt responsible. These assholes were related to Cleo. If my wife and I weren't here, would they have ever discovered the Dixie Reapers or put the women and children here in danger?

Wire and Savior exchanged a look, some unspoken communication passing between them. I had to rely on gut instinct and the unwavering belief that we could pull this off -- save the innocents and protect our own. I hoped those two were thinking the same thing.

As I stood among my brothers, a plan taking shape amidst the chaos, I couldn't shake the image of Cleo's sleeping face, serene and oblivious to the crossroads we'd come to. Two paths lay ahead, each fraught with danger and sacrifice. And whichever one I chose, I knew it would lead me into hell. The possibility of losing my wife, or having to take down the lowest scum on earth. Neither sounded like the best day on earth.

"Joker, are you up for checking out the warehouse with Tempest and Prophet?" Savior asked.

I nodded. "If that's what you need from me."

Tempest walked out and I followed, both of us going to our bikes. Prophet already stood outside waiting for us. I figured the Pres must have texted him or something.

The rumble of our motorcycles cut through the silence as we approached the warehouses. Prophet rode on my left, his eyes scanning the shadows. On my right, Tempest seemed to have a storm brewing beneath his calm exterior.

"Remember, in and out," Prophet whispered.

My gaze fixed on the looming structures ahead. "Like ghosts."

"Let's tear this place apart." Tempest cracked his knuckles.

We got off our bikes and went on foot, nearing the first of the rundown buildings. My heart hammered against my ribs, a reminder of what was at stake. Cleo's face flashed in my mind -- the way she'd looked asleep in my arms, peaceful, a stark contrast to the chaos around us.

"East side," Tempest instructed. Our boots hit the gravel, the sound muted but still too loud for my liking.

We moved as one, the bond of brotherhood guiding our silent steps. Tempest took point, his large frame surprisingly graceful as he skirted debris and puddles of stagnant water. Prophet flanked me. My senses were sharp, ready for any sign of trouble.

"Door's clear," Tempest said.

"Check the windows," I whispered, moving to peer through the grimy glass. Nothing but darkness greeted me. It felt like staring into the abyss.

"Clear," Prophet confirmed from the other side.

"Back to the bikes," I said, a knot of frustration tightening in my gut. We needed something -- anything -- to give us an edge. If they'd been here, they were gone for now. Maybe they'd only been checking the place out earlier.

We retraced our path, heading back to the clubhouse. As the compound came into view, the weight of the upcoming battle settled over me. There was a chance some of us wouldn't come back home. It was a risk we had to take. I couldn't think of another way to keep Cleo and the others safe.

"What did you find?" Wire asked.

"First warehouse is a dead zone," I reported, pushing open the door to the clubhouse.

"Second one?" Savior asked, leaning against the bar with a map spread out before him.

"Same deal," Prophet chimed in, removing his helmet and running a hand through his hair.

"If they were there earlier, they already left."

"Time's running out, Joker," Wire said, his eyes meeting mine. "We can't afford to miss this opportunity."

"I know," I replied, feeling the vise of time squeezing tighter. "We'll go over every inch again if we have to."

"For now let's give Wire time to do his thing. There must be something we missed," Savior said.

I grabbed a beer and sat at the bar, trying not to give in to the urge to run home and crawl into bed with Cleo. I didn't know how much time passed as I waited, thinking of the ways this could go horribly wrong.

"Joker," Wire called out.

I turned, finding him hunched over a laptop that cast an eerie glow on his determined face. I strode over, bracing myself for another curveball.

"What is it?" I asked, leaning in to catch a glimpse of the screen.

"Found the secret auction," he replied, tapping a few keys. "It's not at any warehouse -- it's online. Dark web stuff, heavily encrypted."

"Online?" My brows knitted together as I processed the information. "That changes things. It means they'll be at the warehouse, but who knows where the other two women will be."

"Exactly." Wire's eyes met mine, steady and serious. "They're smarter than we gave them credit for. Harder to trace, harder to stop. We can still stop the one at the warehouse, but..."

My jaw set in a hard line. We were playing a game with ghosts, chasing shadows that knew how to dance just out of reach.

"Can you get us more info? Location of the handoff? Anything?" I asked.

Wire's lips twitched into a sardonic smile. "Already working on it, brother. But we gotta be careful. One wrong move and they'll vanish."

"Keep me posted," I said, clapping him on the shoulder before turning to leave. My mind was a whirlwind of plans and countermeasures, but above it all, Cleo's face floated, serene and unaware of the chaos her world was becoming.

The clubhouse doors open and Dessa wheeled her way inside. The panic etched on her face made my heart stop.

"Savior!" The urgency in Dessa's voice made the hair on my nape stand up. The Pres was already striding toward her.

She wheeled farther into the room, her hands white-knuckled on the rims of her chair, her breaths coming in short, ragged gasps. The sight of her, usually so composed and strong, now frayed with panic, sent a cold shiver down my spine.

"It's Ares," she managed, her words tripping over each other. "She's gone."

"Gone?" Savior asked. "What do you mean gone?"

"I -- I checked her room, and... she's not there.

Not anywhere." Tears glistened in her desperate eyes. "She wouldn't just leave. You know it as well as I do. I even asked Prophet and she isn't with him. He hasn't heard from her all day. It's like she's vanished."

"Fuck. She was at my place earlier, but that was a while ago." The curse came out as a hiss between my teeth. I felt the ground beneath me shift, the foundations of our plans suddenly as unsteady as quicksand. Ares, Savior's daughter, missing could only mean one thing. Those fuckers had her. I couldn't think of any other possibility right now.

"All right, Dessa, we're going to find her," Wire assured her.

"Tempest! Prophet!" Savior barked, summoning them with a tone that brooked no argument. There was no time for second-guessing, no space for doubt. In our world, hesitation was a luxury paid for with blood. Each of us knew it.

"Start a search," Savior ordered. "Spread out, ask around. She's here somewhere. She has to be."

I knew he didn't want to think of what it meant for his daughter to be gone. Especially with everything we faced right now.

"Will do." Tempest nodded, his expression grim as he turned to follow the Pres' command.

"I'll check the cameras," Wire said. "Every angle, every second. I won't blink."

"Joker…" Dessa's voice trembled, gripping my arm with a surprising strength. "Please… Is there a chance Cleo may know something? Was it her family who took Ares?"

"Cleo is at home asleep, and even if she weren't, this isn't something she'd have the answers to. We'll find Ares."

As Dessa nodded, trying to swallow her fear, I

couldn't help but feel the weight of guilt bearing down on me. My woman's family was most likely behind this. If I hadn't come home, if I hadn't married Cleo... Except I didn't regret her being part of my life. It wasn't her fault she had a shitty family.

The clubhouse was a living, breathing organism of fear and tension, the walls themselves seeming to pulse with the urgency of Ares's disappearance. More brothers came to help, but I worried we might be too late already.

"Anything?" I asked.

"Wait," Wire held up a finger without turning, his focus absolute.

I clenched and unclenched my fists. I could tell Savior was doing his best to hold it together. He had to be scared shitless right now, but Dessa needed him. Hell, we all did.

Every tick of the clock was a taunt, every silent second stretching into eternity.

"Here!" Wire's voice sliced through the air like a gunshot, and we all crowded around.

I peered at the grainy image, my gut twisting. There she was -- Ares -- slung over a man's shoulder. He'd kept his face turned from the cameras, almost as if he knew where they were. Just the same, I could tell he wasn't one of ours.

"Got a timestamp," Wire continued, "but after this frame, they vanish."

"No one vanishes without help," Savior said.

"Cleo warned me about her brother. I should have listened."

"Her brother?" Prophet echoed, his tone sharpening with realization. "You think he's behind this?"

"Wouldn't surprise me," I said, the pieces

clicking into place with a dread certainty. "We need to move, and fast. I'm betting she's one of the secret auction items."

"This is war, and wars are won by those willing to do whatever it takes." A determined look settled over Savior's face. If this really was Cleo's family, they'd fucked up in the worst way. By taking the President's daughter, they'd sealed their fates.

My brothers nodded, a sea of grim determination. We were more than a club. We were a force, bound by blood and loyalty. And we would bring Ares home, or die trying.

Chapter Twelve

Joker

The fluorescent lights of the hospital corridor blazed like a thousand unforgiving suns, each one casting white beams on the polished floor. I paced, my boots thudding against the linoleum with a rhythm that echoed the pounding in my chest. Today was supposed to be about hope, about Cleo getting a shot at a longer life with the ventricular assistance device, but dread hung heavy inside me, a nearly crushing weight.

"Joker?" Wire's voice over the phone cleared my mind for a moment. "Any word yet on Cleo?"

"Nothing," I replied, my voice gravelly, my fingers tightening around the phone. "She's still in the OR. It's a five-hour dance with the devil, and we're barely an hour in. This is fucking killing me."

"Shit, man." Wire paused, and I could hear the distant sound of clinking keyboard keys in the background.

"Any news about Ares?" I asked, the words tasting like bile. I hated this -- waiting helplessly while Cleo fought for her life, and Ares... who knew what hell she was enduring. "We have to find her."

"Nothing yet. We're all here for you and Cleo. Leave everything else to us right now. Focus on your wife."

Disconnecting the call, I resumed my pacing. In the empty corridor, there was only the relentless buzz of electricity and the hollow echo of my footsteps. My mind was a war zone, thoughts ricocheting between Cleo's delicate heart and Ares' uncertain fate.

"Excuse me, sir," a nurse interrupted. "You can't be on your phone in this area. Please keep it switched off."

"Right," I muttered, pocketing the device without breaking stride. Her gaze lingered on the ink snaking up my arms, visible from the rolled sleeves of my shirt, before she scurried away.

I felt like a rat in a cage. I wasn't any good to anyone right now. All I could do was wait for Cleo to get out of surgery. I hated feeling helpless.

Another hour peeled away with excruciating slowness. The updates I gave the club over the phone were sparse, punctuated by terse assurances that I'd be there as soon as Cleo was out of the woods. Every time the doors swung open, my heart leapt, only to sink again as it was never Cleo's doctor or nurse. They said no news was good news. I had to hope that was true.

I heard someone approaching and saw Hammer walking toward me. He stopped and clapped me on the shoulder.

"Joker." Hammer's voice was a lifeline. "How's our girl doing?"

"Still no word," I said, my throat tight. "Just asked Wire about Ares."

"Grimm and Tempest are combing through every piss-poor lead we have. Wire is doing his thing on the computer. We'll eventually find her. We don't leave family behind." Hammer leaned against the wall near me. "Stop worrying about Ares and think about your wife right now. You're all Cleo has, but Ares has the entire club searching for her."

I pressed the heels of my hands into my eyes until I saw stars, willing the tension to ebb away. Cleo was my heart, and without her, the world was nothing but shadows and silence. He was right. I needed to put everything else out of my mind.

Time felt like it stretched endlessly. With every passing minute, I lost a little more of my sanity. A glance at my phone showed a little over five hours had passed since they'd taken Cleo into surgery.

"Joker?" A different nurse approached "Your wife is out of surgery. She's being moved to recovery now."

"Is she…" The question lodged in my throat, raw and desperate.

"She's stable. The procedure went well."

"Can I see her?"

"Only family," she said, already turning away. I quickly followed, leaving Hammer behind. He'd most likely return to the compound and spread the word Cleo was doing okay.

The steady beep of the heart monitor filled the otherwise silent room. I stood by Cleo's bed, ink-covered fingers gripping the rail like it was the only anchor in my storm-tossed world. Her chest rose and fell in a steady rhythm. My hand shook as I reached out to brush her hair back from her face.

"I know I should have said this for the first time while you were awake, but… I love you, Cleo."

Her fingers twitched and I hoped it meant she'd heard me. I didn't know how long it would take her to open her eyes. Nor did I know how long they'd let me stay here. Something told me they'd chase me out soon so I wouldn't tire Cleo out once she was awake.

A nurse stopped by giving me a quick smile before she checked on Cleo.

"We'll be placing her in ICU for a few days. If everything goes well, she'll go home in about two to three weeks."

"Does that mean she won't be able to have

visitors?" I asked.

"Family only and one at a time. Visiting hours will be posted in the ICU, as well as the rules you'll need to follow. The nurses there can answer any other questions you may have."

"I'm her husband, but if I wanted other family to be able to see her…"

"You can leave one or two other names."

I'd have to see which brothers would be willing to help check on Cleo. For now, it looked like it would only be me on the list.

My phone vibrated and I realized I'd left it on. The nurse would complain if I didn't shut it off, but I took a quick look at the message that came through. It looked like Wire had an update on Ares.

We found her. She's already been sold.

What the fuck? *But you know her location?*

I didn't understand what was going on. The auction at the warehouse was happening any moment, if it hadn't already. For some reason, Wire kept finding information showing the time had shifted. I wondered if they knew they were being watched and were trying to keep us from interfering. Why had they sold Ares online so much earlier?

I saw he was responding, but I needed to turn off the phone so they wouldn't kick me out. I shut it off and shoved it into my pocket.

Cleo stirred, eyelids fluttering. Her eyes opened, fixing on me as awareness slowly seeped back into them. Confusion clouded her gaze before sharpening into concern.

"Joker?" Her voice was a whisper, hoarse and weak. "You look like hell. What's wrong?"

I forced a half-smile. "Just worried about you."

Her brow furrowed. Cleo reached out a shaky

hand, and I took it gently, her fragility a stark reminder of what she'd been through and what awaited her in the future.

"Talk to me, Joker," she pressed, squeezing my fingers with surprising strength. "It's not just me, is it? What else is going on?"

I couldn't hide the truth -- not from her, not when she looked at me like that. "Ares has already been auctioned off."

"God…" Her lips parted, her breath hitching with the weight of the revelation.

"Hey," I said, brushing a thumb over her knuckles, "we're gonna find her. We're gonna bring her home."

"Promise me," she demanded, her grip tightening. "Promise me you'll save her."

"Always," I vowed. "Right now, you need to focus on healing. Don't worry about anything else."

And as Cleo's eyes drifted closed again, succumbing to the pull of medicine and fatigue, I leaned forward, pressing a kiss to her forehead. With each step away from her bedside, it felt like I was being torn in two -- husband or brother. I wasn't sure I knew how to be both right now.

I strode out of the room, needing to check in with Wire. Once I stood outside the hospital, I read his message. *The buyer already has her. Can't pinpoint their location.*

It felt like we'd not only failed Ares, but Savior and Dessa as well. They had to be going crazy, especially since Ares had already survived this same thing once before. Savior had been the one to rescue her before. I could only hope we'd be able to find her before it was too late.

Hammer and Aura are coming to stay with Cleo.

We're going after her family and the other buyers within the hour. Auction was pushed back for some reason.

I'd no sooner read his message than I saw the two of them walking toward me. Aura gave me a brief hug.

"Thanks for being here," I said.

"I'll text or call with any changes," Hammer said. He motioned me back inside. "Just make sure they'll let me see her."

I got him added to the list of family, then went out to the truck I'd driven this morning. I'd go get my bike, then head to the clubhouse.

* * *

I pulled up to the clubhouse and killed the engine.

"Joker!" Tempest yelled out from the doorway. "Shouldn't you be at the hospital? We can handle this without you."

"I need to be here," I said. I entered the clubhouse and saw they'd pushed a few tables together. I didn't know why they just hadn't gone into Church and used the huge ass table in there.

"Wire's got some leads," Grimm offered.

"Like what?" I asked.

"Not sure what caused the delay but they haven't started the live auction yet," Wire said. "Looks like it's happening any moment."

"Then we need to get to the warehouse," Gears said.

A group of us went outside to our bikes. The Prospect standing guard threw open the gate. I noticed Sticks drove a club truck, which meant he'd be the one transporting the girls we saved tonight.

I hadn't asked about the other secret auction. Had a girl been sold at the same time as Ares? I hoped we could find them both, and soon.

The warehouse loomed ahead. We stopped far enough away we couldn't draw attention to ourselves. Clinging to the shadows, we crept closer.

I peered through a broken window, looking for the girls. They stood in front of a crowd of men, nearly naked, their wrists bound and mouths gagged. There were only two, which meant if Ares had been here, she wasn't now.

Savior had joined us, even though he hadn't originally planned to do so. He stared at the warehouse with hatred burning in his eyes.

"Saint, Warden, you're with me on the west side," Savior said. "Gears, take Tank and Joker to the east. Sticks, you bring up the rear and get those girls out. Tempest --"

"I'm the hammer," he interjected, the gleam in his eyes promising a storm of violence.

"Then let's send these fuckers to hell," Savior said. We split up, a silent prayer to whatever gods watched over men like us clinging to my lips. I needed to end this for Cleo. When she came home, I didn't want her looking over her shoulder, wondering if her brother would attack.

Moving with stealth, we surrounded the warehouse. Inside, the muffled cries of the captive girls reached us, fueling our rage, sharpening our focus.

"Three... two... one..." Savior counted down, and then hell broke loose.

Warden went in and shot the auctioneer between the eyes. Gunfire erupted, the sound deafening within the confines of the warehouse. I moved through the chaos, each shot a promise to Cleo, to Ares, to my brothers. I saw Warden and Sticks extract the girls, and noticed Savior and Saint had Cleo's family cornered.

It was pure mayhem as my brothers took out the buyers one at a time. No one would leave here alive. These sick fucks would disappear after tonight. Pain burned my upper arm. Looking to my right, I spotted the man who'd shot me. I fired off two shots -- head and chest. The man fell where he stood.

By the time I reached Saint and Savior, they'd tied up Cleo's father and brother. Judging from the bruises on both their faces, it seemed the Pres had already started questioning them.

"I'd have been content to never meet my in-laws," I said.

"Where is she?" Savior asked. "Where the fuck is my daughter? Stop playing stupid and just tell me."

Cleo's brother, a carbon copy of the man beside him, spat at Savior's feet, defiance etched into his sneer. "You think you scare us, biker trash?"

"Wrong answer," I said, each word a promise of pain. I pulled a knife from the sheath against my thigh. Their eyes flickered to the blade in my hand. And then, I let loose hell.

The room became an artist's canvas, painted with crimson splatter. I forced myself to hold back, not quite killing him. Blood dripped onto the concrete floor.

"Let's try again. The man asked about his daughter. Where is she?"

"Go to hell!" The old man sneered at us. "You'll never find her. And we'll never say a word to guide you to her. Nothing you do will change that."

"Then how about another question. How did you find Cleo?" I asked.

"Our network is bigger than you think." The man smiled, but it was downright horrid. A chill skated down my spine. "Do you know how many predators there are in the world at any given time?

More than you'd ever imagine. All it took was dropping her photo to a few people, and soon countless men were searching for her."

"She was gone for years. Shouldn't you have given up?" I asked.

"That girl owed me. She ruined everything. I had plans for her. The kind that would have made me richer than my wildest dreams." He spat on the floor. "Fucking bitch should have done as she was told."

"So someone followed her here?" I asked.

"Of course. I've had multiple eyes on your place. Watching my daughter and the rest of you. Mostly used women once we realized you were soft when it came to those you deemed weaker than yourselves. The lot of you aren't as clever as you think."

"Smart enough to catch you," Savior said. He gave me a nod. It was all the permission I needed.

The screams that followed were a macabre duet, as I exacted dues owed in full. I made them suffer for everything they'd put Cleo through. For kidnapping Ares. For destroying countless lives.

When I'd finished, neither man was recognizable. Savior looked like he'd aged a decade. Whatever it took, we'd find Ares. I followed the Pres outside.

Warden and Sticks emerged from the shadows, the two girls in tow. They were safe now, but Ares... Ares was still out there.

"Joker, what about --" Sticks began, but his words choked off as he caught sight of the carnage inside the warehouse. "Never mind."

Those men had seemed like monsters to so many people. In the end, they'd bled like anyone else, and died just as easily.

"Joker!" Savior's voice cut through my reverie.

"We've got to move."

"Understood."

As I walked away, my thoughts turned to Cleo, her heart stitched together by machines while mine was torn apart by vengeance. She would never have to fear them again. That much, I had ensured. I only wished Savior had been able to take his daughter home tonight.

I cast one last look over at the warehouse. Blood smeared the floor, staining the concrete. More covered the walls. Since Savior hadn't told anyone to remain behind for clean up, I had to assume he'd called in a crew.

The roar of my bike cut through the silence as I raced down the moonlit road, the night air whipping past me like a cleansing force. I was coated in filth from the warehouse -- blood, sweat, and the residue of death. Cleo's pale, vulnerable face haunted me, her life hanging by a thread while I waded through the darkest pits of humanity to avenge her.

I killed the engine in front of my place, the sudden quiet jarring. Going inside, I went straight to the bathroom and stripped out of my clothes before getting into the shower. The water scorched my skin, but I barely felt it. Streams of red swirled at my feet, disappearing down the drain, a stark reminder of the bloodshed.

After scrubbing myself raw, I dressed in clean clothes. Even though I knew I probably wouldn't be able to see Cleo tonight, I felt like I needed to be there.

Chapter Thirteen

Cleo

"Joker, you look like hell."

"Feels about right," he said, a smirk playing on his lips "Been through it to make sure you're safe."

I searched his face, trying to piece together the words he hadn't said. It seemed like more than just my surgery weighing him down. "My father... my brother..."

"They won't hurt you or anyone else ever again, Cleo. It's over."

"Good." I sighed, feeling as if a weight had been lifted. I'd been too scared to do anything myself all these years. Knowing Joker had stepped in and handled it, filled me with warmth. Thanks to him, countless people would be safe now.

"The doctor said the procedure went well. You have to stay here a few weeks, then you can go home," he said.

"Hopefully, this will give me the time I need for them to find a heart for me. I'm not ready to leave you behind."

He took my hand, squeezing my fingers. "Don't say such stupid shit ever again. You're not going anywhere."

"May not have a choice, Joker. I'm sorry I didn't tell you before now. If I had, then they could have done this procedure sooner. I was stupid for hiding it."

"Yeah, you were." He smiled a little. "I'm glad things are okay between us now. I can't begin to tell you how much you mean to me, Cleo. Always have. When I was locked up, your letters kept me going."

I winced. "And then I stopped writing. To be fair, I didn't receive anything for several months. By then, I wasn't sure if I should write or not. I didn't know what to say."

"It's all in the past. None of that matters anymore."

"You're too forgiving."

"Only when it comes to you. Rest," he said. "I'm here. I'll keep watch and chase away the monsters."

"You already did." I no longer had my family watching and waiting, trying to find a way to get to me. Joker kept me safe before by giving me his name and telling me to run. Now he'd saved me again.

He lifted my hand and kissed the back of it. "I'll do whatever it takes to keep you with me, Cleo. Even if it means marching into hell and kicking the devil off his throne, I'd do it."

I wished I could hug him right now. I wanted nothing more than to cuddle against him and fall asleep with his arms around me. The weeks I'd have to stay here would be miserable.

"What about the club? Is everyone all right?" I asked. He hesitated and it made me tense a little. "Joker, what's wrong?"

"No casualties on our side. My arm was grazed, but I'm okay."

No. That wasn't all. I could tell he was hiding something. "What aren't you telling me?"

"This isn't the kind of talk we should be having right now."

"Maybe not, but not knowing isn't much better. I'll just lie here thinking of all the things that could have possibly gone wrong."

"Ares... I've tried to keep it from you because I didn't want you to worry. But knowing you, you're concerned anyway. Otherwise, I wouldn't say a damn word right now. We found out your family sold her. Wire is trying to locate her, but…" He ran a hand over his face. "No leads yet."

The heart monitor went crazy as my heartrate skyrocketed. They'd taken the President's daughter and sold her? Would the club blame me for what happened? I couldn't breathe and my chest ached. Black dots swam across my vision.

I heard a siren going off and saw lights flashing, then there were the voices of nurses yelling in the hall. Joker said something, but I couldn't understand him. It felt like I was sinking under water, everything becoming muted. My vision blurred, and then I lost consciousness.

* * *

Three Weeks Later

Home. I was finally home again. It felt like forever since I'd been here. Our house might not be huge, but it was cozy and filled me with warmth. I ran my hands over the kitchen counters before taking a seat at the table. Joker carried in my prescriptions and the few items we'd grabbed at the store. Although, I'd had to fight him when we got there. He'd done his best to make me ride in the electric scooter with the basket on the front. I'd refused, repeatedly. He'd given in, but caged me between his arms, his hands on the shopping cart and me between the cart and him.

Joker set the bags on the counter, and when I stood to help put everything away, he glared at me.

"Sit your ass back down," he said.

"I'm not dead, Joker. I can still help."

"You're not supposed to overdo it. I can't handle you falling out or, God forbid, your heart stopping.

Please, for me, just sit there and let me handle it."

I nodded. I hated that he felt so scared he might lose me, but at the same time, who'd have ever thought such a tough-looking ex-con would be so sweet?

He'd just finished putting everything away when I heard the front door open.

"Cleo?" someone called out.

I recognized the voice immediately. "In the kitchen, Darian."

Except it wasn't only Darian. She had several others with her, including some women I'd only met once or twice in passing. I wasn't sure if they were here to check on me, or throw me out because of what my family had done. My throat grew tight and I felt my eyes burn with unshed tears.

"I'm sorry," I said. "My family... There's nothing I can say to fix what they did. Ares is so young, and now she's..."

"Hey!" Ridley pushed to the front. "None of it was your fault. Some of us have shitty parents. I did. Well, I halfway did. My dad is awesome, but my mom? She tried to use me to secure a business deal for my stepfather. So, if anyone gets it, I do."

"And me," Rin said, stepping forward. "My brother turned me into a whore. Coming to this club was the best thing I ever did. They saved me and gave me a second chance at life."

"A lot of us have brought trouble to the club," Darian said. "But these men push through it and keep going. You're one of us, Cleo. Family. Forget the assholes who were related to you by blood. Having the same DNA doesn't give them permission to treat you like garbage or use you the way they did. You were a victim too."

Joker came over and placed his hand on my

shoulder. "See. I told you no one here blamed you for what happened. I'll leave you ladies to talk. If you need me, I'll be in the bedroom."

"Are we running you off?" Ridley asked.

"No, I want to change the sheets and make sure Cleo will have everything she needs when it's time for her to lie down and rest. Just don't let her do too much, and try to keep the visit short," Joker said.

He walked out and I shook my head. "He thinks I'm going to break."

"You kind of did," Ridley said, "so I get why he's so overprotective. He's right, though. We need to keep this short."

"Dessa wanted us to come by," Rin said. "She worried you'd be blaming yourself for everything. Seems she was right."

Mara came closer and sat in the chair next to mine. She'd been quiet the one time I'd met her. I didn't know why she'd volunteered to visit right now.

"I don't live far. I'm going to put my number in your phone, and you call if you need anything and Joker isn't around. I know the others here are willing to stop by too," Mara said. "I mostly stay home, so I'm the easiest to reach."

"Yeah, this one is a hermit," Darian said, pointing to Mara.

Mara scowled at her. "I'm sorry I'm not a social butterfly. I like peace and quiet."

"You have two kids. How quiet could it be?" Ridley asked. "Although, your two aren't anything like my girls."

"Most kids aren't," Darian said, rolling her eyes.

Mara held out her hand and I gave her my phone. She programmed in her number, then the other ladies added theirs as well. They didn't stay much longer, heeding Joker's words. After they left, I went to the bedroom to find him. He'd already stripped the bed and put on fresh bedding. The dirty ones were in a pile on the floor.

"Don't even think of picking those up," he said. "Put on something comfortable, like pajamas, and get into bed."

"Since when do we have a TV in here?" I asked, eyeing the one mounted on the wall across from the bed.

"I wanted to make sure you could stay in bed without being bored."

"Travis, I'm fine. The hospital wouldn't have released me if I wasn't ready to come home. I'm not going to lie in this bed every day for the rest of my life."

He glowered at me. "If you don't rest, that life could be very damn short."

I didn't want to argue with him, especially when I knew he was only doing his best to keep me safe. I would allow it, to a point. Only if he let me do something first.

"If you want to wrap me in cotton and hide me away here, fine. But first, I need to see Dessa and Savior. Even if it isn't my fault Ares is gone, I feel like I need to apologize to them."

"Cleo, that's not necessary --"

"Please," I cut him off. "I have to face them. It's the only way I'll find any semblance of peace. I know the words won't mean anything to them, and they won't fix anything, but maybe it will alleviate some of the guilt I feel."

I knew it was terrible to say such a thing. An apology should make the wronged party feel better, not the one having to ask for forgiveness. Although, I supposed it could do both.

"All right," Joker said after a moment. "I'll make it happen. Just not today. You've been through enough already."

"Thank you." The thought of facing Dessa and Savior was terrifying, yet unavoidable. The path to redemption -- if such a thing existed for me -- was through the heartache I had inadvertently caused. My family may have done the awful deed, but I'd been the reason they came here.

"Let's get you settled," Joker said. He guided me into the bathroom and helped me change, then kept me steady as I went back to the bedroom and climbed into bed. He handed me the remote and showed me how to work it, then toed off his boots, removed his cut, and lay down beside me.

One step at a time, I repeated silently. In this life of chaos and calamity, it was all I could hope to manage.

* * *

I took a nap for two hours, then convinced Joker to call Savior. I didn't want to put this off any longer than necessary. Even though it would have been easier for me to enter their house than for Dessa to come here in a wheelchair, Joker wasn't going to let me go farther than the living room.

"Are you sure about this?" Joker asked.

I nodded. I wasn't sure what I'd say to them. It wouldn't be enough. All these weeks later, they still hadn't located Ares. I could only imagine the horrors she might be facing right now. Depending on who bought her, was she even still alive? I'd heard my father once laughing about a buyer who paid a fortune for young women and teens, only to torture them to death in less than a month. Had a monster like that bought her?

Joker must have read the resolve on my face because he pulled out his phone, tapping out a message. He stared at it for a moment, then his lips set in a line of grim determination. "They'll be here soon."

"Okay," I said softly, more to myself than to him. I tried to picture Dessa's kind face, not twisted in sorrow, and Savior's strong presence, not clouded by rage. Tried and failed. No matter how many times people said I wasn't to blame, I worried Dessa and Savior wouldn't feel the same way, especially as more time passed and their daughter remained missing.

We heard a vehicle pull into the driveway. Since Dessa couldn't use the wheelchair to come inside, I knew Savior would have to carry her. My pulse spiked, fear clawing up my throat as Joker went to answer the door. I stood, my legs unsteady, forcing myself to breathe evenly.

"Hey," came Dessa's soft greeting, as Savior brought her into the house. He helped her get situated on the couch, then took the place next to her.

"Hi," I managed.

Dessa looked up at me, her eyes rimmed red, and the dam of her resolve crumbled. Tears spilled over, carving wet trails down her cheeks. The sound of her crying, raw and wounded, was the most harrowing noise I'd ever heard.

"God, Dessa -- I'm so sorry," I blurted out, the words tumbling over each other in my urgency. "I wish --"

"Stop." Her hand lifted, a silent plea. "It's not your fault. I've been crying like this for weeks now. But not once have I blamed you for any of it."

But it felt like it was, the guilt nearly suffocating me.

"Look at me, Cleo," Joker said firmly. I glanced

in his direction. "It's not on you."

"Isn't it?" I countered, my gaze flicking between the couple who had become collateral damage in a war they never wanted.

"Your family did this, not you," Savior spoke for the first time since entering. "But it's hard, Cleo. Hard not to want someone to blame. Just the same, neither of us fault you for what happened. You couldn't have known what your father and brother would do."

"I know," I admitted, my own voice hoarse with held-back tears. "And I'll do anything to make this right."

"You can't do anything to erase what happened or bring her back," Dessa said softly, her hand reaching out as if to offer forgiveness or maybe seek comfort for herself.

The words hurt, but I knew they were true. Joker took a seat and tugged me down onto his lap. "I'm going to ask that we keep this short. She's not supposed to get stressed out, but she refused to sit still another moment without speaking to you."

"Please stop blaming yourself," Dessa said. "I have to hold onto the hope we'll find Ares and she'll be okay. It's what keeps us going. And like Savior said, this would be easier to have someone to blame, someone alive anyway. The only people responsible are your dad and brother."

"We won't stay longer. Don't want to tire you out," Savior said. "But my wife is right. Let go of what happened. You're part of this family now. Worry about healing and staying by Joker's side for many years to come. Let the rest of us handle the situation with Ares."

Savior stood and lifted Dessa into his arms. He carried her out of the house and I stood, letting Joker get up. He locked the front door, then forced me back to the bedroom. I'd play along for now and stay in bed for a few days. After that, he would just have to deal with me going about life as usual. I couldn't let this hold me back. If I did, then I'd spend what time I had left not living at all.

Chapter Fourteen

Joker

The clubhouse felt ominous every time I came here these days. Instead of a place to share drinks, laughter, and reminisce, it had turned into Mission Central. Until Ares came home, there would be a cloud hanging over all our heads. I didn't know how the President hadn't come unraveled by now. I knew Dessa was barely holding on, and heard their two younger children cried every night, wanting their big sister back.

The longer she remained gone, the smaller the chance became we'd actually find her and bring her home. At this point, even if we did, I didn't think she'd be the same girl I'd come to know. The brightness of her eyes would have dulled by now, assuming her owner hadn't broken her entirely. How the fuck had the man vanished so thoroughly that even the world's top hacker couldn't find the fucker? Something felt off about the entire thing.

Bull leaned in to whisper to me. "If you need to be home, we can handle this without you. I know you're worried about Cleo."

"I think I'm going to make her feel smothered," I said. "She probably needs a little time to herself. Besides, I know the ladies will help keep an eye on her. Wouldn't surprise me if someone hadn't noticed I'd left and plans to check on her."

He nodded and we both focused on what was going on in front of us.

"I've been scouring every damn lead," Wire muttered. "I won't rest until we find her. If it was my kid out there, I'd want someone to do the same for me. I just don't understand why I can't find a single trace of them."

"Any word from the street?" I asked. "It can't be possible that no one in this fucking town saw anything that day. Sure, we fucked up and let her get taken from our compound. That's on us. But someone had to have noticed her between here and wherever she ended up."

"Nothing yet." Tank sighed and rubbed his hands over his face. "Jesus. There are times I think it would be better if we just burned the world to ash. How can there be so many rotten souls out there?"

"I'm afraid it's only going to get worse and not better," Venom said. "Evil has always existed. The only difference is technology makes us more aware of it. Instead of discovering something months or a year after it happened, we now have access immediately. But I do think the evil in the world is growing. Maybe they just hid better a century or so ago. All I know is, I'm tired of this shit."

I looked around the room as I sipped my beer and my gaze caught on Prophet. He stood apart from everyone else, his demeanor icy. I knew he spent a lot of time with Ares. This had to be hitting him hard. Not a damn thing I could think of to say to him. Even if I did, the words wouldn't make him feel any better. Some things couldn't be fixed so easily.

"Damn man is about to explode," Tank murmured.

Savior sighed, running a hand through his hair. "He's got it bad for Ares. I've known for a while he plans to claim her. He's just been waiting for the right time. She had to get old enough, for one, and then he didn't want to rush things. Now this…"

"Love's a hell of a thing," I said. "It might make

us crazy, but sometimes it gives us strength."

"Let's just hope love's enough," Savior muttered, his gaze lingering on Prophet. "Every damn day I half expect to wake up and discover he's gone, off somewhere searching for Ares. He won't care if he's going the wrong direction. That man would search the world over for her."

He wandered over and I went back to Wire, hoping he'd found something new. Anything. Even the tiniest clue would be welcome right now. He rubbed at his eyes and sighed, then gave me a tired smile.

"While I'm hunting for Ares and the bastard who took her, Lavender's working on another front. She's doing everything she can to find a heart for Cleo. I know this has to be hard for you, being here to support the Pres in regard to Ares but wanting to stay with your sick wife."

My chest tightened at the mention of Cleo. Savior might wake up every day thinking Prophet had taken off, but I lived with a different fear -- waking up to find out Cleo had died during the night. I knew the ventricular assistance device was supposed to buy her more time, but what if something went wrong? What if it wasn't enough to keep her going?

"Tell Lavender thanks. She's a damn angel." I'd take whatever help I could get.

"Will do." Wire nodded. "We're family, Joker. Your fight is ours. We'll help get Cleo through this."

The minutes ticked by and soon another hour had passed. Nothing new. No idea where Ares might be, or if she was even still alive. The not knowing made things worse for everyone. The entire club felt her loss.

"Joker," Savior finally said, his voice gravelly with command, "go home to Cleo. She needs you more than we do right now."

I nodded, my throat tight, torn between the loyalty to my brothers and the fierce need to be with my woman. My cut felt heavier as I stood up, the patches a testament to the life I'd chosen -- a life that was now demanding more from me than ever before. And yet the Pres was telling me to focus on my wife and not his missing daughter.

"Let us know if there's any change with Cleo," Tank said.

"Will do."

I left the clubhouse and went out to my bike, eager to go home. Even if Cleo wasn't awake, these days I even found pleasure in watching her sleep. Anything to prove to me she was still alive and right here with me.

Walking into the house, the first thing I noticed was the smell of food. I wanted to spank her ass for cooking and not resting, but I didn't have the heart to fuss at her. She just wanted to feel normal.

I walked up behind her, placing my hands on her hips. "What's for dinner?"

"Baked chicken, steamed carrots, and whole wheat rolls."

The hospital had given Cleo a list of foods to avoid, and ones they recommended she eat. I was happy to see her eating healthily, even if it meant I had to eat something like this and not a damn cheeseburger. Maybe her diet would keep both of us alive longer.

I set the table and helped her fix our plates. We sat across from one another at the kitchen table, the soft hum of the fridge filling the silence. I didn't know what to say to her right now. I knew she wanted to ask about Ares, but she wouldn't. We had to avoid conversations that might cause her stress, and that was a big one.

"Lavender is doing her computer thing and trying to locate a heart for you. Wire told me today," I said as I took my first bite of food.

Not bad. Not as flavorful as I'd have liked, but I'd have eaten cardboard if that's what it took to keep Cleo with me for many more years.

"She doesn't have to do that," Cleo said. "The hospital will be alerted when there's a heart that's a match for me. I know I'm not at the top of the list, but still... they're doing what they can."

Speaking of doing things, I knew she wouldn't want to sit idle for long. I'd need to find ways to keep her occupied, while also not letting her do too much. I knew she liked reading and puzzles. I'd have to stock up on both types of books. But it left me wondering what else I could do for her. She didn't need to do a lot of walking right now, so we were limited on where we could go.

"Do you like things like museums?" I asked.

"I do," she said. "I've only been to one once, but I really enjoyed it. Why do you ask?"

"There's one not too far from here. They have wheelchairs you can rent, so you wouldn't have to walk through it. I thought maybe we could go on a date in the next few days," I said.

She brightened immediately. "Really?"

"Yeah. I don't want to keep you in a cage, but I do want you to be safe." I finished my food and carried my plate to the sink. "Thank you for dinner. It was good."

She smiled a little. "Liar. I know it didn't have enough seasoning for you."

"You cooked it, and you made something that will help you stay with me longer. That's all I need for it to be the best meal ever," I said.

"Such a sweet talker," she murmured.

"It's just you and me tonight. I'm not expecting any visitors. Anything in particular you want to do?" I asked.

"Well, there is, but you'll say we can't. Although, to be fair, I did ask the doctor, and he said as long as we're careful and kept an eye on my heartrate, or symptoms that I needed to stop, then..."

I held up a hand, knowing where she was going with this. Or I thought I did. "Are you saying you want to have sex? I love you, Cleo, and I love being intimate with you, but have you lost your damn mind?"

She huffed and stared at the table. The dismay on her face felt like someone had sucker punched me. I felt like an asshole, and at the same time, I was too fucking scared I'd hurt her physically. Not that I wanted to cause her emotional pain either.

"I feel like half a person right now, "she said. "I'm here, walking and talking, eating dinner with you, but it's more like a roommate than your wife. It feels like we've gone back to square one."

I reached over and took her hand. "We haven't. I would love nothing more than to be with you in that way, but not at the risk of your health or your life. I'd rather wait until I know it's safer."

She glared at me. I'd never seen such an expression on her face before. Fury. Pain. Hopelessness. It was all there, and so much more.

"What if waiting means you never get to share that with me again?" she asked "What if you keep putting it off and I die tomorrow or next week? I'm on borrowed time, Travis, whether you want to admit it or not."

I felt the blood drain from my face. I got up and

walked off, bracing my hands on the counter. I couldn't look at her right then. If I did, I might fall apart. She needed me to be strong for her. I needed her to know that when she felt like splintering to pieces, I'd be there to hold her, give her whatever she needed. Except, it seemed the one thing she needed terrified me.

"Please," she said. "Can't we at least try?"

"Fine. But the moment your heart rate goes too high, or you feel any discomfort in your chest, get short of breath, feel dizzy, or anything else they said to watch for, then we're stopping. And you'd better damn well not lie by hiding it from me."

"All right." She gave me a soft smile. "Should we clean up the kitchen first?"

"You're not doing anything to exert yourself. I'll pick up the kitchen, rinse the dishes, and then I'll help you take a quick shower. Because I'm assuming you want one."

She nodded. "That would be nice. Getting clean at the hospital wasn't the same as bathing here at the house."

While she sat at the table, I tidied the kitchen. My heart felt like it was hammering against my ribs. If this went horribly wrong, I'd never forgive myself. At the same time, I had a hard time telling her no, especially after she reminded me how little time we may have left together. There was no guarantee the surgery she'd just had would keep her alive until a heart had been found. Not to mention, I wasn't sure where she was on the list. There could be several people ahead of her.

If Lavender did find one for her, I hoped she found a way to guarantee it went to Cleo. Maybe it made me an asshole to bump her ahead of other people, but she was my wife. I honestly couldn't give a fuck about anyone else right now.

After I finished, I took her hand and led her back to our room. I made sure we had the pager handy. If the hospital alerted her about a heart, I wanted to know regardless of what the hell we were doing.

I started the shower and stripped out of my clothes, then helped Cleo undress. The water felt warm when we stepped under the spray. I tried to be as gentle as possible when I washed her. If she weren't so fragile, I'd have done far more, but right now I wanted to get her to the bed. Once we were both clean, I dried us off and lifted her into my arms.

"I can manage to walk that far," she said.

"Humor me, Cleo. I'm trying to give you what you want while doing my best to keep you safe." I paused. Motherfucker. "Protection."

"What?" she asked.

"We don't have protection, and you don't need to get pregnant right now. Shit! I can get dressed and see if one of the single guys has a condom they can spare, or just run to the store a buy a box."

She shook her head. "No. Instead of doing that, why don't you let me please you this time? I've never done that before, but I want to try."

I froze and stared down at her. "You want to suck my cock?"

Her cheeks went scarlet. "Yeah. Is that okay?"

Was she serious? It was like a dream come true, but... why did I feel like I was taking advantage of her? I needed to figure out the easiest way to do this with her. A position that would keep her from straining herself.

"What if I kneel on the floor?" she asked.

"You might hurt your knees." She gave me her *are you serious right now* look. "Fine. But let me get a folded towel or something."

I retrieved two towels from the bathroom, folded them, then stacked them for extra padding. Holding her hand, I supported her as she sank to her knees. She tentatively reached for my cock, running her finger down the shaft and over the head. A shiver raked my spine.

"I may be bad at this," she said.

"I seriously doubt that. If you blew on my dick right now, I might come."

She giggled and the light in her eyes filled me with warmth. I hadn't seen that look in weeks, and I'd missed it. She cupped my balls with one hand and wrapped the other around the base of my cock. Her tongue flicked out and licked the head before she fitted her lips around it.

Holy fuck! I may have been somewhat joking when I'd said I'd come if she blew on me, but when my balls drew up it took everything in me not to blow my load right then and there. Couldn't remember the last time I felt something this incredible, and knowing I was her first? It made this even more special.

She took as much of me into her mouth as she could, then pulled back. Her tongue swirled around the head of my cock before she swallowed me down again. I shut my eyes and started counting. Anything to maintain at least a little control.

"You're killing me," I muttered. "Feels too damn good."

She made a hum of appreciation, and the vibrations hit my dick in just the right way. I cursed and gripped a handful of her hair. Using short, shallow strokes, I didn't even get a chance to warn her before I came, filling her mouth with cum. Some dribbled from the corner of her lips and down her chin.

I pulled out, my chest heaving, and my body feeling like it was on fire. "Swallow, Cleo."

She gulped it down, then wiped the rest off her face. Her hand trembled as I helped her to her feet. Leaning down, I ravaged her mouth, kissing her as if my life depended on it. We were both breathless when I pulled back.

"You're fucking incredible," I said.

The alarm for her heart rate went off, and panic filled me. I swiftly lifted her into my arms and eased her down on the bed. Using gentle strokes, I ran my hand over her hair. "I need you to calm down. Long, deep breaths."

She followed my instructions, and her heart began to slow little by little. Yeah, we weren't having sex anytime soon. Not unless they were sending an ambulance for both of us because I thought I might have a heart attack if anything happened to her, especially if I was to blame.

I eased down on the bed beside her and pulled her into my arms. As long as I had her, nothing else mattered. Sex wasn't everything. At my age, I knew there were more important things in life. Sure, I enjoyed these moments with her, and liked the closeness I felt when I was inside her, or even when we cuddled afterward. None of it was worth it if her heart gave out.

"Love you, Cleo," I murmured.

"I love you too."

Chapter Fifteen

Cleo

"Do you ever think about kids?" This might not be the best time to ask. He was so worried about me dying that I knew it was most likely the last thing on his mind. I still wanted to know how he felt about having a family.

"Kids?" he asked. "Before you came here, I'd figured I'd die alone, except for my club. But yeah, I'd like to have a family with you. I'm worried that even after you get a transplant, your body won't be able to handle a pregnancy."

He made a valid point. One I'd considered myself. "There's always adoption, if you're open to that. I know some men don't want kids if they aren't theirs biologically, but you don't seem like that type of man."

"I'd be okay with that. Might be better to adopt a kid who was a little older. Then you'd have time to yourself while they were in school, and they wouldn't exhaust you quite so much."

"Wire and Lavender were able to find the online auction for Ares. Do you think they could locate children who were being sold?" I asked. "I mean, ones who need a family? Not someone like Ares who has parents desperately searching for them."

"Probably. Not right this minute, though. One of them is searching for Ares and the other is trying to find you a heart. When at least one of those issues is resolved, then maybe we can ask."

I snuggled closer to him. "You saved me, twice now. I want to do the same for someone else. I feel so helpless sometimes. But if there's a child who desperately needs a safe home, a place with loving parents, then I want to give that to them."

"You'd be a good mom," he said. "Not too sure I know how to be a dad, but I'd give it my best."

"I think you'd be amazing at it." I leaned up to smile at him. "You worry about me all the time, and make sure I'm happy. I have no doubt you'd do the same for our kids."

"Maybe they'll take after you and be little angels."

"Or take after their dad and raise hell?" I asked.

"Angels with a devilish streak?" he asked.

I couldn't help but laugh. That sounded pretty perfect. Once we got through the current trials we faced, maybe we could make our dream a reality.

I stared at the pager on the bedside table and wondered if it would ever go off. The one thing I feared was taking my last breath and that stupid thing going off not even a minute later. I worried what would happen to Joker if I really did die. The way he'd looked when he came to the hospital, I wasn't sure he'd be able to keep moving forward. We'd grown close since I'd shown up at the compound. Now I couldn't imagine my life without him, and I wondered if he felt the same.

But if we did have a chance to adopt a child, he'd have a reason to keep living. Was it selfish that I wanted him to have a long and happy life, even if I wasn't part of it? I knew he'd be hurting if I died, but I hoped he'd find a way to keep living. One of us needed to.

"You're thinking dark thoughts again, aren't you?" he asked softly. "I'm not going to let anything happen to you Cleo. Even if I have to rip the heart out of someone with my own two hands, I will make sure you get one."

"Can we try *not* to resort to murder as a way to keep me alive?"

He held my gaze. "When it comes to you, there's nothing I wouldn't do. So no, I won't make that promise. I can't."

I opened my mouth to say something, and he placed a finger over my lips, silencing me. The intensity of his gaze left me spellbound. This man... did he have any idea how much I loved him? I was willing to do anything for him.

"I will do whatever it takes to keep you with me, to start a family with you, and grow old together. Or in my case, older." He smiled a little. "Maybe we'll get two kids. A girl and a boy. I can teach him about motorcycles and how to throw a ball. You can show our daughter how to cook."

I arched an eyebrow. "What if our daughter wants to ride a motorcycle?"

"Then I'll teach her how. Flicker's woman rides one. I have no problem with women having bikes. I guess I just wanted a dainty daughter like her mother." He held me close. "And I'll make sure both know how to defend themselves. Our children will never be defenseless. They'll know how to throw a punch, how to incapacitate someone, and the best ways to break away if someone tries to kidnap them."

"Did Ares not know all those things too?" I asked.

He frowned. "Now that you mention it... I need to make a call."

He dialed Savior's number and put it on speaker.

"Joker, is everything okay?" Savior asked the second the line connected.

"Fine, Pres. You're on speaker. Cleo just asked if Ares knew how to protect herself, and it made me wonder... how exactly did those fuckers get their hands on her?"

"We're not sure. Found the spot in the fence where they cut it. We were so busy chasing our tails, we missed them breaking in. Won't happen again. I don't care if I have to electrify the entire damn fence, I refuse to let this happen to any more of our women and children. Every time we think we've built a fortress, someone proves us wrong, and it's pissing me off."

"Could she have been threatened or drugged?" Cleo asked. "I know my brother. He'd have done anything to get what he wanted. If he took her from your house, or had been watching your place, then he'd have known you have two smaller children."

Savior heaved a sigh. "And Ares would have done anything to keep them away from kidnappers. She overheard me talking about Cleo's family. I'm sure she had some idea as to why she was being taken."

"Is the fence still cut?" Joker asked.

"No. It's been mended. Not the greatest fix, but it will have to do for now. The entire fence may need an overhaul. We'll discuss security once Ares is safe. Listen, I need to go. Wire has a few potential leads he's chasing," Savior said. "I'm hoping we might actually have something this time."

Joker ended the call and stared up at the ceiling. "Why didn't any of us question this sooner?"

"Because everyone has been focused on the fact Ares was gone, and not so much on the how." I threaded my fingers with his. "I have to believe she'll come back to us sooner or later. It's too cruel to put her through this twice only to have it end badly."

"Let's hope you're right."

Someone pounded on the front door, and I jolted. Joker slid out of bed and pulled on his boxers and jeans. I quickly put on pajamas so I could see what was going on as well.

"Who the hell?" Joker muttered as he walked into the front part of the house.

I followed him, my own pulse quickening not with fear but with an inexplicable sense of urgency. The knock came again, more desperate this time, demanding our attention. Had they found Ares? Or had something else bad happened?

Joker swung the door open, revealing Lavender, her eyes wild and cheeks flushed with what could only be excitement or terror. Maybe both.

"Got news, Cleo," she gasped out, chest heaving as if she'd run all the way here. "Leads... on a heart."

My world halted, teetered on a precipice between hope and the crushing weight of skepticism. A lead meant a chance... even if it wasn't guaranteed, there was a possibility I'd have a new heart soon.

"Come in, Lavender," Joker said, stepping aside, but she shook her head.

"No time. The heart I found is in a patient currently on life support. A friend has family who works for a hospital a few hours away. The family is deciding if they're going to donate the organs. We should have an answer by tomorrow."

"Thank you," I whispered, my throat tight. "I don't like that someone had to die for me to live, but..."

"It's not one hundred percent for sure, but you're a match if the heart is still good." Lavender smiled. "I'm going to stick close to the computer. Once I get the call, I'm going to do what I can to make sure that heart is on a helicopter and heading this way. Keep that pager handy! You may need it."

She took off, running for her vehicle. Was this really happening? I stared at Joker, almost too scared to hope this could be for real. I'd thought I'd have to wait months, and possibly never get a heart. But Lavender had found one for me.

I looked up at Joker, his gaze fierce yet vulnerable, a mirror to my own turmoil. And in that moment, I allowed myself to believe. To trust in the possibility of a life where my heart didn't merely sustain me but thrived within me -- where the world was more full of opportunities, and we could build a life together.

"Ready for some cinematic distraction?" he asked. "Maybe something funny?"

"Yeah," I murmured, letting him lead me over to the couch.

He chuckled softly, thumbing the remote until a comedy splashed across the screen. As the characters on-screen bumbled through their fictional lives, I leaned into Joker's side, allowing myself a moment of levity. His arm wrapped around me, a steel band of protection, and I closed my eyes briefly.

A sharp rap at the front door shattered the illusion, our heads snapping toward the sound. Was Lavender back? Joker's body tensed, his posture shifting from relaxed to alert in an instant. The atmosphere crackled with tension, a stark contrast to moments before. It seemed movie night was over.

"Who is it?" Joker called out.

"Brother, it's Bull. We need to talk -- now!"

Joker's eyes locked with mine, a silent conversation passing between us. He squeezed my shoulder gently before rising, his movements calculated and precise. He got up to open the door and let Bull inside.

"Found something," Bull said. "It's Ares. There's a lead. A real one this time."

"Where?" Joker asked.

"Wire is still working on it. Everyone is at the clubhouse. You up for joining us?" he asked.

"Go," I urged Joker, my voice steady despite the chaos swirling inside me. "I'll lock up and stay here with the pager just in case. If anything happens, I'll come get you."

"Or you could just use the phone," he said.

Bull shifted, restless energy rolling off him in waves. "Time's wasting, brother."

With a final, lingering look, Joker followed Bull into the night, the roar of their bikes filling the quiet a moment later.

I stood at the window, watching until the red taillights disappeared into the darkness -- a prayer on my lips for Ares. *Please, let it really be her this time. Bring her home*!

* * *

Joker

Wire's fingers danced over the keyboard, his eyes flickering with a focused intensity that burned through the dim light. I didn't understand anything he was doing, but if it led us to Ares, then I wanted him to keep going.

"What do we know so far?" I asked.

"Georgia," Bull said. "Some bigwig with a taste for young teens and women bought Ares. Wire's trying to tap into security feeds."

"Damn it." Why did this have to happen to her? Hadn't she suffered enough already?

"If there's a camera in that place, I'll find it," Wire said, not even pausing in his typing.

The clubhouse thrummed with the pulse of urgency, every brother's attention riveted on the mission at hand. The weight of their collective focus was like a physical force.

"Come on, come on," I muttered under my breath, pacing the length of the room. If this was another dead end, I wasn't sure Savior could take it. None of us could. Ares was family.

Minutes dragged by, each one an eternity, stretching until they were thin and taut enough to snap. The sharp click of keys filled the room.

"Got something!" Wire shouted. All of us descended on him.

On the screen, pixels shifted, revealing the grainy image of a mansion, its walls a silent testament to the secrets they kept. Wire's hands flew over the controls, coaxing the feed to reveal its hidden truths. It looked like the bastard had several set up. Wire flicked through them one at a time.

"Come on, baby," Wire whispered, his voice a mixture of technician and sorcerer calling forth images from the digital ether.

Suspense knotted in my stomach, a snake coiled and ready to strike. The ghostly images on the screen flickered, teasing us with the promise of answers just out of reach. She had to be there.

"Anything?" Savior asked.

"Wait…" Wire's words trailed off as he shifted to another feed, giving us a glimpse of pure hell.

"Is that --?" Bull began, but no one finished the sentence. We didn't need to.

Our silence was a shared language, spoken in the glances we exchanged, the set of our shoulders, the tightening of our fists. The image on the screen held us captive. We'd finally found her. I only hoped she hadn't been completely broken.

"Get the location," I said. I eyed Savior. His face had turned nearly purple as the rage built inside him. He stared at his daughter and the signs of the abuse she'd suffered.

With a loud roar, he picked up a chair and threw it across the room. The wood shattered on impact. He lifted another and smashed it as well. Flicker and Saint grabbed him.

"Easy, brother," Saint murmured, his hold tightening. They dragged him toward the door, away from the screen that continued to display a nightmare we'd all be reliving for a long time to come.

"Let me go!" Savior roared.

"Shh, we got you," Flicker coaxed, his tone soft, a counterpoint to the chaos. "We're going to get her back, Savior. Right now, we need you to cool down and think about this logically."

They took him outside before he could demolish the entire clubhouse. Not that any of us would blame him.

"Almost got it," Wire said, his fingers a blur. "Found the exact coordinates!"

"Prophet," I turned to him, seeing my own reflection in his stormy gaze. Yeah, he had it bad for Ares. If anyone looked even more murderous than Savior, it was him. "We're bringing her home."

"Like hell *we* are." Prophet growled, the promise of violence a palpable thing in his voice. His hands trembled where he'd fisted them at his sides, and I knew he was barely holding back. Usually, he was one of the calmer members of our club, but not right now. Vengeance filled him as he stared at Ares' battered body.

Around us, the air crackled with the energy of men who knew the stakes, who lived and breathed chaos and retribution. This was more than a rescue -- it was a reckoning, and we were the judges, the jury, and the executioners. Didn't matter which brothers went to get Ares, they'd make sure justice was served in the most brutal way possible.

I looked at the computer screen again. Ares was there, her form small and broken as she huddled in the corner, knees hugged tightly to her chest. Her once vibrant eyes had lost their flame, replaced by a haunting emptiness that dug its claws into my soul. Blood smeared across her skin, and bruises had already formed on every visible part of her body. They hadn't even allowed her to keep her clothes in the dank cell where they'd dumped her after doing God knew what to her.

As Wire scrambled to sever the connection, I watched Prophet. His face was a mask of stone, every line etched with a cold, seething anger. It wasn't just the sight of Ares that ignited his wrath -- it was the knowledge that someone he loved, someone we all loved, had been defiled by a monster's touch.

"Close it, Wire!" I barked. I didn't think Prophet would keep it together much longer. We needed that screen out of view immediately.

"Trying!" Wire's fingers danced frantically across the keyboard, but it was too late. Prophet had seen everything, and he was two seconds from losing his shit.

"Prophet, man," I began, reaching out, but he shrugged off my hand. The look in his eyes was one I recognized -- the calm before the storm, the eye of a hurricane poised to unleash devastation upon anything in its path. In that moment, I knew he would tear the world apart to set things right. And God help anyone who stood in his way.

The steady thrum of my heartbeat echoed in my ears, a relentless drumbeat that seemed to resonate with the tense atmosphere hanging thick in the clubhouse. Wire's fingers halted their frenetic dance across the keyboard, and he turned slowly, a slip of paper clutched in his grasp.

"The mansion's south of Atlanta. Only building within fifty miles. Heavily fortified."

"Let me see," I demanded, snatching the paper from him. The scrawled address was a death sentence written in neat block letters -- a place where innocence was marred and devils roamed free. But not for much longer. Soon, something told me the place would be nothing more than ash and soot.

"Prophet," I started, but he simply pivoted on his heel, striding toward the door with a purpose that silenced any words I might have uttered. He'd seen the address, and I knew damn well he was going after her.

"Damn it," I muttered under my breath, watching as the door closed behind him.

"Wire, tell me you got more than just the location," I said. "We need some intel to keep Prophet safe, and he's going to need backup."

"Look at this," Wire gestured back to the screen, bringing up a satellite image that revealed the extent of our problem. Tall fences. Security cameras. Guards patrolling with dogs. It was clear: this was no mere mansion -- it was a fortress designed to keep people out -- or perhaps, more accurately, to keep them in.

Jesus fucking Christ! This was bad. "He's walking into a Goddamn suicide mission."

"I'll go after him," Warden said.

"Anyone else?" I asked. Foster lifted his hand. Kid was only a Prospect, but he was also the son of a patched member. I glanced at his dad and Bull gave a slight nod of his head, giving permission. "Then you and Warden haul ass after Prophet. Once the Pres has his head back in the game, maybe we can get you some backup from other clubs."

"Already alerting Outlaw and Shade. I'm sure the Devil's Fury and Devil's Boneyard will help."

"Let them know we need all the firepower and manpower they can spare. If Savior gets pissed I overstepped, then I'll deal with it later."

"Done. They should be mobilizing soon."

Savior came back inside, looking as if part of him had died. Saint and Flicker stood with him.

"Fury and Boneyard are sending extra men," Wire said. "And Prophet lit out of here like his ass was on fire. Warden and Foster went after him."

"Good." Savior sighed. "Thanks for doing what I couldn't. That's my baby girl, and I'm sorry to say I couldn't be both father and President just then."

"We've got your back," I said. "And soon, you'll have Ares at home."

He closed his eyes, and I knew the words had given him at least a little comfort. Now I had to hope I hadn't just lied my ass off.

Stay safe and wait a little longer... they're coming for you.

Epilogue

I tiptoed from the bedroom and out into the living room. Cleo's heart transplant had been a huge success, so far. I dreaded the possibility of her body rejecting the heart. The doctor seemed to think things would be fine now. He said in rare occurrences the body could reject it years later. I refused to believe we'd have to face that nightmare, not after everything we'd been through.

Opening the front door, Lavender and Wire waved at me, but my attention focused on the child in front of them. A seven-year-old boy. He seemed small for his age. They'd managed to save him from a trafficking ring by funneling funds into an account to purchase him at auction, only for them to later hack the seller and take every penny in every account they could find. In this particular boy's case, his parents had been the ones to sell him the first time. No idea if it was for drugs or just because they were greedy fucks. Either way, there wasn't anywhere for him to go, except here.

I went down on one knee, watching and waiting to see what he'd do. He took a slow step toward me, then another. Stopping about two feet away, he stared at the ground.

"Are you my owner?" he mumbled.

"No. I'm your dad," I said.

His head jerked up and his eyes went wide. "What?"

"The man behind you is my brother, Wire. The

people here call me Joker, even though I haven't had a whole lot to laugh about lately. I know we're not related biologically, but if you'll let me, I'd like to give you a home and a family."

His eyes narrowed slightly. "Why? What do you want in return?"

"Only for you to grow up healthy and happy, and I hope you'll be good to your new mom. She's a bit fragile."

"A mom?" he whispered, almost like it was a prayer. Looked like I'd found the magic word.

"She had a bad heart and needed surgery. She's mostly healed now, but I still worry about her. Do you think you'd want to live here with us? Help me watch over her?" I asked.

He nodded slowly and inched a little closer. "Can I see her?"

"She's asleep. Why don't we get you cleaned up a bit, and then you can help me wake her up?"

He tensed and I realized my mistake. "I didn't mean I'd be washing you or anything. You're seven, right?"

He nodded again. "That's what they told me."

Shit. Did the kid not even know when his birthday was? How long had he been in that hellish place? How many times had he been sold? I glanced at Lavender and she slightly shook her head. I had a feeling this kid hadn't had parents in a long-ass time.

"Well, at seven, you're big enough to clean yourself. You have your own bathroom. They told me what size you wear so I bought you a few things. I had to be sneaky, though."

"Why?" he asked.

"Your mom doesn't know about you yet. But she really wants a little boy."

"Why didn't she have one?" he asked.

"Well, remember how I said she had a bad heart? Even though it's been fixed now, it's still not a good idea for her to have a baby. At least, not for a little while longer. I honestly would prefer that she never have one because I'd be too scared I might lose her."

He tipped his head to the side. "Will she like me?"

"She's going to love you. Do you have a name?" He paled and looked away. All right. Clearly that was a trigger. "Would you let me name you?"

"What name would you give me?" he asked.

"How about... Caspian."

"That's a funny name." The boy smiled. "I like it."

"Have you ever watched *Chronicles of Narnia* or read the books?" I asked.

"No. I wasn't allowed to watch TV or read."

Motherfuckers! I hoped Wire and Lavender completely wrecked their lives.

"Well, Caspian is a Prince in one of the movies. Maybe we can watch all of them later. So, you're all right being called Caspian?"

"Yeah." He held out his hand and I grasped it before standing.

I gave one last look to Wire and Lavender before heading inside with my new son. I showed him the room I'd set up in secret, gave him some clean clothes, and showed him to his bathroom.

"I'll wait in the living room. When you're finished and dressed, meet me in there and we'll go see your mom." I shut the bathroom door and walked off, making sure I stepped loud enough he could hear me leaving.

I flipped on the TV and sat on the couch. After

making sure we had access to the movies I'd mentioned to him, I put on something random. I heard footsteps and thought Caspian must have finished quickly, until Cleo came into the room. Shit. So much for letting our boy wake up his new mom.

"Did you have a good nap?" I asked.

"Yes. Why does it sound like there's water running in the bathroom?" She started to head to the hallway, and I reached out to snag her hand. She paused and looked down at me, her brow furrowed.

"Sit. There's a surprise for you."

"And it requires the water to run?"

I nodded. "It does. Just be patient. I promise you'll like it."

She huffed and sat beside me, leaning her head against my shoulder. It wasn't more than ten minutes later that Caspian walked into the room wearing his new pants and shirt. He had socks on, but hadn't put shoes on, which was fine. If the kid wanted to run around barefoot, I didn't care.

Cleo stared at him so intently I wondered if she was even breathing. I waved my hand in front of her face. "Cleo, you all right?"

"There's a little boy in our living room," she murmured.

"Well, he's not just *any* boy." I cleared my throat. "Cleo, meet our son, Caspian. He's seven, and he agreed to live here with us."

Her hand went to her mouth, and she approached him slowly, going down to her knees in front of him. Caspian watched her, seeming uncertain what to do. Cleo's hand trembled when she reached for him, lightly taking hold of his fingers. It was all the boy had needed. That simple touch gave him the courage to hug his new mom.

"I'm not hurting you, am I?" he asked. "Dad said you'd had your heart fixed."

"No, you're not hurting me. This is the best hug ever."

"I know I should have told you," I said. "Ridley and the other ladies knew what was going on. It's why they kept asking you over to their homes or taking you out to eat. It gave me time to get his room ready and buy enough clothes that he'd have some stuff here when he arrived."

"Toys? Books?" Cleo looked at me. "Did you get everything he'd need?"

Caspian hugged her tighter and I saw tears trickling down his cheeks. I felt a little jealous since he hadn't hugged me yet. But from what Wire and Lavender had told me, he'd been abused mostly by men.

"Caspian, why don't you show your mom your room," I said.

He took her by the hand and led her into the small hallway, then into the bedroom. I'd removed the items I'd had in there previously and now the room contained a twin bed, small desk, and dresser. She'd asked about toys, and while I'd made sure he had something so he wouldn't be bored, I'd thought she might enjoy taking him shopping if she felt up to it. The doctor had told her to exercise several times a week so her heart would stay healthy, but an all-day trip to the mall might be a little much this soon after her transplant surgery.

A small bookshelf stood beside the desk. The shelves were empty since I hadn't known how well he could read. Now I had to wonder if he knew how to at all. We'd have to get him caught up so he could attend school. Wire had said he'd handle the paperwork once we had a name for him. He'd heard me call the boy Caspian, so I had a feeling by tonight, the boy would legally be Caspian Clemons.

I'd thought most boys enjoyed cars, so I'd bought a handful as well as a playset for them. A tub of Lego blocks was on top of the bookshelf. I didn't have any idea if he'd like building things with them, but at least he'd be able to give it a try. And lastly, I'd gotten a coloring book and crayons, which were on the desk. Since the club had known what was going on, they'd given me a stuffed bear, which I'd placed on his bed.

"How many outfits does he have?" Cleo asked, opening the closet and dresser drawers.

"For now, two sets of sweats, two pairs of jeans, and two shirts. Plus socks and underwear. I also got him a pair of tennis shoes. Anything else I thought we could all buy together." I folded my arms and leaned against the doorframe. "Not today, though. Tomorrow we can have a family shopping day if the two of you are up for it."

"I don't need anything else," Caspian said quickly. "This is more than I've ever had."

I stepped into the room and reached out to ruffle his hair. When he flinched, I drew my hand back. "This is only the beginning, Caspian."

Cleo looked at me, her eyes misty with unshed tears. "You've given me the best present ever. I know we talked about having a family, and adopting because of my heart, but…"

She muffled a sob and I pulled her into my arms. "It's fine, Cleo. You're allowed to cry whether it's because you're happy or you're sad. Same for you, Caspian. Tears aren't a sign of weakness. Not in this house."

He came closer and tentatively hugged me. I

placed my arm around him and hugged my wife and son. I knew this was a huge step for the boy.

"Let's pop some popcorn and watch a movie," I suggested. "We'll take it easy at home today and let Caspian settle in."

"I love you," Cleo murmured, going up on her tiptoes to kiss me.

"Love you too." I glanced down at Caspian. "And even though you just joined our family, I can say with complete confidence your mom and I both love you. I hope you'll come to trust us and will be happy here."

When I'd gotten out of prison, I hadn't been sure whether or not I'd have a place to call home. Not only had my brothers welcomed me back with open arms, but I now had a family. Whatever came our way, I'd protect them, even if it cost me my life. They meant everything to me.

* * *

Savior

If it were anyone else, I'd have completely lost my shit by now. Prophet and the others had managed to rescue Ares from the hell she'd landed in, except then he'd disappeared with her. It had taken him a few days to reach out and make sure I knew she was safe. However, he wouldn't tell me where they were.

I stared at the message on my phone, wondering when I'd get to tell my family Ares would be returning to us. *She needs more time. I refuse to rush her healing process to make everyone else feel better.*

As much as I wanted to demand he bring her home, I knew he was right. Prophet was only thinking of what Ares needed. I had to consider Dessa and our other children, as well as the club. There were many who were anxious for her return.

Keep her safe and tell her I love her.

I would have given anything to see her, to talk to her. If Prophet didn't think she was ready, then I'd trust his judgment. For now, I'd bide my time and wait. I only hoped it didn't take much longer. I missed my girl and wanted her home.

Always. His response made me snort. Thanks to Ares I'd never hear or read that word the same way again. The girl was obsessed with *Harry Potter*. And Prophet knew it. The fucker had done that on purpose.

I decided to record a short video and send it to him. When he thought Ares was ready, he could show it to her.

"Ares, I know you're hurting and you need some time to sort through everything you're feeling and the things you experienced. I failed you as both a father and the President of this club, and saying I'm sorry will never be enough. What I can say is that I love you, I miss you, and the moment I realized you were still alive was the first time I was able to breathe since the day you disappeared. Come home to us when you're ready. We love you, and we'll be patiently waiting."

I ended the video and sent it to Prophet. *When you think she's ready, show her this.*

It only took a moment to get a response. *She doesn't blame you, or the club.*

Of course, she didn't because that's just who Ares was. My strong, independent, beautiful girl. For now, I'd keep putting one foot in front of the other, even though it felt like a piece of my heart had been ripped out.

He'd bring her home. Of that I had no doubt.

I just had to be patient and wait.

Harley Wylde

Harley Wylde is an accomplished author known for her captivating MC Romances. With an unwavering commitment to sensual storytelling, Wylde immerses her readers in an exciting world of fierce men and irresistible women. Her works exude passion, danger, and gritty realism, while still managing to end on a satisfying note each time.

When not crafting her tales, Wylde spends her time brainstorming new plotlines, indulging in a hot cup of Starbucks, or delving into a good book. She has a particular affinity for supernatural horror literature and movies. Visit Wylde's website to learn more about her works and upcoming events, and don't forget to sign up for her newsletter to receive exclusive discounts and other exciting perks.

Harley at Changeling: changelingpress.com/harley-wylde-a-196

Bad Boys Multiverse
  A Bad Boy Romance
  Dixie Reapers MC
  Devil's Boneyard MC
  Hades Abyss MC
  Devil's Fury MC
  Bryson Corners
  Owned by the Mob
  Reckless Kings MC
  Devoted Guardians MC
  Savage Raptors MC
  Underland MC
  Devil's Boneyard MC Audio
  Dixie Reapers MC Print

Dixie Reapers MC Audio
Hades Abyss MC Audio

Changeling Press, LLC

ChangelingPress.com